SHE TOOK MY BABY

SHE TOOK MY BABY

STEENA HOLMES

bookouture

Published by Bookouture in 2026

An imprint of Storyfire Ltd.
Carmelite House
50 Victoria Embankment
London EC4Y 0DZ

www.bookouture.com

The authorised representative in the EEA is Hachette Ireland
8 Castlecourt Centre
Dublin 15 D15 XTP3
Ireland
(email: info@hbgi.ie)

ISBN: 978-1-80550-244-9
eBook ISBN: 978-1-80550-243-2

Thank you
To all those who hold secrets close to their hearts, remember this:
Secrets that destroy can also refine.
Choose your secrets, and choose them wisely.

Ayla Marie, this one is for you.
You are enough and you always have been.
In fact, you are more than enough. You are amazing, brilliant, a bright light always on the side of others; you have a heart of gold and a passion for good. You are an amazing woman and I am so proud of you. Xoxo, Mom

ONE

TRINA EMMET

PRESENT DAY

I'm a prisoner with no escape. Trina Emmet, inmate 001, living out a life sentence without parole or hope of redemption. Everything I've done has led me to this moment; everything I will do is because of what I've done, and no matter how much I want to change things, I can't.

I'm a mother, but they won't give me my child. That's the worst sentence a woman can ever live, in my opinion.

My prison: the Bullseye Ranch. My cell: an eight-hundred-square-foot cottage that once was promised to be my castle. My crime: I have no bloody clue.

Today is, was, my official due date, and in the past three weeks, I've endured an endless loop of a living hell, and there's nothing I can do about it. Three weeks ago, I rushed up to the main house to help my friend who was in early labor, and in the midst of the chaos, I ended up falling down the stairs and going into early labor myself. Just like I swear I heard the sound of my baby after he was born via emergency C-section, I also believe I was pushed down the stairs—both things everyone tells me I imagined.

An alarm goes off on my phone with a reminder to take my medication. I shut it off and toss the pill down the toilet.

Dr. Harmon says they're to help with the healing after such a traumatic delivery experience, but all they do is make me feel tired and groggy with huge memory lapses, and I don't like the feeling at all. It's been three weeks and I'm healing just fine, *thank you very much.*

My sentence is also definitely not self-imposed. I may live on the largest ranch in Western Canada, nanny for one of the wealthiest ranching families around, but I'm very much in exile at the moment.

Apparently, and this is something I don't remember doing, I tried to take my best friend's newborn son and screamed at her for stealing my baby.

Now, they don't want me up at the main house, or around their children. At least, not until I'm better.

I rub my empty womb and lightly touch the stitches over my deflating skin. My body is still healing. My chest aches. A warmth spreads across my breasts moments before soaking through my shirt.

I'm told eventually my milk will dry up, but I don't want it to.

They keep telling me my little girl died in my womb from the crazy fall down the stairs. My head wants to believe them, but my heart won't accept their version of the truth. Thanks to the ultrasounds, I know I was having a boy, not a girl. If a child died, and that's a big if, it wasn't my son.

I don't remember much from that night three weeks ago, but what I do remember is waking up and hearing the beautiful cries of two newborn babies. I know I heard my baby, but everyone—the doctor, my friends—they all tell me I imagined it.

I look about my cottage, at the comfy, cozy vibe I've created over the years, and I don't want to be here, but I haven't been cleared to drive, and no one will take me anywhere, no matter how often I beg.

After pumping, I shuffle my way back to my chair on the back deck when there's a knock on the door. "Go away," I call out, knowing exactly who it is and not wanting to see him.

I should have known the man opening that door wouldn't respect my wishes and leave. He's not the type who typically hears someone tell him no.

"Trina, what are you doing up? You need to be resting." Marcus Eaton closes the door behind him.

"I have been resting. All I do is rest." My tone is friendly, but I'm not sure I could hide my weariness even if I tried.

Getting a visit from Marcus Eaton, the man in charge of everyone and everything at this ranch, is not just a regular, everyday occurrence; at least, for most people, it's not. Any time slot in his calendar is highly sought after, and yet he's been here. Day after day for the past three weeks. Him and Wyatt. Personally, I prefer Wyatt's company.

My feet slide along the floor before I pull out a chair and drop into it.

"You're just exhausted. You did too much today, didn't you?" He eyes me with a thoughtful gaze and I feel exposed. "Did you take your pill? It's around that time, isn't it?"

I only nod.

He smiles. "Good. I can talk to the doctor about weaning you off it, if you think you're feeling better."

"Does that mean I can come back up to the house?"

He sets the bag he's carrying down on the counter, ignoring my question. "I brought lunch—I thought we could make it together, but why don't you just sit there, and I'll make it instead." Most people would say that as a question, but not Marcus. He very rarely asks for permission and never apologizes and is always in control.

"That's very kind of you but completely unnecessary," I say, masking the hurt I feel.

"Of course it's necessary. Don't think I haven't heard how you are refusing to eat anything we send down. Why is that?" There's a slight rebuke in that sentence.

"I have plenty of food here," I say instead. "I don't mind cooking for myself."

He cocks his head, and those emerald eyes of his dull a little while he gives me the briefest of nods. He realizes I didn't answer his question and respects that.

Color me surprised.

"Most of this was pulled from the garden just this morning. I know a chef's salad is your favorite," he says, pulling out produce from the bag, holding it up so I can see. "I also brought your mail." He pulls out some letters from his pocket and sets them on the counter.

"Why won't you eat anything Mabel sends down?" Marcus asks, obviously not letting the topic drop. He takes over my kitchen and pulls out a cutting board.

"I eat."

One of his brows nudges upward in disbelief. "Not enough. You're wasting away. I'm worried."

My hand goes to the small round of my belly.

"That's why I'm here. That's why Wyatt comes at night. To make sure you're okay."

He slices open my exposed heart with his words. "You asked Wyatt to check in on me?" That hurts. I thought Wyatt came for me, because of me, because of us and what's between us. But if he's only here because he's told to be... that changes everything.

"That man might be in my employ, but when it comes to you and Rosalind, he doesn't take orders from anyone. It's why he's here, to be honest. Because he looks after you two almost as well as my brother and I do."

By the look on his face, I can't tell if that's a good thing or not.

"If I didn't know he spent his evenings here with you, then I'd have someone else down here, and you know it."

"So you're the day shift, he's the night shift, got it." It's hard to keep the sarcasm from my voice. "But you're a busy man, and I don't need a babysitter anymore."

"I'm not sure you're aware of what you need." Marcus gives me a cutting look. "Although, you certainly seem more spirited today, which is nice to see."

I'm about to give a biting reply, but the look he gives me has me clamping my lips together to stop from saying anything else.

"Would you like me to stop sending people down?" he asks. At least twice a day, he sends someone from the house down to make sure I'm okay, to clean, do laundry, and weed my small garden. I'm rarely alone.

I nod. "I'm okay, honestly."

"Is the lie for me, or yourself?"

Ouch, that hurts.

"I'll stop hovering if that's what you would like."

As a thank you, I pull myself to my feet and shuffle over to help make lunch.

"Go sit back down," he tells me. "I've got this."

Not once, while he's in my kitchen, does he pull out his phone or look at his watch, even though I'm sure he's received a dozen or more calls, emails, and texts while he's been here. He's attentive, chatting about everything and nothing, giving me time to relax, which I know is a dangerous position to be in.

No one should ever be relaxed around Marcus. He's not known as a shark for nothing.

It's not until we're sitting at the table that I bring up the one subject I know he doesn't want to discuss.

"How is Rosalind? How is..." I pause, my tongue not wanting to utter his name yet, "the baby?"

He sets his fork down and wipes the edges of his lips with his napkin.

I press on despite his silence. "You know this is the longest we've been apart, right?" She's a sister to me. Her family is my family, and we've been together for years. I came on as their nanny when the twin girls were born, and there was never any plan of me leaving.

"And you know the reason for that," he says, leaning in, elbows planted on the table.

"No, I don't. I only know what you've told me happened."

He scowls. "Trina"—he lets out a long sigh and leans back in the chair—"she needs some time. She's still afraid there will be a repeat of last time."

I wish I could promise there will be no repeat, that I won't accuse my best friend of stealing my son, but I can't promise that. Not when I still believe I heard the cries of two babies and I know someone has kept my baby from me.

It's the *why* I can't figure out. Why would she do that to me? We grew up together. We survived foster homes together. We've been through more than most friends have. It doesn't make sense.

While she gets to nurse her baby, count his fingers and toes, and rock him to sleep, my heart is shredded as I sit here with empty arms. I never got the opportunity to hold my baby, to count his fingers and toes, to kiss him and tell him I love him.

"I'm sorry." He grabs hold of my hand, lifting it from my lap. His touch is gentle as his thumb strokes my skin. "I know it's hard. I know it's unfair, but I have to respect her wishes."

"What about the girls? Can I at least see them?"

The way he pins his lips together, I already know the answer. "On that, I'm the one who is saying no. It's too soon for you to go back to work as their nanny. It's only been two weeks."

The echo of pain in his voice speaks to the pain in my soul, and tears trickle down my face as I stare into his eyes.

"It's been three weeks, actually," I correct him. "And today is, was, my official due date."

He looks like he's going to say something but doesn't.

"When do you go back to China?" He was away on a business trip the night I gave birth.

"I'm going to stick around for a bit," he says. He points to my plate. "You've barely eaten anything."

I pick up my fork then set it down again. I'm not hungry.

"You need to eat more, Trina. I wish you'd let us take care of you."

I swallow hard. He wants me to give in and accept that help, but I can't.

I believe someone poisoned me and then pushed me down the stairs the night I gave birth, and that's the real reason my baby isn't here.

Marcus was the only one not there on that fateful night and that's the only reason I trust him right now. I know too much about him, about the mask he wears, to trust him for anything else. In fact, one day, I plan on making sure everyone sees the real man behind the mask, if it's the last thing I do.

TWO

With Marcus gone, I tidy up the kitchen, wipe down the counters, and flick through the mail he brought down with him.

Travel brochures, junk mail, bank statements, and a letter from the Nova Clinic, with a return address in Switzerland. However, it's not addressed to me; it's addressed to Marcus, with "Urgent" stamped in red. It's probably related to the breeding program they run with their cattle.

I have three options for what I can do next. I can leave it here till Marcus comes back tomorrow. I can call for someone to come down and get it. Or I can take it up to the main house myself.

I like the last option. The only problem is that, technically, I'm not welcome back there yet. Marcus made that crystal clear earlier.

Not like it's going to stop me, though. This gives me the perfect excuse to see if I can find proof of my baby, because so far, the only proof I have that I gave birth is the scar around my abdomen. I don't even have a birth or death certificate yet.

Stepping outside, I head toward the main house. Nothing

has changed, and yet it looks different. The pathway feels longer, the wraparound porch less welcoming, and for some strange reason, it no longer feels like home. Not like before.

My steps slow as I crest the small hill, and I find I'm not alone.

"I thought that was you. How are you, love?" Mabel, the housekeeper, stands on the top step of the porch. "Are you ready to be out and about already? Don't rush the healing, trust me on that." She hurries down and gives me a hug. Mabel is the grandmother of the ranch. "You look too pale." She tsks as she climbs the stairs, pausing when she sees I'm not following. "Come sit. I'll grab you a tall glass of fresh cold tea I just made this morning. We can have a little chat and catch up." The smile she gives me is motherly and I find myself relaxing.

"Marcus left this by mistake," I say, holding out the letter. "It's marked urgent so I thought…"

"He left with the girls for a run into town, and Mrs. R is resting," she says as if noticing my hesitation to sit. "It's just you and me for the next hour." She points to the chair.

She takes the letter and heads inside while I sit down on one of the rustic rockers on the porch and lean my head back. I lightly rub the scar on my belly and wince at how sensitive it is right now. I close my eyes as I think back on the last time I sat out here.

Rosalind and I had sat out here, our swollen feet resting on a stack of pillows, our hands resting on our enlarged bellies. We were both carrying differently. With her tall frame, she was all belly and barely looked like she'd gained any weight, whereas with my shorter body, the weight gain went everywhere and I resembled a wine barrel.

We were both quite exhausted. Rosalind's wheelchair sat off to the side. She was officially on bed rest but couldn't stand being stuck in the house for another minute. It was my first day of official maternity leave, but it felt weird being up here on the porch instead of playing with the girls.

"Think she'll be able to handle them?" Rosalind looked out to the front yard, where the temp nanny was waving around bubble wands with the girls.

"All I know is better her than me," I replied. "I could shut my eyes and fall asleep right here," I said with a yawn.

"Don't you dare do that, Trina Emmet. You know how contagious those are, and there's no way I'm going back up to my bed, so you better cut it out." Rosalind shook her head at me.

"How are you feeling?" I asked her.

"Like I've been hit by a boat." She rubbed her stomach while wincing. "I don't remember being in this much pain with the girls, and I was double the size with them."

"But everything is still okay? What did the doctor say?"

"As long as this little one cooperates, I should go to term, which in and of itself will be a miracle."

"Wouldn't it be something if our little ones were born on the same day?"

"A dream," Rosalind said with a smile. "We always do seem to do things together, don't we?"

I chuckled because it was true. Most of our life, for as long as we'd been friends, we'd always done things hand in hand.

"And what about you? Did your check-up go okay? I can't believe how easy your pregnancy has been compared to mine."

"Easy? I had morning sickness for six months."

"You know what I mean. I can't wait for this little girl to be born."

"Have you decided on a name yet?" Between the two of us, we kept a running list of possible names but narrowing it down had been hard.

"Josephine Kathleen, after my mom. How about you?"

I couldn't even hide my grin if I wanted to. "Jack Douglas,

after my father." He died when I was young, but the memories I have, they're full of love.

"Can you imagine four kids running around this place? Trent and Marcus will need to create their own man-cave just to escape." Rosalind smiled at the idea and I wasn't sure if it was the idea of four kids running around, or the fact Trent, her husband, would even want to escape – he loves children. In fact, both the brothers do.

Neither of us said much after that. Marcus had been an awkward topic between us recently.

The screen door claps as it closes, jolting me from my memory.

"I made a fresh loaf of lemon bread this morning. I know that's your favorite. It's even drizzled with that lemon cream glaze that you like." Mabel walks out onto the porch, tray in hand.

I take the glass of iced tea and hold onto it. Mabel takes a sip before she sets her cup down. She's watching me, so I feel like I need to drink except—

Her phone dings and her attention is taken from me to her screen. The smallest of smiles plays on her lips.

"Good news?" I ask.

Her head jerks up and she blinks rapidly.

"Your phone," I say. "You were smiling at whatever you were looking at, so I assumed..."

She clears her throat and looks around. "My, um, my oldest daughter just moved back home," she finally says.

"That's great," I say, keeping my voice light. "I know how much you've missed her not being close by." Mabel has two daughters, one on the East Coast and one who lives up north. In all my years here, I've never met either, but I've heard a lot about them.

She looks away. "They should arrive later tonight."

"They?"

"She—"

There's a cry from the upstairs window that stops her. We both glance upward.

"Oh, that poor little thing. All he does is cry. Breaks my heart to hear him." Mabel gets to her feet. "He's probably hungry, and Grace is down at the barn again. I better give her a ring." She mutters this last part.

Off to the side of the house, Mabel's name is called. We both glance over to see one of the ranch hands standing next to a teenager.

"Is that Matty?" I can't believe my eyes. Mabel's grandson from her youngest daughter, whom she's raised since he was a newborn, has shot up like a weed in the past few months.

"Mr. M says he's old enough to start being a proper cowboy." Mabel's voice comes out in a rush, and I notice she's clenching her apron tight between her fingers. She pauses then looks at me. "Will you be okay for a moment? I hope nothing has happened." She leaves before I can utter a sound, rushing down the porch steps.

The crying upstairs doesn't let up.

A familiar ache spreads in my chest, a warm tingling sensation, and I groan. I glance down and, sure enough, I'm leaking.

I debate heading back to my cottage, but the intensity of the cry increases, and I make my way into the house and climb the stairs toward the nursery. The calls are a siren, drawing me in, even though I know there will be hell to pay if I'm found.

Seeing the poor little thing in the crib just about breaks me. Why hasn't anyone come in to see him? His face is red, and he's bundled up so tight. I immediately unwrap him and let his little arms and fists flail about.

Baby Jack looks up at me, and I can't help myself, I pick him up. The moment I do, his cries disappear as he snuggles into the crook of my neck, his face burrowing close.

Having him this close, the ache in my heart eases and my soul whispers two simple words.

My son.

My feet automatically take us to the rocking chair. There should be a bottle around, but there's no bottle and no nurse. Jack nuzzles my breasts with frenzied movements and so, without thought, I nurse him.

It feels... right. Even though I've never done this before, he latches on without issue, and the let-down in my chest is a welcome relief.

I can't stop the tears from falling as I stare at the precious thing in my arms.

I don't let myself think, I just feel. I feel the weight of him in my arms, the light tugs as he drinks... I feel a sense of peace I didn't know I'd have, and instead of dwelling on it, pondering it, wondering if my nursing him is the right thing to do or not, I just let it happen.

The cracks in my heart fuse together, the broken pieces become one again, and every fiber in my body tells me one thing and one thing only.

He is mine.

My fingers trace down his tiny face, feeling the softness of his skin, and I realize something: He has light hair. Light hair with reddish highlights. Like mine.

Jack. My son. My body and heart have always known he's mine, and now I understand, I believe, that of course I tried to take him.

He is mine. He belongs with me. I belong with him.

How could I not remember this? Holding him like this? Being with him? A sob rips through my chest, pushing out from my throat and filling the room as I struggle with the truth.

This is my son, and she took him from me.

Rosalind took my baby.

I play with his fingers as he wraps his tiny digits around

mine. I'm startled by the color of his eyes. They are cornflower blue. Like mine.

He stares up at me, and I swear he's smiling even though I know he's too young for that. I memorize his features, his every perfection.

I glance over at the door and, for a moment, just a brief moment, I'm filled with a hatred toward Rosalind, for what she's done, for how she's stolen my baby from me and hasn't said a single word to me since then.

Instead, she's blocked me from her house, from her children, from her life.

My teeth grit as I push down that growing anger and focus instead on this moment with Jack. I don't know how many moments like this I can get with him, but I need to do everything in my power to make sure I get them.

I glance up at the tall armoire in the corner and freeze. There's a camera there, pointed right at me. I blink a few times and slowly check the rest of the room, hoping to not make it obvious.

There's another one on the dresser, pointed right toward the crib.

They know I'm here. Or they will know, if they don't already.

Why two cameras? We never had any for the girls when they were born.

The realization of my life hits like a slap to the face. They stole my baby from me and now they're doing everything to make sure I don't take him back.

Except, I will. But to do that, I'll need to find proof that he is my son before I can do anything. But who do I trust to help me?

I lean my head close to his, taking in his smell. All the nights when my heart has broken into a million little pieces fade away as I rock him to sleep.

Returning him to the crib is the hardest thing I've ever done. Walking away from him feels like I'm abandoning him, but I know the Eatons. I know what they're capable of. I know that to get my son back, I'll need to do things I never thought I could.

When it comes to the Eatons, "fair" isn't a word in their vocabulary.

THREE

"What are you doing here?"

I spin around, heart roaring in my ears, palms slick, and find Rosalind in the doorway: hair pulled back into a loose ponytail, cardigan buttoned wrong, her summer dress creased like she fell asleep in it. She clutches her sweater like she expects it to hold her bones together.

"You're not supposed to be in here," she says. "Why are you?" Her eyes are wide, mascara smeared, lips trembling.

I step away from the crib.

"Rosie, I—"

She cuts me off like she's snipping a thread. "Are you here to take him again? Scream at me about what a terrible friend I am? Do you... do you still hate me?" She flinches, as if realizing the brutality of her accusation.

I probably deserve it. I don't remember ever telling her I hate her; in fact, I don't remember doing anything like what she says, but the possibility hangs in the air like the aftershock of a gunshot. I close my eyes, try to bring up the memory, but there's nothing.

My heart thuds as her words hit like arrows. But then I see Jack, how peaceful he looks, and I don't apologize.

I may not remember saying the words, but I understand why I would have.

"I'm not angry with you," she says, voice dropping, and she steps into the room with a kind of wavering resolve. "I want you to know that. I'm not angry with you." She repeats herself, as if the extra syllables can plug the holes where forgiveness leaks out. "I don't blame you, not at all."

My throat is too tight to let any of the words I want to say escape, so all I do is nod. Nod, and remind myself to keep my cool, that if I want to get my son back, I need to be smart about my next words.

"It's so good to see you." I infuse my voice with warmth and hope she doesn't hear the lie. Stepping away from the crib, it feels like I'm wrenching my own teeth out, one by one, but I do it. She needs to see me retreat. She needs to believe I'm harmless, that the only thing I'd ever cradle too hard is my own regret.

She glances at the crib, then at me, then back at the crib, before she pivots and leaves the room. "Come with me downstairs?" It's not a request. She expects me to follow, and I do, but not before one last look at Jack—his lashes so long they could sweep a heart clean off the floor.

She heads straight through the kitchen to the back porch. By the time I make it there, Rosalind has slumped into a wicker chair, grabbed the nearest blanket, and wrapped it around herself like armor. The chair looks too big for her, as if she's shrunk since having the baby.

"Where is Mabel or that baby nanny?" she mutters, talking to herself more than to me. And then, after a long drag of silence, "This feels awkward, doesn't it?" There's a flicker of the old Rosie in the way her mouth lifts on one side, like she's working up the energy to be kind.

My tongue is a slab of stone in my mouth.

She leans forward, elbows on the blanket, her hand reaching out, and for a second I imagine she's going to beg my forgiveness, admit she knows what happened and help me get my son back. That together, we'll find a way to rewind the last few weeks and give us all a different ending.

Instead, she just says, "You know I would never take your baby from you, right?" She presses her palm against the back of my hand, fingers clammy and unfamiliar. "I'm so sorry, Trina. I know what it's like to lose a baby. I don't blame you for what happened. I want you to know that."

My hand recoils before I even think about it. "And yet, somehow, I'm banned from the house and I'm not even allowed to see the girls."

She sighs, a sound that's become her signature. "And yet, here you are, so it's not all that bad, right?"

"I came to return some mail, and I heard Jack crying." Here I am, explaining myself even when she hasn't asked me to.

"It's okay. I won't tell Marcus," she says softly. "We just... we both need time. Time to heal, to adjust."

The words make my stomach twist. I picture all the times I've had to explain the concept to the twins: how healing means the scrape stops bleeding, but the pink skin never looks the same. Healing doesn't erase the wound; it just covers it so you're not always aware of the pain anymore.

"And the girls? How are they?" I miss them more than I thought possible. "They must think I abandoned them."

Her face brightens, but only slightly. "They don't think that at all; get that out of your head. They're good. Honestly. And so in love with little Jack. You were right—they're amazing with him. They miss you, too, to be honest. They keep asking if they can go down to visit."

"Please let them."

She looks down at her hands then up at the view beyond the porch, where the Alberta sky threatens rain in the next few hours. "I'll miss them if they leave."

The words catch me off guard. "Miss them?" I lean closer, pulse quickening. "Why? Where are they going?"

She doesn't answer, just keeps staring at her own clenched knuckles. Eventually she tells me, "They might visit their grandmother for the summer."

Everything goes sharp at the edges. "But... that's not what we planned," I say. "We had the whole summer mapped out, remember? The girls, summer camp, the two of us. I was going to come back in a month. Light duties, you said." My voice rises, and it's only when she flinches that I realize how tightly I'm gripping the armrest.

Her lips thin. "This isn't about you. It's for them. For all of us." She's lying, I know it, but I can't figure out why. There's a hole in her logic, and it pulls at me like a riptide.

"This is because of me, isn't it?" I don't hide the accusation. "Because you don't trust me around them anymore."

She still won't meet my eyes. "It's because we both need time. You need time to mourn, and throwing you back into the family after everything that happened, after losing your baby—"

"Don't." My word is sharp as a snapped bone.

"Don't what?" She blinks, the question raw, an almost challenge.

My left eye twitches as a throbbing pain lands behind it. I try to relax my jaw, knowing the clenching is what's giving me a headache, but the more I try to relax, the more tense I become. I rub my thumb along my forefinger and push myself to my feet.

There's so much I want to say as I look down at her startled face. Her brows furrow together in a question but I press my lips tight, refusing to say a single word.

Don't you dare talk about my son as if he's dead. Don't

pretend to understand what I'm going through. Don't gaslight me right now.

I say nothing. Instead, I walk away.

FOUR

I find myself down at the barn, leaning against a wooden post as the cowboys exercise the horses. The summer sun beats down on my shoulders and I feel a slight burn on the scar that peeks out from the top of my sundress. Years ago, an ember from a fire that changed my life burned into the skin just above my breasts. A slightly faded phoenix tattoo now covers it.

Growing up in the city, I read books about living on a ranch, watched the old Western movies, but to actually live it... I would come out here, watch the cowboys move cattle into the chute as dust billowed around them in thick clouds kicked up by the hooves and the steady shuffling of boots. In the beginning, I'd pinch myself to make sure I wasn't dreaming.

I don't pinch myself anymore.

The horses scare me. The men stink worse than an overripe bag of garbage left in the sun for too long, and the dirt clings to your skin, making you feel like there's always a layer of something on you.

And the smell. Most of the time, the smell of manure has me gagging. I swear that's why I had morning sickness for so long.

Moving here, back then, was a dream come true. Who knew girls like us, with our background, could live a life like this? When I first agreed to come to work for Rosalind and help raise her twin babies, my answer was immediate. I never told her I had ulterior motives for coming. When she first introduced me to the boy who swept her off her feet, there was something about him that seemed familiar. Familiar and off.

Rosalind and I have been friends for a very long time, but she has no idea that I didn't just come here to be a nanny to her children. I came to prove just how evil the Eaton men really are.

"Well, if this isn't the best sight of the day." I turn around and find Wyatt coming toward me on his horse. "I was wondering if you'd come." He gives me his boyish smile complete with dimples before jumping down. He ties his horse to the fence post, pulls off his hat and kisses my cheek.

"And miss that stench?" I wrinkle my nose and push him away. "When did you last shower?" He looks like he's put in a hard day. His hat-head hair is starting to curl at the edges which means he'll be bugging me for a quick trim soon.

He sniffs his armpits and shrugs. "Oh, honey, that's just the smell of a hard day's work, that's all. We cowboys wear this stench with pride."

I do my best to smile but it's hard. He rests his tanned forearms on the wood behind him, leaning back so his face stares up at the sun, and his quiet presence puts my soul at ease.

"What's going on in that pretty little head of yours, TeeTee?" His use of the girls' nickname is what I needed. "Are you okay? You look a little piqued. Why don't you let me get one of the trucks and drive you back?" His dark green eyes narrow as he looks me over.

"I saw Jack," I admit. Of all the people who are in my life, he's the only one left I know I can trust completely.

"Huh. Is that so?" He doesn't sound too surprised. "And how was that?"

"It was good." There's a sigh in my voice that I know he hears. The corners of his lips twitch. "He's perfect."

He says nothing.

"And no, I didn't try to take him again."

His head cocks to the side and I feel bad for saying that.

"I'm going to call the doctor." My voice is so quiet that I'm not sure he hears me. But the quick dart of his head as he looks me directly in the eyes tells me he has.

"What's wrong? Are you feeling okay?" The concern in his clipped tone is so very clear.

"No, no, nothing like that." I swallow hard. "I never received a birth certificate."

The way he cocks his head: He doesn't understand. Of course he doesn't. Why would he?

"Seeing Jack, I..." I stop because I don't know how to word the feeling in my heart. Giving voice to what I know deep down... it makes it real. Telling Wyatt, it places the burden on his shoulders as well.

The last thing I want to do is put him in the middle.

"Say it." The quiet authority in Wyatt's voice is all the bolster I need. Maybe he's thought it as well. Maybe he knows what happened but hasn't wanted to say anything without proof, too.

"Jack is my son." The wind carries my words far away from me, from my heart. Anyone other than him would tell me it's crazy talk, that it's just postpartum depression or something.

"Do you really believe Rosalind would steal your baby?"

I take a little too long to answer.

Wyatt holds out his palm. "Hand me your phone," he says.

I unlock it and pass it over. I watch as he pulls up the number for the doctor's office and hits the dial button. He hands it back.

"What...?" I'm baffled as I hold the phone up to my ear and listen to it ringing.

"Ask them. You need closure. You need to know for sure and you also need permission to say it out loud, so that you don't think it's all in your head. So ask them."

It keeps ringing and then I get the voicemail option. "This is... um, Trina Emmet. Ahh... I need a copy of the birth certificate of my baby. It's been three weeks. You can email it to me; I think you have my email on file." I rattle off the address, just in case, and then quickly hang up. When I turn back, I notice Wyatt watching me with an intensity that scares me.

"I'm not crazy," I say.

"Never said you were."

"But you don't believe me?"

He rubs his hand over his face, leaving dirt streaks in its wake. "I won't choose between you and Rosie, you know that."

His words are a dagger to my heart. His stance has always been the same: He's never chosen one over the other, always supported and loved us both equally, and I've always known that, but...

"Are you keeping an eye on me because of what happened? Is that why you come by every night, because Marcus or maybe Rosalind told you to?"

He snorts. "Whatever gave you that idea?" he asks. "Marcus wouldn't order me to go see you. He knows better than that."

His reassurance wraps me in the warmth of his love but it doesn't escape me that he doesn't comment on Rosalind.

"That doesn't answer my question."

His lips thin, his expression serious. "Am I worried about you? Yes. You need closure," he repeats. "And you need someone to believe in you, believe that you're not imagining things. I'll always have your back, you know that."

"Why didn't you say anything?" I ask.

"That I've been worried? I tell you that almost every night when I visit."

He does? I try to search my memory, but there's nothing.

"I bring you bags of groceries so you eat, and pick you wild-flowers to put a smile on your face. We watch stupid romcoms every night, just so I can hear that sarcastic giggle of yours. I'm an action man, not a wordsmith, Trina."

That's true. He has done all that. Now that I think about it, I've seen him more than anyone else. Even more than Marcus.

"Thank you," I say, "for checking in on me like you have. I do appreciate it."

He barely gives me a nod. I know Wyatt well enough to know there's more being said with his silence than with his words.

I think about the nights he comes by, when we sit on the couch watching TV and not speaking. I think about how he lets me curl up beside him, his arm around me, my head on his shoulder, as the tears fall and I use his shirt as a tissue. How he came and lay beside me in bed when I couldn't move because of my grief.

He looks like he's about to say something but stops.

He stares at something behind me, and a wedge of anxiety takes hold of my spine and causes goosebumps to crawl over my skin.

FIVE

The sound of boots scuffing against dirt has me turning, one hand gripping the post for stability.

One of the Eaton twins is walking toward us. Damn it. Rosalind must have told him I was at the house, in Jack's room.

"Bet he's here to check in on little Matty," Wyatt mumbles.

"How is Mabel's grandson doing?" I ask, relieved at the momentary change in subject.

"He's a natural, go figure." Wyatt sighs, then straightens as Trent lifts a hand and waves.

"Hey, boss," Wyatt calls out. When it comes to Trent, Wyatt has no problem giving the man his due. It's obvious he respects him, and I've never seen Wyatt attempt a power play with Trent, unlike with Marcus.

"I just received a call from Officer Jardin. One of the crew got in a bit of a mess last night at the bar. Can you go pick him up?" Trent looks out over the horses in the exercise pen and shakes his head. "He can pay me back for saving his ass by mucking out the stalls for the next week. If he can't handle that shit, he can't handle my horses. Got it?"

Wyatt replaces the hat on his head and nods. "The new guy,

right? He had the night off, but when he didn't make it back this morning, I figured he'd slept in his truck."

"Well, he slept in a cell instead."

"I'll handle it," Wyatt says, his lips a firm line of disapproval. He's been here almost seven years, and it didn't take the men long to realize he keeps a tight hand on his crew.

"Make sure he learns the lesson this time. This is strike two, and I don't like using up favors on stupid stuff like this. Next time, he can rot in that cell. He's just lucky I'm the one Jardin called and not Marcus."

Wyatt rubs the back of his neck. "The kid is a handful. He might need more than a week of horseshit duty, but I'll get it figured out."

Trent steps away while he answers his phone. Wyatt swears softly under his breath. "I knew hiring that kid was a mistake, but he's a Marcus hire. Any other ranch and he'd be in jail already."

"The power of the Eatons at work," I say, repeating a phrase he's said to me often. Some of the staff like to joke that the Eatons are so rich, they could get away with murder if they wanted, and they're probably not far off.

He nods. "Some days I don't know if I want to thank Rosalind for getting me this job or curse her." His words are serious, but I see the hint of a smile that plays at the corners of his lips.

"You curse Rosie? That would be the day. Go on, go deal with that, and then come by later tonight if you have time," I tell him.

"You'll let me know if the doctor's office calls?" Wyatt takes off, holding the reins of his horse. He looks over his shoulder, and I give him a thumbs up.

I glance over at Trent and notice he's watching me. He's serious, his eyes searching mine with something that looks like concern.

I feel like I need to apologize for getting caught, but that's the last thing I want to do.

"Anything I need to know about?" he asks, his voice warm but weighted. "About the doctor?"

"I..." I pause, judging my words, making sure I say the right thing. "I never received a birth certificate for my baby." When his eyes narrow, I can't tell if this bothers him or if he's upset. "Unless it was sent to you and just misplaced?"

He shakes his head. "No, I haven't received anything yet. Why don't you let me follow up on that for you, okay?"

"Isn't that odd? I mean... shouldn't we have something by now?"

He gives me a quick look before I hear the shuffling of stones beneath his feet. "It was a complicated night, you going into labor like you did and, well, losing the baby. The documents are probably still being processed, that's all."

That's all? That sounds like a weak excuse, and he knows it.

"I know you were up at the house," he says. I catch my breath and wait for the consequence. "It's... it's okay."

The air rushes out from my lungs with a woosh. "I will never hurt Jack." It's a promise I will carry for the rest of my life.

"I know."

Trent Eaton is a man I admire in more ways than I've ever let myself admit. For being from one of the wealthiest families in Western Canada, he's very down to earth, relatable, and even... fun, if that's the right word to use. He knows how to relax and ease tense situations yet still get to the truth of matters when needed, which is probably why he's the face of the company while Marcus is the one who runs everything.

Together, they are a powerful dynamic.

"How did Rosie seem?" One simple question, and yet his whole countenance changes. It's like my answer carries the weight of his world.

"Tired," I say, feeling like I need to be careful. "Why?"

"I'm worried about her." He exhales, running a hand over his jaw. "She's... having a hard time, and I don't know what to do. I've never seen her like this before, and honestly, it scares me."

I swallow hard and don't know how to respond, so I just say, "I heard about the girls going away for the summer."

"Yeah, it'll be quiet here this summer. Different."

My heart crumbles a little at that. "Can I see them before they leave?" I hate that I have to beg to see the girls I've practically raised.

"Are you sure? It's not too soon?"

"I'm sure. I don't know what I'm going to do without them being around, you know? We had so many plans for the summer."

A cowboy whistles in the background. I watch the men in action as they guide the steers around the pen. I know their job isn't easy, and that it can be dangerous and even life-threatening, but right now, it looks almost simple.

I also see little Matty, not so little anymore.

"Nice to see Mabel's grandson out there," I say.

There's a look on Trent's face I can't quite read. "He'll be around for the summer."

I thought Matty was well liked, but I'm not getting that from Trent's tone right now.

"It's crazy how much he looks like you and Marcus—have you ever noticed that?"

He glances over toward where Matty is standing, almost mirroring Trent's stance right now. Trent must notice because he straightens and pushes his shoulders back.

"He looks like every other wannabe cowboy who comes here to learn," Trent fires back.

"Sorry, I didn't mean..." I don't finish my sentence because Trent walks off, leaving me to stand alone. He pulls out his phone and starts talking, his back to me, so all I can hear is the rise and fall of his voice.

When he returns, I bite my lip to stop myself from apologizing again for my obvious gaffe.

"Can I ask a favor?" Trent asks, taking me by surprise.

"Sure," I reply, though I have no idea where this is going.

"It's about Rosalind. She... needs help, but she won't ask for it. You know how she is, stubborn to the core, believing she can do all things, all at the same time."

I nod because I do know my friend. Or, at least, I thought I did. The friend I knew wouldn't have stolen a child.

"What does the doctor say?"

Trent sighs. "Postpartum psychosis. I had to do some late-night googling to understand that diagnosis. I figured she was depressed, you know? But it's more than that..."

Psychosis? That's serious. "Is she a danger to herself? To the girls? To the baby?" My insides twist with worry.

Trent's face falls. He isn't just worried—he's burdened. He carries it in the way he holds himself, in the exhaustion behind his eyes.

"If by 'danger' you mean completely ignoring Jack, then yes. She doesn't believe he's real. She'll only hold him if Marcus or I force her to. She blocks out his cries... Basically, she acts as if he doesn't exist. That's not... that's not Rosalind."

This is shocking. That's the exact opposite of the woman I know and respect, but it also explains why she didn't check in on Jack today when he was crying.

"I'm not sure what I can do to help," I say.

He shoves his hands into his jean pockets and bows his head. "Maybe just... keep an eye on her?"

"When I'm not allowed to be at the main house?"

He doesn't say anything, not for a while. We stand in silence until he turns, and I can see that he's wrestling with whatever he's about to say next.

I look back at the cowboys in the pen, watching them work in harmony. My life, until coming here, was anything but harmonious. The only real stability I've ever had has been with Rosalind. Before, when we were teenagers, and now, as adults. My life is so tightly woven with hers that I don't know where I begin and she ends. Or I didn't, until now. Now, I'm not sure I know who she is at all. But maybe she doesn't either, if she's dealing with postpartum psychosis.

"We both love Rosalind, right?" His voice is small, his question full of loopholes.

"We do."

"Then can we agree to put her first? Above everything else? I need... I need my wife to be okay, and the only person she's ever really trusted is you."

"She has Wyatt, too," I remind him.

Trent half chuckles. "You don't have to remind me. But right now... I know it's a big ask, considering, but..."

Considering? Did he just say that? Considering what? That he stole my child?

At the same time, I realize the open door for what it is.

If I say no, I'm blocked from the house, from my son.

If I say yes, I'll have full access to him, and to find the proof that I need. And to even find out why my best friend stole my son and thought I wouldn't notice, or that once I did, I'd be okay with it.

"Your family is my family. It's always been that way and you know it," I remind him. "Of course I'll be there for Rosie."

And for Jack, too.

SIX

ROSALIND EATON

Jack's little fist is clenched tight around my finger as he stares up at me with eyes that remind me of Trina. He's perfect. Perfect and beautiful and he has an old soul vibe to him, something so different than when my girls were born.

When he looks at me, it's like he's reading me, judging me, trusting me, and a spread of warmth wraps around my heart, just like it does whenever I'm with Trina.

She is someone who has always loved me, always been on my side, through thick and thin, and I don't know what I'd ever do without her.

These past few weeks have been hard.

"But we're going to get through it, aren't we, little one?" I reach for a little black lamb and hold it out for him. He lets go of my finger and reaches for the sheep, and I know the smile on my face illuminates the room. How can it not? He's so perfect.

There's a thud of the back screen door and then heavy steps on the old wood floors. I set the lamb down and quickly leave Jack's room, keeping tight to the wall and making it into my bedroom before the heavy tread starts up the stairs.

I settle in the chair, drape a blanket around my legs, and grab the journal, opening it to a blank page.

I calm my breathing and I wait. Wait and listen. But there's no sound, no noise, just blissful silence. It takes me a few moments, but I let myself relax.

I'm supposed to use this journal to acknowledge my feelings, to find a way to drag the emotions from my mind to my fingers. The first step in accepting how I'm feeling is to acknowledge it, or so Dr. Harmon says.

But how am I feeling right now? I have no idea. There's nothing.

Just like there's been nothing for the past three weeks, ever since that night.

It's the only way I know how to survive this.

I'm told I died that night. My heart stopped for exactly seventeen seconds. Seventeen seconds when I no longer existed.

I struggle to wrap my head around that.

I was dead. Now I'm not.

Death changes a person. It's changed me, and not for the better. That fog within my brain refuses to lift, and there's no vibrancy with life anymore.

I should be outside playing with our girls, but even thinking about being with them, seeing them, and spending time with them exhausts me.

When did my own children start exhausting me?

Never. Until now.

There's a cry from the other room, but it doesn't last long. Someone is there with Jack.

I pick up my pen and write: *Seventeen seconds. That's how long it takes to lose yourself. To come back... wrong.* I set the pen down and close my eyes.

The quiet is nice. Days have been merging lately. The present mingles with the past until I'm not sure which is which.

"Rosalind."

My breath hitches, and my shoulders push back as I take a second to prepare myself before forcing a smile.

"Rosalind."

My name is called again, this time with a hint of expectation. I twist and see my brother-in-law, Marcus, standing there, holding something in his arms.

I sigh. Why does he keep doing this? Why do I let him?

"Didn't you hear little Jack crying?" His Prince-Charming-like face frowns, and he gives a little *tsk-tsk*. "I thought we talked about this, Rosalind," he says, his disappointment with me very clear.

"Marcus, I'm tired," I say.

"Your son is crying." Marcus crosses the floor and sits on the edge of the bed, holding his arms out toward me.

I take the object from his arms, just like he wants me to.

"There you go," Marcus says, adjusting the blanket around the baby. "I think he's hungry. When did you feed him last?"

"We have the baby nurse for that," I remind him.

"Grace is only here to help, but you need to be feeding him. It'll help with the bonding." Disappointment laces through Marcus's words. "I thought we discussed this?"

I don't look down at the thing in my arms. I can't. It's like I'm physically unable to tilt my head.

"How is your journaling going?" He takes the notebook from my lap, frowning as he looks at the words I wrote. He slowly closes the notebook and sets it on the table beside me.

We're about to have a conversation I have no interest in having.

"Rosalind, you remember what the doctor said, don't you?" His tone is calm, but the accusation is still there.

Once upon a time, we had a good relationship. In the beginning, it was easy—how could it not be? Marcus wanted Trent to be happy, and I made Trent happy; thus, the three of us were all happy.

Until we weren't, and somehow, the fault is all on me, although I don't think that's fair.

It takes two people to screw something up. In our case, it took three.

"I'm trying, Marcus." I don't look down. Why would I? It's only a doll in my arms.

I heard of these reborn dolls used in therapy. That's what's happening here, but no one will admit it. So I play along with their games—to a point.

I don't think anyone understands how much this hurts me, them pretending like what happened didn't. I died and they took my child from me, even though everyone around me—the doctor, my husband, our cook, even the baby nurse—tells me otherwise. But I know the truth, and it's like a shadow-filled cavern inside me that is never-ending, completely engulfing.

"Rosalind?"

Startled, my eyes pop open.

"Didn't you hear anything I've said?"

I blink twice. "I'm sorry," I say as meekly as I can.

He's displeased. "We just want to help you get better."

"I know." My lips tremble as I unsuccessfully struggle to withhold my tears. "I'm just so..." I can't finish the sentence.

"Look at your son." Marcus kneels in front of me, one hand on my arm, the other on my knee. "Look at little Jack. Can you do that for me, please?"

I shake my head a little. "Don't, Marcus, please." I'm begging. I know I am. I don't understand why they are all doing this, why they are all forcing me to act and be how they want me to be.

I wish he'd leave me alone.

I hate how he comes into my room as if he has every right to invade my privacy. I hate how he believes he can command me to do whatever he wants, to feel whatever he imagines I'm supposed to feel.

I hate how he intimidates my husband, that it's always Marcus's decision that carries more weight.

And the hold he has on me disgusts me, destroys me, and even demoralizes me to the point where I'm not sure I'm even who I say I am.

What happened to the me before all of this?

Did she die on the delivery table?

"Where is Trent?" I glance toward the doorway. He was here this morning and promised he wouldn't be gone long. For a man who promised not to leave my side, he's hardly been here lately.

"He's handling a meeting for me," Marcus says with a sigh. He takes the doll from my arms and holds it close to his chest. With gentle circular movements, he rubs its back.

"Why?"

He looks at me funny, like who am I to question him, and yet, I do.

"He was supposed to be here for at least a month. No business trips, just family time. You both agreed." There's a challenge in there, however weak it sounds.

"This client is... a bit of a problem, and Trent has a better connection than I do with them. He smooths things over where I'm like sandpaper." Marcus turns and stares out the window. "I've never handled this client well. When Trent saw the meeting on the calendar, he offered." He looks my way again. "Rosalind, why is this an issue now? You knew this."

No, he didn't tell me he'd be away again. I would have remembered. "When will he be back?"

He shrugs. "Soon, I'm sure. Why don't you go outside and spend some time with those nieces of mine?"

I feel myself sinking deeper into the chair as a wave of

exhaustion flows through me, like a growing tsunami about to pull me under.

"They have a nanny for a reason." I manage to get the words out before my lashes flutter closed.

I wait till he leaves. I wait longer until I know he's gone, down the stairs, outside, and I listen for his truck to pull away. Then I return to Jack, just like I left him, lamb close to his side, except now he's sleeping.

He's perfect. He's perfect and beautiful and I will do everything and anything to protect him.

SEVEN

TRINA

Don't trust anyone.

After my morning walk through the gardens, I came home to find a note shoved beneath my door.

Don't trust anyone.

What the... My heart seizes for a split second as I spin and look around, but there's no one here. I look at the note again, clutched tight in my hand. What does this mean?

Don't trust anyone. Names and faces whirl through my mind as I think about who I do trust, and honestly, that list is very small right now. But who left this?

I think about texting Wyatt, but I'd rather ask him in person, see his facial reaction when he reads the note. This isn't in his handwriting, that I do know.

My phone pings—it's a text from Rosalind.

Will you join me for iced tea on the porch?

Will I join her? Hopefully she'll have Jack with her.

Honestly, I miss our closeness. It only takes one look to know immediately what the other is thinking. Sometimes we'd sit side by side and not say a word, and yet feel like we'd had an hour-long gabfest.

I miss that friend. The friend I thought would be there by my side, raising our babies together. Where did she go? What happened that she would betray me like this?

I fold the note and place it in my pocket. Don't trust anyone.

That includes Rosalind.

Each step toward the main house reminds me of that night three weeks ago, the night when everything in my life changed.

I'd just put up my swollen feet to relax and catch up on a show I'd saved when my phone went off. Mabel, in a panic, told me Rosalind had gone into labor and needed me.

All feelings of exhaustion disappeared as I pulled my sweater on and trudged up the walkway.

It was too early. She was weeks away from her due date. She'd worked so hard to make sure nothing harmed her baby. When the doctor put her on bed rest, she carefully limited her activities. Trent wouldn't let her lift anything heavier than a coffee mug. She only walked small distances and sat outside as much as she could. She did everything right to give her baby the needed time to grow within her, and yet, it still wasn't enough.

I stop and gaze up at the house, at the window that is partially open.

With the window open that night, everyone across the yard could hear her screams.

That night is now my living nightmare.

I'm at the part of my walkway where I can clearly see the porch but I can't be seen, and the first thing I notice is Rosalind, pacing back and forth, holding Jack in her arms.

He's snuggled up tight to her chest and her head is lowered enough I can't see her face, but the way she coddles him, I can imagine.

My heart twists at seeing him, excitement building at the thought that perhaps I can hold him again, when the screen door opens.

Rosalind immediately drops her arms into a loose hold and I want to yell out for her to be careful, that she'll drop Jack.

A woman rushes over instead and takes Jack from her arms. I can't hear what's being said, but Rosalind shakes her head and the other woman leaves.

Jack is gone.

That interaction felt... off. That woman looked... familiar.

"Trina," Rosalind calls out, now noticing me. "You came," she says once I'm close enough to the porch for us to talk without yelling at one another. "I wasn't sure if you would." She sounds different. Pensive and withdrawn, exhausted and sad all rolled into one.

"Is everything okay?"

"Yes, of course, why wouldn't it be?" Rosalind pours me a glass of iced tea and holds it out. I reach for it, but I don't take a sip.

"Was that the baby nurse I saw?" I ask, clearing my throat.

"Grace? Yes."

"How is she?"

"With Jack? She's fine." Rosalind shrugs. "A little overfamiliar at times, but Trent likes her and Marcus apparently vetted her before she arrived, so..."

"Overfamiliar? What does that mean?"

"Sometimes she says things, suggests things, which is fine, but it comes across as... I don't know, condescending, maybe? Trent thinks I'm being too sensitive, that she's just here to help. Her and Marcus seem close."

That last part doesn't surprise me. "And is she? Helping?

Do you like her?" I have so many questions, but I need to know who is taking care of my son.

"It really doesn't matter if I like the woman or not, does it? As long as she does her job."

That doesn't sound like her. She's a micromanager, knowing all the details about everyone around her.

"Have you used her before? She looks familiar."

"What? Grace?" Rosalind shakes her head. "I don't think so. But Marcus says she came with glowing reviews."

"Did you read those reviews?"

"What's with the questions, Trina? She's fine. She was hired to take care of Jack, so she's doing exactly that." There's a tone of exasperation in her voice and I know it's time to drop the subject.

"I was... hoping to see him again?" I'm hesitant to bring it up, but it would be weird if I completely avoided the topic too.

"It's his nap time. How are you healing?" She points to my stomach, changing the subject.

I lightly touch the area. "Pretty good. I had a bit of an infection from the surgery, but that's gone now."

She nods. "Same." She cradles her stomach. "Who would have figured we'd give birth the same night, in the same way, with the same outcome?" She says this last part quietly, as if not wanting me to hear her.

But I do.

"You had a C-section, too?" Why didn't I know this?

I try to recall everything that happened that night, but it's all a blur.

"You didn't know?" She leans forward. "I thought for sure Marcus might have mentioned it."

I shake my head. "No, no one said anything."

She shrugs, like it doesn't matter.

"Did they tell you I died?"

This has me sitting forward, gasping. "Died? What do you

mean died? Like *dead* dead, or there were complications and you could have...?"

"*Dead* dead."

"What the actual—" How could no one have told me this?

"Crazy, I know. The doctor says I can't have any more children, now, too." Her lips pin tight as she looks away.

I'm still trying to wrap my head around this news—that I almost lost my best friend, and no one told me. Not Marcus, not Trent, not even Wyatt. Then what she said hits me.

I heard two babies crying that night. Every time I close my eyes, I still hear those cries. If she has my baby, what happened to hers?

"Rosalind, what did you mean about the same outcome?"

She starts. "Oh, of course. Right..." She sighs. "Of course. Sorry, I shouldn't have said that." Her voice is devoid of any emotion, and a shiver runs up my spine.

I lean forward. "Rosie, did something happen?"

She blinks rapidly, like she's trying to focus on my words and can't. She turns away and stares out into the yard.

"Are you okay?" My voice is lowered, softer, hoping to penetrate whatever shields she has in place. Maybe if I can get through, I'll get the truth. "Rosie, you know I'm here, right? That no matter what happened, we can face it together?"

Her eyes close and a tear trickles down her cheek. "Except, you weren't, were you?" she barely whispers.

"I'm so sorry, love, I really am." I think about how scared she must have been, to have found out she died while giving birth. I can't even imagine...

"They say dying changes you. But they never say how." She fills up her lungs with one long breath and opens her eyes. "And please, don't apologize for anything that happened that night." Her dismissive tone almost hurts. "What you went through, what we both went through... You never have to apologize to me. Sisters never apologize, remember?" She swallows and the tears fall faster now.

I wish someone had told me sooner. I could have lost her forever, and I can't process that.

Maybe they felt I couldn't handle it. Maybe they thought they were doing me a favor.

"Can I ask you a question?" Consider this a little test. I've never known Rosalind to lie to me.

"Of course you can."

"What happened to your baby?"

It takes her a moment to respond. "Nothing happened to my... Trina, what's going on?"

"When I woke up, there were two babies." I see the skepticism on her face. "I heard two distinct cries. I know I did."

She looks like she wants to say something, but she bites her lips together instead. She stands and walks to the edge of the porch, leaning on the railing.

"Did you? I don't know, Trina," she says, not looking at me. "I wish that were true, I really do." A shudder runs through her body. "I can only tell you what I was told. But I think you already know that answer, don't you?"

"That I was hearing things. That my baby died. But... I know that didn't happen."

She turns then, shaking her head. "I wish I had a different answer for you." She lets out a long breath. "Let's talk about something else, okay?" She waves a hand in the air, like she's dispelling whatever tension there is between us.

Rosalind has never been one for tension.

I squash everything I want to ask. Like why she didn't answer my question, like why she says she won't lie, but then she won't tell me the truth, either.

"The girls have missed you. This has been the longest you've been away from them since they were born, isn't it?"

"It is. I'd love to see them."

She nods. "I'll make that happen."

"Where are they, by the way?" I'm surprised neither one of them has come running out to see me.

"Marcus took them down to the barn to see all the baby animals."

We sit in silence for a little bit. There's a distance between us and we've both put up boundaries, something that's never been there before.

"When will Dr. Harmon be back?" I haven't seen him in a few days, not that I'm complaining.

She shrugs. "Trent has him here almost every other day, it's ridiculous."

"But you're doing okay, right? And Jack is too? No issues?"

"Again with all the questions. Seriously. We're all fine. I'm fine. He's fine. The girls are fine. We're all completely fine, okay?"

"I just want to make sure, that's all."

"Jack is fine, Trina." There's something in her tone that feels off. She might as well be talking about one of the foals in the field for the amount of emotion in her voice.

"Do you trust me?" she asks.

I hesitate a little too long.

"Seriously? I've always had your back, Trina. Like you've had mine. I can't believe you right now. I need..." She stops, biting her lip until there's blood.

"I can't do this, any of this, if you don't have my back." There's something in her gaze, a shadow of the woman I know, screaming at me to take notice.

"Rosie, I—"

"If you won't trust me right now, then we have nothing."

As I sit there, trying to understand where she's going with this, she leaves me, stomping into the house with a flash of anger I'm not used to seeing on her.

I hear the sound of footsteps on the wood, drawers opening and closing, and then the screen door slamming open.

She reels her arm back and throws something my way. It hits my chest before sliding down to my lap.

A keychain with one key attached.

The whole world goes silent for one beat, two, and in that lull I realize she's trembling so violently she looks like she might vibrate right off the porch. Her eyes bore into me, wild and wet and unblinking.

"If you don't trust me, then go." She's shrieking now—not a sound I've ever heard from her before, not even in the worst moments in the group home, not when she broke her wrist twice in one summer, not when she realized her firstborn son was gone. "Take Jack," she yells, voice cracking on his name. "If you honestly believe I stole him, then take him! Take him and go"—her voice shreds itself, fracturing into a rattle of air—"and don't ever come back." The last syllables collapse into a whisper, all the oxygen gone from her lungs, everything deflated, devastated, as though she's just confessed to the thing she's most afraid of.

She stands there, hunched and gasping, a wild animal driven into a corner. Her tears, huge and hot, streak her cheeks and soak into the thin gold chain around her neck. I want to cross the porch, wrap her in my arms, hold her together the way I used to when she would wake up from nightmares, but I'm paralyzed, pinned by guilt, by my own confusion, by the sudden, inescapable certainty that I've made everything worse, not better.

I look at the key, then up at her. For the briefest moment I see her as she used to be—brave, loyal, terrifyingly clever—before the layers of perfection and power and domesticity settled over her like coats of paint.

The screen door slams open and Trent is there, all six foot four of him, hair sticking up where he's run his hands through it, shirt half-tucked and boots leaking dirt onto the mat. "Rosie, what the hell?" he says, but in the next instant he takes her in, her hunched shoulders, her streaming face, the way she's clutching at the porch post like she'll slide off the world without it, and his voice turns gentle. "What happened?"

The way he's holding her, with her face hidden against his chest, rocking her like you'd rock a toddler who fell off his bike, it pinches my heart knowing I'm the reason for this breakdown. Rosalind mumbles something into his shoulder. I can't hear, but I do notice the change on his face as he continues to stare my way. It's just us, him and me, and there's no accusation or blame in his eyes, just the naked question: *What did you do?*

I cover the key with my hand. The answer must be written all over my face because I see the exact moment his expression hardens.

"Maybe it's better if you leave," he says, low and quiet, but there's no room for negotiation. He's physically holding Rosie up now with both arms, her knees wobbly, and she's sobbing, really sobbing. He leads her back inside, closing the door in a slow, soft motion that is more final than if he'd slammed it.

What the hell just happened?

I sit there for a long time, the scene replaying in my head until I notice something about the key. It looks like a house key, one Mabel would have, to unlock any door in the house.

Why would Rosalind toss me this? I think back to our conversation, to what was said and what wasn't said, to what could have been code, but I can't find anything.

And yet, I know her. She wouldn't have thrown me this key unless there was a reason.

EIGHT

The key digs into my palm. For the past thirty minutes, I've been sitting on my front porch, creating a plan of where to go and how to get there in the main house, now that both Trent and Marcus are gone.

I watched them drive off the property in separate vehicles, even waved as they passed by, all casual while my thumb traced the metal ridges in my lap.

It's been two days since I last saw Rosalind.

Yesterday, Marcus suggested I give her some space. Wyatt even brought it up last night when he was here for dinner.

I get it. Of course I do. I saw, firsthand, that my friend isn't okay. She disintegrated before my eyes, became a shell of a person I didn't recognize.

I'm worried about her.

She died on the delivery table and I only just found out. She has postpartum psychosis, and from what I've read online, she should be under medical care, not left at home even if loved ones surround her.

It makes me wonder if her dying, if that's why she's so

different. Something like that can fundamentally change a person.

It also makes me wonder what else I'm not being told.

The walk up to the main house always feels longer than it should. It's not the distance but the way it looms on the rise, windows glinting in the sun. I climb the porch steps and am hit with the feeling of being a trespasser. The memory of being asked—ordered, really—to stay away from Rosalind hasn't left me. It prickles that they believe I'm going to harm my friend who is so obviously broken.

I pause, and it's not because there's someone there to greet me but because there's a lock on the door, a matte black keypad that wasn't there the other day.

Is that there because of me?

I reach for the handle on instinct, giving it a quick jiggle, but it doesn't budge. My fingers brush the keypad, and for a second I consider knocking—like a visitor—but the idea fills me with shame. They locked me out. Someone locked me out.

I stand there and stare at the numbers. My mind cycles through possibilities—the girls' birthday, Trent and Rosalind's anniversary, the old gate code—each one a different permutation of numbers that means something to somebody in this house. I try 1111 first because that was always Rosalind's go-to whenever she set a code: the easiest combination, a gesture of trust rather than security. The pad flashes red and gives a sharp electronic beep. I try the girls' birthday next: 0114. Beep. Red. Denied. I try 8888, the old code for the tack shed—Marcus has a thing for repeating numbers—knowing it won't work but hoping anyway. Beep. Red. Still nothing.

I check my phone, scanning for a text or email, anything to suggest the new code. I scroll back through the last week, fingers trembling, but there's only a string of empty reminders, a news article about postpartum psychosis, and a missed call from a number I don't recognize. No code. No explanation. Just silence from the people who are supposed to be my family.

I lean back against the siding, the sun hot on my face, the wood cold at my shoulders, and I want to scream, to call Trent or Marcus and demand to know why I'm locked out, but I already know the answer. It's about me. It's about the baby. It's about her.

I wipe my hands on my jeans and press 5225. Jack's name in numbers. The pad flashes green, a quiet click as the lock disengages, and for a heartbeat, I just stare at the handle in disbelief. It worked. I'm in.

It's all quiet other than the low hum of music that fills the space. I slowly make my way through the house, trying every door on the main floor, but none of them are locked.

I wonder if this key is for the office upstairs.

One step at a time, I make my way up the stairs and pause at the landing.

I'm only met with silence.

I'm halfway toward the closed office door when I hear Jack crying through the partially opened nursery door. I freeze, sure that I'm about to get caught. My gaze scans the hallway, looking for any cameras, but I see none.

Jack keeps crying; the sound is heart-wrenching, and I hate that no one is responding to him.

I wait it out, listening for any sound of movement from Rosie's room, the girls' room, or even from the nursery itself, but there is none.

Finally, I can't handle it anymore. I pivot, the key unimportant, and walk into the nursery, where my little boy is crying in the crib, his arms flailing about.

I pick him up, holding him close, and he calms.

"I'm here, little one, I'm here," I whisper as I rock him in my arms. The ache I felt in my soul is gone and I lean my cheek against the top of his head, breathing in that new baby smell that's so intoxicating.

"Shh," I hush over and over as I rub his back in small circles. I make my way to the rocking chair and sit, holding his small body tight to mine.

I hear a noise. Rosalind stands in the doorway, arms across her chest. I can't quite read her.

"What are you doing?" she asks, her eyes wide.

I glance down at Jack and smile. "I'm holding—"

"Put it down. Put it down now." She rushes forward, hands outstretched like she's going to take the baby from me.

I tighten my hold and lean back as far as I can in the chair.

"Stop," I say, with more force than I intended, and she does. Her knees touch mine, she's that close, but her hands drop, and she stares at me with such a look that I feel shamed and bewildered at the same time.

"How can you?" She barely whispers the words before her hand covers her mouth, and she backs away, one step at a time. "I thought you, of all people... that you wouldn't go along with this... with him, especially after everything... I thought I knew who you were." A sob rips through her. She turns, rushing away.

I don't move, not until I hear her bedroom door slamming shut. Jack stirs in my arms, and I continue to rub his back, but I'm not sure if I'm doing it to soothe him or myself.

What is she accusing me of? I've never seen that look in her eyes before, like I've broken her heart, betrayed her trust.

Climbing to my feet, I go to put Jack back down in the crib, but he instantly fusses, so I bring him back to my chest and hold him close.

I make my way back out into the hallway, Jack in my arms. Knocking on her door, I call out her name.

"Go away."

"Let me in, please?"

"Are you holding... it?" Her voice is nearer now, just on the other side of the door.

It?

"Please open the door, Rosie." I gentle my voice, hoping to coax her to listen.

The door slowly opens, and at first, her eyes are soft, but they harden when she notices Jack in my arms.

"Why?" The word comes out in a hard breath.

"I tried to put him down"—I give her a smile—"but then he started fussing."

Her brows scrunch together. "Stop it, Trina. Give me the stupid doll." She holds out her hand.

I hesitate. How do I do this? What do I say? How do I handle this?

Adjusting Jack so he's lying in my arms, his face visible, I swallow hard.

"He's not a doll, honey," I say with as much gentleness as possible. "Look, you see how his lips move?" I touch his hand with the tip of my finger. "See how he grabs onto me?"

Her gaze flickers down then up to mine. "How did you do that?"

"I didn't. He did. He's not a doll, Rosie." My voice breaks and eyes well as I watch her tear her gaze from me back down to Jack.

His lips pucker as I lightly bounce him in my arms, and little mews escape his mouth. I make little shushing sounds and he settles.

"No. You're making him..." She reaches out and touches Jack's fingers, gasping in shock. "But he's..." She pulls back. "I don't understand," she mumbles, stepping backward into the middle of the room.

I open the door and follow her. "He's real," I say, hoping that if I say it enough, if she sees him move enough, she'll believe it.

"He wasn't," she says, hitting her rocking chair with the back of her legs. She drops hard.

"What do you mean?" I come in closer, keeping my steps small.

She looks up at me with wide eyes that are suddenly full of tears. "He wasn't…" she repeats, her voice hijacked by tears. "I sat here, here, and Marcus"—she pauses, trying to find some control, never taking her gaze off of me—"he brought my baby to me, placing him in my arms, except he wasn't a baby, he wasn't Jack." Her voice rises with hysteria. "He was a doll, Trina, a doll."

I glance down at Jack. This is not a doll. This is a precious little peanut who rests peacefully in my arms.

"That doesn't make sense, Rosie."

Shaking her head back and forth, she wipes her face and swallows hard. "You, of all people, know how he likes to play games. You never trusted him, not for the longest time, remember?"

I remember. I remember thinking he was the man who'd taken advantage of Rosalind when she was a teenager and left her pregnant. I remember vowing to get revenge and then hating Trent when I first met him because I thought he was Marcus, not realizing they were identical twins. I remember the fights Rosie and I would get into over it all.

She never remembered the guy who took advantage of her. We'd been young, at a party, and of course there was alcohol involved. I saw her climb the stairs with someone who looked an awful lot like the Eaton boys, but she swears it was someone else.

I've always known the truth. That's why I'm here. I've never told Rosie that, though. I've let her believe I've dropped it, that I've been wrong in believing the Eaton boys could be so evil.

"That was different, Rosie," I say even though it tears me apart to do so.

"Maybe it wasn't. I swear it, Trina, Marcus handed me a doll and pretended like he was real. Sometimes when I go check on him, it's just a doll in the crib. I think they're in on it together, him and the baby nanny he hired." Her voice breaks with a loud snap, like a dried-out twig.

She's exhausted. Moving to kneel by her side, I take her hand and place it on Jack's chest. "Do you feel this?" I ask. "A doll doesn't breathe."

She blinks fast and furious, hiccups now rattling through her body.

"He's real..." She barely gets the words out before tears flow down her cheeks.

She doesn't ask to take him, and I don't offer to give him up, so instead, we sit there, together, and the quiet starts its healing process in our hearts.

I think about her words, her accusations toward Marcus. I want to say that he would never be so cruel, but I know better. Marcus can be a lot of things, whenever it suits him. Charming, irresistible, manipulative, and definitely cutthroat.

But making her believe her child is a doll? That's heartless.

NINE

Shortly after I leave the house, dust rises as a black SUV makes its way up the long driveway. It stops beside me and the side passenger door pops open.

"Trina!" Tears swell and gather on my lashes as Riley and Addison jump down from the vehicle and run toward me. The hollow in my heart fills at the happiness on the girls' faces. I half bend, opening my arms, waiting for them to plow into me.

"Girls..." Marcus calls out, his voice a low growl, and the girls slow, stopping just short of me. "Thank you," he says as they whip their heads to look back at him. "Remember what I said." There's a hint of strictness to his voice that has me standing tall and giving him a look.

"I told them they had to be gentle with you," he says with a shrug, "or the next time we go for ice cream, I'll be the only one eating and they'll have to sit there and watch me."

It's hard to hide my smile, considering the girls' eyes are wide with disbelief.

"He won't, right, Trina?" Riley whispers. From the way she looks over her shoulder, she's not sure if she believes him or not.

It's crazy how much I've missed them. "Has Uncle Marcus

ever lied to you?" It's really, really hard not to let a smile creep onto my face.

Her body straightens as her lips quirk like she's actively trying to think if he's ever lied.

"He does tease us a lot," Addison says.

I nod. "That's true." Marcus heads our way, his movements silent, like he's stalking the girls. At the last minute, he roars and scoops the girls up in his arms, their squeals ringing in my ears as I laugh.

This man is multifaceted. Over the years, my feelings for him have become complicated. I started off hating him, but seeing how he is with his nieces, that hatred has disappeared and something else has filled its place. I can't name that new "something," though, because I can't quite put a finger on it. Respect? Admiration? Caution? There are multiple versions of him, depending on the situation, and I guess I like some versions more than others.

Once he releases them, the girls rush my way, smothering me with hugs and chattering up a storm. I keep them close, brushing my hand down their hair, nipping their cheeks with my fingers, all the while listening and trying to keep track of the stories they're telling me.

"Okay, okay." Marcus finally steps in. "Why don't you go pick some wildflowers for Trina? I think she needs a new bouquet to replace the dead one sitting on her kitchen table." He gently pulls the girls away from me and points toward a bed of wildflowers on the other side of the driveway.

I smile, loving how the girls race off to the field to pick me flowers. "How do you know they're dead?"

"You know me better than that," he teases. "I see everything."

I want to laugh but the way he said it, I realize he's not joking.

He glances up toward the lighted window. "You were coming from the main house?"

I only nod, not knowing what to say. I could make up an excuse—anything is better than the truth.

"Rosie probably appreciated the company. Trent hated having to leave again."

"I'm worried about her," I say.

"We all are. How was she?"

I shake my head. "Not good. She thought Jack was a doll."

He heaves a sigh. "You were with Jack?" His brows nestle together.

"He was crying, and no one was there to take care of him." I'm not going to apologize for this.

"Where was the baby nurse?"

He's going to be upset about this next part, but there's nothing I can do about that. "Rosalind let her go."

His frown intensifies before he pulls out his phone and dials. "Grace? It's Marcus. Yes, I'm back. Hey, would you mind helping the girls with their bath tonight? Yeah, thanks. See you soon."

He shakes his head as he pockets his phone. "She'll be back here in a few minutes. This isn't the first time Rosie has done this. Typically, Grace knows to call me right away, though."

"What do you mean this isn't the first time?" I feel like I'm wading through a swamp when it comes to knowing what's going on in that house right now.

"She's fired Grace a few times now. The doctor says she's confused. I've got it handled."

Which is his way of telling me to drop it.

"When do the girls leave again?"

"In a few days. Why?"

"I asked Rosalind if I could see them. She said it was okay, but I didn't realize they'd be leaving so soon."

He gives me a funny look. "Rosalind said yes?" He sounds surprised.

"Is that an issue?"

"Well, it really doesn't matter anymore, I guess."

"And what is that supposed to mean?" He's not making sense.

He rubs the back of his neck and glances away, shuffling his feet in the dirt. "She didn't want you to be with the girls alone, that's all."

I blink several times, digesting his words, not believing them.

"Does she not trust me with them? Are you serious, Marcus? I've only watched them since the first day they were born." My heart hurts find out this. He has to be making this up, but when Marcus gives me a slight nod, tears fill my eyes.

"It's not you, Trina, trust me."

I reel back like he hit me. "It's not me? What else is it, then?"

"The psychosis. We just have to be patient, that's all. Anyway, it's a moot point now, isn't it?" he says, changing the subject. "You look... different."

"Really?"

He looks at me like he's seeing me for the first time. "You were smiling."

"Don't I always?"

He leans back on his heels. "Not lately."

Inhaling, I take a few minutes to think about this and realize there's only one cause for that smile. Jack. But I won't say that.

The girls rush toward us. "Daddy's coming," they say, pointing toward a vehicle driving up.

Marcus pulls out his phone, takes a quick look, and shakes his head. "That's Grace. She's going to help with bath time," he tells them. The girls pout, their cute little faces puckered up with disappointment. He hands Riley the bag he'd set beside him. "When you're ready, we'll start reading this new book."

"Oh, what book did you get?" I lean forward so I can see inside the bag. I can't see the cover, but it's a thick novel.

"It's a story about dragons and princesses and fairies," Riley says, her eyes wide with excitement. "It was my turn to pick, and I've been waiting foreeevvvver to read this one." She draws out the word while glaring at her sister. "This book is even longer than the last one."

Addison has her arms crossed over her chest, but she doesn't say a word. She doesn't need to, though. The girls might be identical in most things, but when it comes to story time, they have very different reading preferences. Riley loves anything associated with fairy tales, mythical creatures, and princesses. Addison prefers stories and characters she can relate to, set in modern times.

Grace steps out of the car, waves at the driver, and heads our way.

"Sorry, Mr. Eaton," she says, holding out her hands for the girls. "I meant to call you, but I got sidetracked." She turns to me. "Hi, I'm Grace. You must be Trina." Her smile is warm, but her eyes are ice cold.

"The girls are ready for their bath," Marcus says. "I appreciate you helping us out like this."

"Not a problem. The girls are darlings. So is Jack, the easiest baby I've ever taken care of." She reaches out and lightly touches Marcus's arm. "Anyway, nice to meet you, Trina."

The way he smiles at her, it reminds me of a night when he smiled at me like that too. A night when we sat shoulder to shoulder, watching the sun set in Santorini. A night full of prosecco and laughter, of infinity pools overlooking the Aegean Sea, of careful caresses and smoldering heat. Everything that happened that night had been a surprise and completely wrong. I hated him, hated myself, hated that it had happened at all.

Learning I was pregnant, however, that changed everything. I didn't stop hating him, but I couldn't regret what happened between us because it meant I was going to be a mom.

Grace turns to take the girls into the house, but I notice the way she glances toward me.

Her eyes are daggers, and if we were alone, I'm sure I'd be dead.

TEN

I take the final sip of my coffee just as there's a knock on my door. I know exactly who it is, having watched them skip down the walkway from my kitchen window.

The smile that grows on my face is full and light as I turn the knob.

"Surprise," the girls shout as they jump on the spot from excitement.

"Oh my goodness, you grew at least an inch," I say, kneeling so I'm on their level and opening my arms. They almost bowl me over as they rush forward and wrap me in love, and I adore every painful second of it. My stomach muscles don't, but I do.

"We didn't grow that much, you just saw us last night," Riley teases me, giving my side a little poke.

"Careful, girls, remember what your mother said." Grace stands behind them, holding a basket in her arms. The animosity from last night is gone, but there's no genuine smile.

I look around to see if she's brought Jack, but it's just her and the girls. "It's all good, Grace," I tell her as I rise to my feet. "What did Mrs. Eaton say?"

"They need to be gentle, and if you look peakish in any way, the girls are to leave you alone." Grace's voice has barely any tone inflection. Her outfits tend to match her personality, and today, she's wearing a beige sundress with a white summer cardigan over top.

"Leave me alone? Are you kidding me?" I reach for the basket in Grace's arms, but she steps back.

"I'm also not to let you carry this as it's quite heavy." She pushes past me. "Where should I set this up?"

"Did you bring bubbles?" I ask Riley, knowing full well she did. Blowing bubbles is her favorite thing to do.

She pulls a small container from her pocket and holds it up high.

"Then I think it's obvious we should go outside. What do you say?" I follow the girls, who rush ahead. Riley opens the French door and waits until we've all walked past before she closes it. I smile in thanks and pat her head gently. She's only four, but she tries so hard to be older.

Grace sets the basket down and stands there awkwardly.

"I think we'll be okay for a bit," I tell her. "I'm sure you need to get back to Jack."

She shakes her head. "I'm to stay and help, and make sure you don't overdo it."

"Says who?"

"Mrs. Eaton."

"Well, then, Mrs. Eaton can go suck on a sour candy," I mumble as I glance toward the main house. I don't need a babysitter, for Pete's sake.

"What's that?" Grace asks, her brows arched high.

"You don't need to stay," I say in the kindest way possible, but she hears the hint of steel in my voice. "The girls and I have a lot to catch up on."

"Sorry, but I can't do that. She was very specific." She lifts her chin a smidgen, and I can see the hunger in her eyes for me to argue.

Why does she hate me so much?

"Addison, can you spread the blanket? Riley, how about you take out the food and get it ready? I'll be right back."

I head into the house and wait for Grace to join me before I close the door. "Do we have a problem?" I ask.

Her eyes widen, but I see beyond the pretend surprise.

"I don't know you, and you certainly don't know me enough to dislike me, so I'll ask again, do we have a problem?"

With three slow blinks, Grace's face morphs from naive to haughty. She looks around my living room and shrugs, one that says, *Meh, it's fine.* "You seem to have done well for yourself," she says. "As for a problem, I can't imagine why you'd ask that. I'm doing as I've been told. You of all people should understand that."

Me of all people? What is she talking about?

"Who are you?"

"A simple baby nurse, here to... look after Jack and keep him safe." The smile she gives me is like a hot knife to the soul, and I do everything not to flinch.

"Now, we really shouldn't be leaving the girls outside on their own, don't you think?" She walks around me and opens the door, planting the biggest, fakest smile I've ever seen on her face. "We don't have much time before we need to get back, so if I were you, I'd enjoy this time with the girls while you can."

That feels too much like a threat, but for the life of me, I have no idea why.

"Momma says you need to eat," Addison says as she holds a plate of food out for me. There are crackers and cheese, cut fruit, and small cucumber sandwiches all laid out. "She says if we can get you to eat all of the food on your plate, then we get to make a cake with Mabel after." The way her eyes widen, the excitement that twinkles, how can I disappoint her?

"What kind of cake?" I sit down beside her, my legs tucked beneath me, and notice how Grace takes a seat in the far corner of my back porch. I hold the plate in my lap but don't eat, hoping to distract the girls from noticing. While I know there's no way anyone would have tampered with the girls' food, I still feel cautious.

"Cherry chip with raspberry frosting," Riley mumbles around a bite of her sandwich. "We can bring you some."

I lean forward and lightly touch Riley's nose. "My favorite kind of cake."

"Mine too." Addison gets up on her knees and adds more cheese to her plate.

I've been excited all morning to see the girls, and even though the babysitter has tagged along, I'm not going to let her spoil this visit. They are as much a part of me as I can imagine; it's like they share my DNA, even though that's impossible. I've been with them since they were born, and while I may not be their mother, in my heart, they're my family.

"Are you still sad about your baby?" Riley leans in close, resting her head against my shoulder. "Mommy is sad."

I run my hand down her long hair and untangle the ends with my fingers. "I'm still sad," I say, pulling an elastic band from my pocket. "Here, let's fix that crazy hair of yours."

Once I've fixed her hair, I pull her close and plant a kiss on the top of her head. "Why is your mommy so sad?" The news isn't surprising, but I'm curious about the girls' reasoning. Despite their age, the pair are very intuitive and observant. Riley shrugs as I finish braiding her hair.

I give it a quick little tug. "Shrugging isn't an answer," I say, making sure there's a smile in my voice since she's not facing me.

"She cries a lot and doesn't play with us anymore," Riley whispers.

"Oh, honey." I wrap my arms around her and hold her close. I don't know what to say. Should I apologize for Rosalind, or maybe offer an excuse?

I do neither. "Does it make you sad when she's sad?"

Riley nods. "Mommy should be happy. But little Jack cries a lot, and Mommy stays in her room all the time. He's sad too. That's what Mommy says." Riley grabs a stick and draws random lines on the ground. "Everyone is just... sad."

She looks up at me with doe eyes as if begging me to fix everything.

"We miss you," Riley says, climbing into my lap and leaning in. I ignore the pain against my stomach and wrap my arms around her.

"I miss you, too," I whisper as I kiss her forehead.

I spend the rest of my time ignoring Grace and focusing only on the girls. I notice she heads inside for a bit, but I assume that's to use the washroom. She eventually comes out with a glass of water and stays in the background while I play games, blow bubbles, and tell stories, and my well is slowly refilling thanks to their love.

"Okay, girls, we need to get back." Grace stands and clears up the dishes from our picnic. "Your mom wants us back now, and Jack is awake."

"You can leave the girls here. I'll bring them back." When Rosalind texted this morning that the girls were coming down, I was to have them until lunchtime. I still have over an hour with them.

She shakes her head. "No, actually, I can't. I was given very specific instructions and will be in trouble if I don't bring the girls back now."

That doesn't make sense to me at all. Rosie knows how much I love these girls.

"Mrs. Eaton will not be upset that you left the girls with me, I can promise you that. I'll walk them back when it's time." There's a level of authority in my voice that I know she hears. Her lips purse, and her brows inch together as I see her wanting to argue with me.

"It's not Mrs. Eaton who instructed me to get the girls," Grace says softly.

"Who then?" None of this makes sense. "Trent? Marcus?"

After a very brief pause, she nods. "Mr. Eaton was passing along the message, but he made it clear Mrs. Eaton wants the girls home."

"Do we have to?" Riley looks up at me, imploring me to let them stay.

"I will walk them up," I repeat to Grace. This time, there is no room for arguments in my voice and even though she didn't specify which brother she was talking about, I already know who. "I think I'm more than capable of taking care of the girls."

"But Mrs. Eaton—"

"Tell her it was my idea if you need to. Or tell Marcus. I don't care. If either one of them gets upset about that, they can talk to me personally, all right?"

I glance at the girls. Addison has a sneaky smile, which makes me a little worried, but Riley looks up at me like I'm her hero.

Grace's phone buzzes. She glances down at it. "This is on you then."

"This is getting ridiculous. Just go."

Why would Rosalind have told Marcus she didn't want me to be with the girls all morning, especially after saying I could have them till lunch? What is going on with her?

ELEVEN

ROSALIND

Walking into the bright kitchen, where the mid-morning sun casts the room in a glow, I find Trent standing at the counter, coffee mug in hand, staring down at his phone.

"When did you get in?" I ask, startling him. He quickly puts his phone screen down on the counter.

"A few hours ago," he says. "You were sleeping so soundly, I didn't want to wake you. Where are the girls?"

"Down visiting Trina," I tell him.

Trent slowly lowers his cup. "By themselves? But I thought…"

I catch how he's watching me, unsure of who I am today. I get that. Sometimes, most of the time, I don't feel myself.

"Grace is with them. They should be back soon, actually."

"So you still don't trust her?"

I nibble my lip and think about how to respond. "It's not that I don't trust her. I just… It's for my own peace of mind. She's still healing, and you know how rambunctious the girls can be." Even I hear the lie, but thankfully Trent doesn't mention it.

He brings the coffee cup up to his lips, and I can tell his mind is going a mile a minute.

"What are you thinking?" I ask.

"It's only been three weeks," he says, finally.

That's not an answer, and he knows it.

"I've been worried," he finally admits. "I've been doing a lot of research online in the middle of the night when I can't sleep."

"What kind of research?"

"About postpartum psychosis and—"

I stop him. "Wait, what? Psychosis? Who said that?" My heart quickens at the thought. Is that what's happening with me?

"Dr. Harmon. He, uh..." Trent starts to rub the back of his neck, and I know whatever he's about to tell me, it's bad. "He mentioned a clinic on the coast that deals with this. Marcus even thinks it might be a good idea."

"A good... idea?" I can't believe what I'm hearing.

He doesn't answer for the longest time, and that's all I need to know.

"What kind of clinic?" My brain is in overdrive as I take in all this. They believe I'm so unwell that I need twenty-four-seven care at a facility. I don't know how I feel about that.

"It's called the Briar House. It kind of reminds me of a wellness retreat center, complete with the thermal pools and massage therapists."

While he's talking, I take out my phone and immediately look up this clinic. It looks nice, coastal, expensive, and very private but...

"You won't let them send me, right? I'm not... I don't need that..." I'm looking at the reviews and reading one where they do electric shock therapy. I look up at my husband in panic.

"I don't need to go there, Trent. I swear it. I know I'm a bit off, but I just had a baby and..."

He takes the phone from my hand. "Shhh," he says. "No decision has been made yet."

Yet.

He glances toward the quiet baby monitor on the counter. "I've been worried, that's all. You weren't like this with the girls," he admits.

What do I say to that? I'm sorry? I am. I'm more sorry than I'll ever admit but this isn't all on me. Surely he can see that, can't he?

His phone vibrates on the counter.

"Are you home today?" I ask.

He nods. "I told Marcus I'm not handling any more meetings or clients for the next week."

"I thought you weren't supposed to do them anyway? I mean, I've seen Marcus more than you lately."

He shrugs. "That wasn't the plan, and I'm sorry I haven't been here like I promised I would be."

"Just say no, then."

"I wish it was that easy. Last night was unavoidable, unfortunately. The client requested me personally. Seems he and Marcus don't see eye to eye on a lot of things, and this deal is rather... delicate. We have a lot riding on it."

I sigh. I've never been one to step in between the two or push myself into the business in any way, but his being home for the first month was important to me, and it was something we had discussed as a family.

"As long as you're not avoiding me." It's hard to say this, to show so much insecurity. I've never liked being a weak person.

He hugs me close. "You and our family are the only things that really matter to me. I'm sorry I haven't been here for you like I promised I would be."

I feel his kiss on the top of my head at the same time his phone buzzes again.

A slight frown appears, and there's now a tenseness of his shoulders.

"Do you need to deal with that?"

He kisses me one more time. "I love you," he whispers before he answers the call and walks away.

I stand there, alone in the kitchen, and look out the window. What has happened to us? We used to be so tight, so close, but ever since I gave birth, my husband has hardly been here. It's like he'd rather be anywhere else than with me.

What have I done?

Deep down, I know the answer to that. I've done nothing wrong.

I head up the stairs and pause at the landing to catch my breath when I hear two voices. When did Marcus arrive?

I head toward Trent's office and pause just outside the door. Their voices rise and fall and there's a level of tension between the two I'm not used to. When there's a break in their conversation, I poke my head in to find Marcus sitting on the edge of Trent's office desk, Jack in his arms.

Sometimes, their similarities are overwhelming. As identical twins, only the slight differences make them stand out as individuals. When they are tired, Marcus will limp from an old soccer injury, whereas Trent likes to tilt his head to the right.

All conversation stops the moment they see me.

"I didn't realize you were here," I say, stepping into the room.

Trent is staring down at his phone, his fingers dancing along the screen. He glances up briefly and gives me a quick smile.

"I've been here for a while," Marcus says. "Little Jack was fussing so I figured I'd hold him till Grace gets back. She's on her way."

"I didn't hear him."

Marcus shrugs. "It's all good," he says. "I was there and he's fine." He glances down at the baby, one finger trailing down Jack's face.

I look to Trent but he's still focused on the phone in his hand. His desk is a mess, and I automatically tidy up the mail that's been tossed about.

"It's okay, you can leave it," Trent says.

He's too late. I stack it all in a pile and set it to the side, and that's when I notice an envelope with the Nova Clinic logo on it. The same clinic the three of us visited last year during our family vacation.

"Everything okay?" I wave the letter toward Trent, who snatches it from my hand and tosses the letter in a drawer. "Trent?"

"It's nothing. Just..." He pauses as if searching for the right words.

Marcus interjects. "Just some test results I asked for last time we were there. They were supposed to email them."

"Test results? Are you okay?"

"Just testing the swimmers, that's all." Marcus gives me a sly grin and I grimace in response.

Jack's body arches as he yawns.

"Can I have him, please?" I ask.

"You want to hold him?" Marcus sounds surprised.

I pause and wonder if maybe I shouldn't have offered.

Marcus gives me that suave smile of his, the one that might weaken any other woman's knees but makes my stomach roll. "Of course, he's your son, I just..." He glances toward Trent, like he's looking for help. "You don't usually want to, that's all."

I say nothing. I only hold out my arms and Marcus places Jack in them. I'll admit, the hold is awkward and being watched makes me nervous.

"Where are you going?" There's a slight rise in Marcus's voice as I walk away from him.

"To the nursery." I glance over my shoulder and I see a flash of concern cross his face.

As I leave the room, I hear Marcus ask my husband a question. "Have you called the doctor?"

My steps slow as I wait for his reply.

"Not yet," Trent says. "But this is good, don't you think?"

"I'm just worried," Marcus says. "What if she relapses? What if while she's taking care of Jack something happens again? Should she be alone with him?"

"She's not going to relapse," Trent says, full of confidence. "My wife is back now. She says she's okay and we need to trust her that she is."

"You know what the doctor said, though." Marcus's voice is clear with doubt and worry.

I stop and wait. Considering I have no idea what the doctor said, I want to hear the answer.

"She's okay," Trent says with a firmness I more than appreciate. My husband has my back, and that's all that matters.

"So what happened last week, then?" Marcus asks.

There's no answer from Trent.

Last week? What happened? Standing there, with Jack in my arms, I try to remember, but I can't. My brain is fuzzy, my memory unclear. There's a haze over the past few weeks. The last clear memory I have from before giving birth to Jack is sitting with Trina on the back porch, talking about what the next few months would look like.

But anything since then... it's not there. It's like it's been erased.

Jack moves, his little arms and legs resisting my hold.

Is he resisting me? Does he not like being in my arms?

I rush toward his bedroom, needing to put him down in his crib. That's where Grace finds me, standing beside his crib, watching him.

"Oh, hello, Mrs. Eaton," she says, folding a blue onesie and adding it to a drawer. "Oh, and there's the little man," she coos. "Is everything okay?"

She waits for my reply, but I don't have one. All of a sudden, I feel like I'm about to float away, like all it will take is a small gust of wind from the open window and I'll be gone.

"Here, why don't I help you back to your room?" she says, taking my arm. "You must be tired," she suggests, and I nod. "You have the life you've always wanted but you're not thriving, are you?" Her voice is low, and I'm not sure I heard her right.

"Excuse me?"

"You poor thing. You've always needed someone to take care of you. Well, it's a good thing I'm here. Don't you worry, I've never let anything bad happen to your children and I'm not about to change now."

Her voice is soothing, but I don't understand what she's saying. A wave of exhaustion hits me like a brick house has fallen on me, and all I want to do is lie down.

She tilts her head, her smile never slipping. "Careful, Rosalind, Mabel already has two things that belong to you, you poor thing."

She helps me lie down in bed.

"What did you say?" My voice breaks.

Grace only lowers her lashes, tucking the throw around me. "All I said was you need to be careful, you poor thing. You're so very tired lately, aren't you?"

She starts to hum a song I haven't heard in years.

A song I thought died with the person I killed.

TWELVE

TRINA

I'm missing things. For the life of me, I can't find a bracelet I bought in Santorini last year. It was a simple rose gold chain with a small cross on it. I found it at a little bookstore and wore it all the time, but I don't remember seeing it after I went into labor.

That's not the only thing I've misplaced. I'm finding books on the wrong shelves, my wool basket set in different places around the house—even though I always keep it by my chair—and lately, I can never seem to find either my charging cord or my portable charger for my phone.

I'm also missing a set of keys from the key hook. They're for the main house, an extra set. Those I must have misplaced because I don't remember seeing them for a long time now.

It's like my mind is playing tricks on me, my memory a sieve. I know this is normal, that eventually I won't have to go through every single drawer in my kitchen to find the measuring spoons, but it's getting a little frustrating.

My phone dings with a message, and I give up the search. The message is from an unknown number, and it's an audio recording.

I hit play.

A voice sings an old children's rhyme that I haven't heard in years. First they hum a verse then they sing it. "My mommy told me, if I was goody, that she would buy me, a rubber dolly..."

I drop the phone, and it lands on the floor with a thud.

That's a song from my nightmares. In one of the foster homes I grew up in, Marilyn, the foster parent, would hum it under her breath constantly. And when she drank, she'd sing the lyrics, creating her own weird ones about the kids who lived with her at the time.

I still remember the one she made up about me: "My Trina is sneaky, she skipped the curfew, she stole the mickey, and got in trouble." It was all true. She was there waiting for me, sitting at the kitchen table when I attempted to sneak in through the back door ninety minutes after curfew. Rosie was with me, drunk as a skunk, puking the whole way home, too. Marilyn was fond of dishing out punishments. Her favorite was locking you in the "spare-spare" bedroom, which was really a crawlspace under the stairs. I stayed in there for four days that time, a combined punishment for both stealing the alcohol and letting Rosie get drunk.

I pick up the phone and type a reply:

Who is this?

The message comes back as undeliverable.

There's a knock on my door. It's Wyatt.

"What's going on?" he asks the second I open the door. "You're white as a ghost." He leads me to the kitchen table and pulls out a chair for me to sit.

I hand him my phone. He plays the message, a frown appearing on his face.

"I don't get it."

"That's... that's..." I can't get the words out. My heart is racing so fast my chest hurts.

"I know what it is; I just don't get why someone sent it to you." He goes into the kitchen and pours two glasses of water, downing his in one long gulp. I sip mine slowly.

I rack my brain thinking of who would send this, my mind going a million miles as I think back to that time in our lives. My hand instinctively covers my burn, my fingers lightly tracking the raised edges covered by my tattoo.

"There's no one..." I don't finish my sentence.

Wyatt gives me a sharp look and that's all the answer I need.

"Have you heard from Rosie this morning?" he asks, turning one chair at the table around and sitting down. He rests his forearms along the back of the chair.

"No, why?"

"That new nanny, Grace, she was out on her morning walk with Jack and mentioned she's a little worried about her."

I want to say something, but I stop myself. I might not like the woman, but I also don't know her enough to judge.

"There's something about her," Wyatt continues. "I think she's after Marcus."

I nod. The memory of her touching his arm the other day flashes to mind.

"As long as it's not Trent, I don't care who she goes after." It's not that I'm worried about Trent cheating on Rosalind; it's more being worried about what she would do if she knew someone was after her husband.

Rosie has a temper, and she doesn't care what burns in her wake.

"That's my point. I caught her flirting with Trent this morning. She can't tell the difference between the two, and someone needs to warn her."

I chuckle, a very catty, sarcastic puff of laughter. "Well, that sure isn't going to be me. The woman doesn't seem to like me for some reason."

Wyatt sighs. "What did you do?"

"Nothing."

"I doubt that." He cocks his head. "I'm tiring of cleaning up this family's messes," he mumbles.

As much as I want to, I'm not going to say anything, keeping my thoughts to myself for once. Wyatt is considered a fixer for the ranch, often being sent off to clean up messes the Eaton family view as dirty laundry. I've never liked it, but I've said my bit to him, and he's told me to mind my own business. Not in so many words, but even so, I know when my opinion is unwanted.

"Did you know Rosie doesn't want me alone with her girls?" The ache in my heart is wrapped tight around my words.

"That's not true," Wyatt says.

I nod. "It is. I wasn't even allowed to be alone with them yesterday. Grace was there to babysit." I grit my teeth, remembering her hovering. "What did I do?"

"Nothing." He sounds so sure, so concrete, but I can't trust that.

"Then why punish me like this? I would never hurt her family, she knows that. Those girls, I love them like they're my own blood."

"Maybe it's just a leftover feeling from when you took Jack?"

I pinch my lips together, and he shrugs. From when I took Jack? My son? I'm being punished for something they did to me, not the other way around. I'm seething with anger and I'm surprised Wyatt doesn't notice. He's more focused on Rosalind.

I think about the note that was left, and the key Rosalind threw at me and as much as I want to say something about that, I don't. Don't trust anyone. Does that include Wyatt? He's always said never to make him choose between Rosalind and me... is that because he'll always choose her?

Deep inside, I know the answer.

"What have they told you about Rosie?" I ask him.

"They're worried she has postpartum psychosis," I say when he doesn't answer me.

"She'd be in the hospital if that were the case, right?"

"With this family? And air out their dirty business for everyone to read about? I think they're trying to keep it contained."

Wyatt slowly nods. "Explains why the doctor is out here so much."

His phone rings. He pulls it out and groans before answering it. "Yeah?" He frowns as he listens. "Do what you need to do, I'll be right there." He hangs up. "Need to head down to the barn. The kid got kicked by a horse." He shakes his head. "It's a freakin' rite of passage, it seems. Why can't anyone listen?"

"Kid?"

"Matty. Mabel's grandson. He'll be fine. Got it in the shoulder and knocked it out of joint." He leans down and plants a kiss on my head. "I'll see you later. Will you do me a favor? Go up and check in on Rosie? Don't let that message bother you. Had to be a prank call, you know?"

Don't let it bother me? How can I not?

It's not a very popular children's rhyme—at least, not now. So why would it be sent, intentional or not?

And whoever sent it, was it just to me, or did they send it to Rosalind as well?

I head up to the main house to check in on Rosalind, like Wyatt asked. That childish song plays over and over in my head, mocking me. I really hope Rosalind didn't get it as well; this is probably the last thing she needs to deal with right now.

I'm lost in my own thoughts as I push open the back door

and step into the kitchen, but I immediately stop short when I hear laughter.

Not Rosalind's laughter—Mabel's. A sound as bright and as girlish as I've ever heard. She's at the table, sitting across from Grace, cheeks flushed, both leaning in like old friends, teacups tight in their hands.

"You've always had such a way with the little ones," Mabel says. "Even when—" She falters at a nod from Grace. Mabel half turns in her chair and the silence that follows is quick and sharp.

Grace recovers first, smiling sweetly. "Mabel was teasing me for spoiling Jack. I can't help it. Babies need love and comfort—it's not something you ration."

I force my feet to move, shutting the door behind me. "I'm looking for Rosalind," I say, my words a little slow as I struggle to comprehend what I just walked into.

"She's upstairs resting," Mabel says, her voice a shade too brisk. She busies herself with the sugar bowl. "Grace was just keeping me company."

My gaze flicks between them. Company. That's one word for it. They look quite comfortable together, like this isn't their first tea break, like Grace isn't new at all.

It took Mabel quite some time to warm up to me when I first arrived. I think my first tea break was probably not for a good six weeks.

Grace tilts her head, still smiling. "You look pale, Trina. Are you all right?"

I swallow hard, the message on my phone burning like a brand in my pocket. "I'm fine." I turn to Mabel. "Has anyone called you yet?"

A flare of alarm flashes in Mabel's eyes. "No, what's going on?"

"Wyatt was at my place when he received a call—your

grandson got kicked by one of the horses and his shoulder got knocked out of the socket."

Mabel springs into action. "No one has called. That boy..."

"We'll go down together," Grace says, getting up from the table and setting her cup in the sink. "The baby is sleeping, but I have his monitor with me. Come on," she says, placing her arm around Mabel. "I'm sure he's okay," she whispers as they leave the kitchen together.

I'm left standing there, perplexed at the level of familiarity between the two women.

My phone buzzes and, to be honest, I'm a little nervous about checking it. Will it be another message? I swallow hard and pull it out of my pocket and my heart drops when I read what's on the screen.

THIRTEEN

Please come help me.

It's from Rosalind.

I race up the stairs, calling Rosalind's name.

"I'm in here," she says.

I nudge open her bedroom door and see her sitting in her rocking chair with Jack, holding him at arm's length. The poor thing looks uncomfortable. His face is all scrunched up, and I'm not sure if he's about to belt out a cry or if he's about to fill his diaper.

"Hey," I say, entering the room. "I thought Jack was supposed to be sleeping?"

The look on her face is one of full relief. "Oh God, thank you. Please, please take him." She awkwardly stands and holds him out to me.

I don't hesitate. "Hey there, little man," I say, bringing him in close and kissing his forehead. I pat his bottom, but it feels like a regular, unfilled diaper. I watch him as he rests in my arms, and his face relaxes as he snuggles in toward my chest, letting out a little sigh.

He is the most adorable thing ever. Not being with him, not seeing him, holding him... I haven't wanted to admit it, but it's been killing me.

"I just saw Grace downstairs," I say. "She seems to think he's sleeping in his crib."

She shrugs. "I turned his monitor off. It's not my fault she hasn't checked to see if the video is on or not. He was crying and she wasn't around, so I brought him in here."

"Well, she's not here now. She and Mabel are down at the main barn. I guess Matty got hurt."

She whirls toward me. "Is he okay?" Her eyes widen slightly.

I give a half-nod. "Wyatt said he got kicked in the shoulder by a horse. He didn't sound too worried." What's with everyone all of a sudden being concerned about the kid?

She paces in the room, back and forth, back and forth, finally stopping at the window. "It's times like this I wish I still smoked."

I snort. "Liar." She's only ever smoked one cigarette in her life, and she swore she'd never do it again.

"You know what I mean." She won't look at me.

"What's going on?" I go to stand beside her, one hand on her arm, and I look at her—really look at her.

She's been crying.

"I thought..." She shakes her head, and I can see her trying to find the words. "I thought I was better, that a switch flipped in me and I was fine, you know?"

I nod because that's what she needs right now, but honestly, I have no idea what she's talking about.

She glances at Jack for a moment. "I overheard Trent and Marcus and I guess... I have times when I can't remember anything. And Jack... he doesn't always seem real to me. I don't want..." She slumps down on her bed, resting her head between her hands. "I don't want to hurt him, Trina."

I barely heard her say the words. I almost don't think she wanted me to.

Hurt him? How could she? I glance down at him and I can't wrap my head around what she's saying.

How could anyone want to hurt a sweet baby? Especially this one?

When I have him in my arms like this, I don't just want to protect him, love him, and hold him close; I do. I do love him. How can I not? We're connected, even if everyone around us is trying to keep us apart. I will find the answers I need and I will get my son back.

"You said you saw him as a doll. Do you still?"

A look of anguish covers her face. "I want to say no, but that would be lying." She looks at me with horror in her eyes. "Sometimes I'll blink and he's... he doesn't look the same. He doesn't look like my son."

That's because he's not! I want to shout this out but at the same time, I see the honesty in her eyes. Does she not know? She has to. Is this a game where she's just playing me?

"I know that sounds horrible," she says, "that I sound crazy..."

Yes. Yes, it sounds horrible. Yes, you sound crazy. No, you shouldn't be alone with my son. Those are all things I want to scream at her, but I push all those emotions down into a small box hidden deep inside me and lock the lid closed. Now is not the time.

I lightly bounce little Jack in my arms, tap-tap-tapping his bum while I do so. The action is natural, and I can tell he loves it. I saw a video that suggested movements like this remind babies of when they were in the uterus.

"You're so good with him," Rosalind says, sadness lacing her voice. "What is wrong with me, Trina?" She leaves the bed and goes to stand by the window again, staring out. "Where is the woman I used to be? She's gone. I can't even feel her anymore... This never happened with the twins."

I glance down at Jack and his eyes are closed. I should return him to his crib, encourage Rosalind to have a nap, and then search through the upstairs for the proof I need. Instead, I carefully arrange some pillows on Rosalind's huge king-size bed and nestle Jack in between them.

There are tears pooling on Rosalind's eyelashes. I'm so torn. My heart breaks for her brokenness; at the same time there's a hatred inside of me that continues to grow anytime I'm around her.

I've never hated her before. Never. I've always looked at her like a little sister, needing protection from the evil world. She's always been fragile, especially after what happened to her as a teenager, and I've always sworn to be there for her. But this... this is a line she's crossed that I don't think we'll ever recover from.

And yet, I can't stop wanting to be there for her either.

I hate myself right now. For being so torn.

"She's still there, Rosie," I tell her, taking her hands in mine. "That strong, vibrant woman who's full of love and joy... she's still there."

Rosalind shakes her head. "I don't feel her. She's gone."

I rub her hand. "No, sweetie, she's not. She's just protecting herself because she's hurting. Sometimes we do things, say things, we don't always mean when we're hurting, and I think that's where you are at."

This is me giving her the chance to right her wrong. To admit to what she's done so together we can find a way past it. Her breath calms after a while, and when she lifts her head, she's able to give me a wobbly smile. "Self-preservation and all that?" she says, trying to sound like everything is fine.

I nod. "Exactly." I wait for her to say the words I'm so desperate to hear, to tell me Jack is my son.

"Did you know Dr. Harmon wants to send me to some retreat center on the coast? A psychiatric treatment center for postpartum psychosis?" Rosalind says instead, her voice fragile and small.

During the pregnancy, I read up on all the things that could go wrong, just as much as I read up on all the ways to be prepared for labor, delivery, and life with a baby. Everything I read on psychosis scared me, to be honest. Sure, they have a lot of up-to-date methods for treatment, but it's still scary.

"Do you feel you should go?" I ask, unsure if she needs my support of her decision or my honest reaction.

She shakes her head. "No." She takes my hand in hers and holds it tight. "This is where I need to be. Everything else will fall into place." She rubs her face, swallows hard, and stands taller. "I'm just emotional, that's all. The things we women go through—from our periods, to prenatal and post, then eventually perimenopause, and then menopause... I swear, it's too much at times."

She's trying to make light, I get that, but what she's going through is very real.

"You need to tell the doctor then. Tell him the truth, okay? He can't help if he doesn't know everything," I remind her.

"Sometimes..." She trails off, not finishing as she grabs a light sweater and bunches it in her hands.

"Sometimes, what?" I'm not letting her off that easily.

She shrugs. "Nothing. Just a feeling I have, you know? But it's nothing. Just me being... broken me, I guess."

I have to be honest, her not admitting things to me, it's frustrating. She's holding back, not sharing everything, and I don't understand why.

"Mrs. Eaton?" Grace is at her door. "Oh, you're not alone. How about I take Jack and settle him in his crib?" She walks in and heads toward the bed.

"He's fine where he is." My voice is a little sharp.

Her look is even sharper. "He should be in his crib," she says as she bends down and picks him up.

"Rosalind?" I glance toward her, fully expecting her to back me up, but she continues to stare out the window and ignores me.

I follow Grace as she takes my son to the nursery.

She sets Jack down, lightly patting his bottom. He fusses a little before falling back to sleep. "Is there something I can help you with?"

"Trina?" My name is being called, which stops me from answering.

When I leave the nursery, I distinctly hear the door closing behind me with a soft thud. Everything in me rankles at the sound, at her in there with my son.

"Trina?" Rosalind calls for me again. I take a moment to center myself, breathe in deep, hold it to the count of five, and then release it.

Earlier, Wyatt said he's tired of cleaning up the Eatons' messes, and I'm starting to understand. In a house where I used to feel like family, now I feel less like a beloved sister and more like hired help.

And if that's the case, this place no longer feels like home.

FOURTEEN

ROSALIND

The house is quiet. Almost too quiet.

I notice Trent's office door is slightly ajar, and I hear the muffled voice of my husband. Wanting to check in with him, I head over and push the door open. All conversation stops as the room snaps into silence. Marcus, Trent, and Dr. Harmon all turn toward me. Serious looks flicker into forced smiles.

I'm an intruder, catching them on a secret. Marcus steps back, hands in his pockets, dark eyes assessing me. Trent looks from me to Marcus, then at the doctor, a nervous energy about him.

The silence in the room right now is unsettling.

Trent's office is orderly and rich with warm wood and a masculine scent. Wall-to-wall bookshelves are filled with binders and leather-bound volumes, neat and freshly dusted. Photos in elegant frames dot the shelves—me with the girls, the girls with Trent, Trent and Marcus, the men with their parents, but none with Jack. I'll have to change that. Normally I love coming into this room. It's nothing like me, everything like Trent, and when I'm in here, I feel safe, like I've just wrapped a warm blanket around myself and could stay in here all day, reading a good book.

Not now, though. Right now, I feel like I've stepped into the middle of something I have no business being a part of.

Trent's posture stays rigid, with Dr. Harmon adjusting his stance, crossing and uncrossing his arms. They both avoid my gaze. Only Marcus seems comfortable, finally stepping forward, all charm and concern.

"Rosie," Marcus says smoothly, a touch too casually, "is everything okay?"

I nod. "Of course, sorry, I didn't realize you were here. You're not here to see me, are you?"

Dr. Harmon shrugs. "I don't mind checking in with my favorite patient. Besides, we were—"

"We had some business to discuss," Marcus says, interrupting him.

My brows furrow. What kind of business do they need to deal with that includes the doctor?

A sense of unease winds its way around me as I glance toward the doctor and Marcus, both of whom seem to be purposely avoiding my gaze.

Without thinking, I blurt, "You're not here because of Trina, are you?"

"Why would you say that?" Dr. Harmon asks.

"She didn't mean it. She was just overcome and..." I wince at how pathetic I sound, how high and breathless my voice becomes as the words plop out, fast-paced. I catch my lower lip between my teeth. "I mean, I don't blame her, and I know no one else does either, right?" The men all stand there watching me blather on, no one interjecting, saving me from looking like a fool.

Marcus's face softens, a careful expression of sympathy. "Of course we don't. What happened, there's no textbook on how to handle this."

I nod. "Exactly. She just needs time. We all do. Maybe she just needs some time away, that's all."

"We were just discussing that, actually," Marcus says. "There's a clinic on the coast. They specialize in postpartum cases like..."—his pause is slight but weighted—"this."

"The same clinic you were thinking of sending me to?" I shake my head. "The coast might be nice. She's not experiencing postpartum psychosis, though. It's grief." I glance toward the doctor, expecting him to agree, but his head tilts while studying me with a clinical intensity. His eyes flick to Marcus and Trent again, and I see a hint of something there. Apprehension? Hesitation?

What am I missing?

The doctor clears his throat, pulling my attention back to him. "I'm more focused on you right now, though, Mrs. Eaton. How are things going with Jack? Have you bonded with him yet? Stopped believing he's a doll?"

The questions hit me like a cold wind. The shift in focus is sharp and unexpected, throwing me off balance. I need to be careful.

"Has his birth certificate come in yet?" I ask. "I want to get started on his baby book and I'd like to add a copy to it." I don't answer his questions directly. Do I believe he's a doll? No. Do I believe they want me to believe he's a doll? Yes.

Marcus's eyes are on mine, unwavering, measuring. The room spins slightly, my thoughts scrambling to catch up. My cheeks burn under their watchful stares.

"Not yet," Marcus finally says.

"But soon? The girls' didn't take this long, right?"

Dr. Harmon interjects. "Shouldn't be too much longer. You know how the government is—they can be slow as honey when they want to be. Now, about my question?"

"I know Jack isn't a doll," I finally utter, swallowing hard and hoping they believe me. Trent plants a light kiss on the top of my head while Marcus and Dr. Harmon exchange another look, a silent conversation that leaves me on the outside.

"The clinic." I don't say it like a question because it suddenly hits me—they are planning to send me. The thought grips me, cold and certain, unraveling the fragile hope I cling to.

Marcus gives a one-shoulder shrug, slow and deliberate. "All we're doing is discussing options."

I steal a glance at my husband and see the frown. "Options? What's going on? I don't need to be sent away."

A curtain falls over his eyes. "Marcus and Dr. Harmon were just discussing other possible ways to help," he says, glancing toward Marcus.

"Me? Or Trina?"

He doesn't answer, but that's all the answer I need.

"I'm getting better," I whisper, knowing they don't believe it, believe me.

I'm not even sure I do. There are moments, hours, and even full days when I don't recognize myself. I'm trying not to stress over it, though. Postpartum is a beast and an ugly one at that.

I step back, the edge of the door digging into my spine. They've already decided, I realize. I wrap my arms around myself, a frail barrier against the swell of panic.

"I just need time," I whisper. "Please? Just a little more time?"

Marcus approaches me, reaching out but not quite touching. "Rosie," he says, soft and persuasive, "this is only temporary."

I look to Trent, to my husband, who should be standing up for me, fighting for me, and being my victor in this amphitheater of carnage.

All he does is nod.

"I'm getting better," I tell him, begging him to believe me.

"We just want what's best for you," Dr. Harmon says.

Best for me? To send me to a place where... what? I'm

poked and prodded? Placed on medication and subjected to electric shock therapy? No, thank you.

"It's only temporary," Trent says, but that's all he needs to say. That's the final nail in my coffin.

Temporary sounds awfully a lot like forever.

I leave the men to finish their meeting and head outside, taking a nice leisurely walk around the grounds, something I haven't done in a long time. By the time I make it back to the house, more than an hour is gone, and inside, I find Mabel and the doctor sitting at the kitchen table, having what looks to be an intense conversation.

"It was all so sudden," Dr. Harmon mutters. "Do you need me to pop down and check on the little one?"

"I'd appreciate that," she says, staring down at the cup she holds in her hand. "She's a precious little one, so quiet. Barely cries. She's a contented little thing," Mabel continues. "Good thing, too. Imagine me taking on a screaming baby at my age? Raising Matthew was hard enough."

A baby? Did I hear her correctly?

"It'll be worth it, you'll see."

Mabel sighs. She looks like she's about to say more when she stops, as if she realizes I'm here. Her face goes beet red as she pushes herself to her feet. "Can I get you anything, Mrs. R?" Her voice wobbles a little.

"Ahh, Mrs. Eaton, you caught us." Dr. Harmon sets down his cup of iced tea. "I was just having a nice catch-up with Mabel while waiting for you. Did you know, her iced tea reminds me of what my grandmother used to make."

"You were talking about a baby?"

She nods quickly. "My new grandbaby."

A sickening feeling lodges in my chest as I realize this is just one more area I'm failing in. I pride myself on knowing everything about our staff's lives, especially those who work so closely with us, like Mabel.

"Oh, don't worry too much about it, Mrs. R," Mabel says, pouring me a glass of water. "You've had so much on your plate. You remember my oldest daughter has been trying to adopt for some time now—well, everything happened all at once. That's why she finally moved back here." The way her face beams, I can tell she's happy.

I offer a smile. "That's wonderful."

"Ah, Mrs. Eaton?" Dr. Harmon calls out. "I was hoping for a few moments of your time," he says, pulling a container out of his bag.

"What is that?" I eye it with suspicion.

He gestures to a chair. I don't want to sit, but I do.

He pushes the container toward me. It's a cloudy-looking powder. "What is it?" I ask again.

"A herbal supplement. Last visit you complained about all the pills you are taking. This will replace most of those supplements. It's all very safe." He has this smile that makes me want to tear out his eyes. "Why don't you try some?"

"I don't know if—"

"Just add one tablespoon of this to your daily smoothies and you'll see a marked improvement in a matter of days." He nudges the container again. His boast is too unbelievable, and that's when I realize he's feeding me a line, but why? For what benefit?

"How about I make you one now?" Mabel suggests. She gets up, taking the powder with her. I twist in my chair to watch her add one scoop into the blender, along with some fresh orange juice.

I turn and feel the doctor's eyes on me. I can see the doubt swirl through his eyes as he watches me, feel his lack of confidence in me.

Mabel passes me the glass. Dr. Harmon watches me closely.

My hand shakes, making small ripples on the surface. I bring the glass to my lips and drink. The powder doesn't just taste bitter, it leaves a chalky trail along my tongue, my throat, the back of my teeth. I almost gag on the first swallow.

I put the glass down, but he nudges it back toward me.

"Another few sips. It's worth it, don't you think? For you to feel better? To want to be there for your children?"

I raise it to my lips again, cringing against the sharp, almost metallic flavor.

"That's a girl." His patronizing tone has me biting my tongue. He doesn't mean to be, I know that.

"Your husband and brother-in-law want what's best for you. We all do. I know how important your family is. This will help you be yourself again." He leans back, assessing my expression, my reaction to everything he's saying. "It's only temporary."

Temporary. There's that word again.

I force myself to take another sip.

"I need to head down to see Trina, but I'll return in a few days and we'll reevaluate your progress. How does that sound?"

I nod, not trusting myself to say what I'm really thinking. Like, *That sounds like you think I'm a risk to myself, to Jack, to my entire family.* Like, *There's so much you don't know, so much that's going on beneath the surface.* But I don't say that. I don't say anything.

FIFTEEN

TRINA

Doomscrolling through videos and curated photographs, my attention isn't on the screen but rather the key in my lap.

I need to find out what it unlocks.

The only way to do that is to get time alone in the main house, when neither Eaton boy is there and Rosalind is off on a walk or napping.

I stop scrolling when I come to a photo of people I went to school with. I scan the names and see that Sarah Clemmens is tagged. I remember her. We were in the same classes and she was at that party Rosalind and I were at.

I click on her profile and go through her photos, one at a time, to see if she's ever posted any #throwback images. I stop when I come to one that looks oddly familiar. It's a bunch of people I recognize, standing in a kitchen corner—the same kitchen corner from that party we all went to.

Bingo.

My heart skips a beat as I write her a message. My fingers shake a little, clicking on the wrong keys, but that's only from excitement. It's taken me a long time to find everyone who was at that party when we were only seventeen. People are married or divorced; some are online, others aren't. Not many remember that party, but a few do.

All I need is one.

I introduce myself, mentioning how we all went to the same party once upon a time, and I was wondering if she remembers seeing either of the Eaton boys there.

I click send and then I wait.

I close my phone, knowing it could take forever for her to reply, if she even does. Of all the messages I've sent over the years, I've only received a few responses. I'm probably going to be stuck in her junk folder, and she'll never see my message.

Thirty minutes later, I get a reply.

I stare at Sarah's message, reading it over and over, not believing that finally, someone has responded with a yes.

Funny you should ask. I was just going through some old photos, saving them to the cloud, and came across ones from that year. I even have a photo of one of the twins—not sure which one, though. I think it's the shy one, but I could be wrong. I even have one of you and your friend. I hear she married him—who knew, right? I'll attach them here. Hope you're doing well.

When the images download, the first one I see is of me and Rosie, standing in a corner, both holding red tumblers in our hands. We were so young-looking then, having no idea what the road ahead was going to look like.

The next image is like a wrench being churned in my stomach. An Eaton twin, standing with a group of guys, beer bottle in hand, and he's staring right into the camera.

I know right away it's Marcus. He likes his beer whereas Trent prefers the hard stuff. Trent once told a story about the first time he'd ever had beer—it was in a contest with Marcus to see who could drink the bottle the fastest. Marcus won, of course, and Trent threw up so much he never drank another. If memory serves, they were thirteen at the time.

The first thing I do is save the photos.

The next is send the one of us to Rosie with a short caption: *We were so cute.*

I knew it. I knew he was there. I've always known it, deep down, but now I have the actual proof.

Not that it does me any good anymore.

When I started this quest to prove to Rosalind just how evil the Eaton brothers are, I never expected it to take this long. Nor did I think we'd be in this place—her married to one, with three babies, and me... well, me having a one-night stand with the other and getting pregnant.

This won't change Rosalind's mind, but I can use it as leverage.

Knock-knock-knock.

I set my phone down and head to the door to find Dr. Harmon. A cool breeze sweeps around my ankles, and from the way the clouds are rolling, with their dark centers, a prairie storm is on its way.

"How's my favorite patient doing this afternoon?" Dr. Harmon asks by way of greeting. "I was just visiting with Mrs. Eaton and thought I'd stop in before leaving. Mind if we have a little chat?"

That's when I realize I've just been standing in front of the half-opened door.

"Of course," I say, stepping out of the way.

He settles in at the kitchen table, takes a look at my phone, but if he has a comment about the photo still on the screen, he doesn't say it. "How are your stitches coming along?" he asks instead.

I turn my phone off and turn it over, face down on the table. "Fine, other than being slightly itchy, which I assume means it's healing."

He nods. "Good, good. We don't want that infection coming back."

No, I definitely don't want that.

"And your"—he looks casually toward my chest—"breast milk? Is it still decreasing?"

I clear my throat and fidget in my seat. "Well, it was but then..." I stop and glance toward the house. "I met Jack," I admit.

He pauses, and it takes a moment for what I'm not saying to sink in. "Ahh, yes. So you fed him then?"

I nod.

"Well, I don't advise it, but that is between you and the Eatons, I imagine. If you continue, your production will likely increase."

"I'd wondered," I murmur.

"Yes, yes, hormones and just how a woman's body responds to a baby. It really is quite spectacular."

His head tilts and I wonder what he's trying to see in my eyes. The happiness I felt holding Jack? How complete my little baby made me while I nursed him?

"I'd advise that you continue pumping," the doctor says. "The baby needs to bond with Rosalind, and if you nurse him, then, well..." He then sighs. "It's the way things are, I suppose. Grieving new mothers have nursed the children of others since, well... I imagine since time began. Have you been to see that therapist I mentioned?"

I shake my head.

"Please do, even if it's just over the computer. It will help you avoid getting, well, confused. You don't want to transfer your emotions onto that baby—it's not fair to you or him. Grieving is a monstrous creature and will surprise you at the worst times. Talking to someone will help." He pulls out his notepad and writes down the therapist's name again, along with the website address.

Transfer my emotions? I've wondered if the doctor knows about the Eatons taking Jack from me, but it doesn't sound like it.

"I'll look into it," I say without making any promises, because talking to a therapist about losing a child that was in fact stolen is not something I plan on doing. "About the birth certificate?" I'm hoping that's why he stopped by.

"Ahh, yes," Dr. Harmon says. "Unfortunately, receiving those documents takes time, and they haven't come in yet."

"How long does it take for a birth certificate to be issued?"

"With the way our government is, I've seen it take anywhere from eight to twelve weeks."

"So nothing has been issued for... the death certificate, either?" The death certificate meant for Rosalind's baby, not mine.

Is that why my baby was taken from me? Because Rosalind couldn't handle losing another baby?

I feel for her, I do, but that doesn't excuse her actions.

Dr. Harmon fiddles with his bag and it feels like he's purposely not looking my way.

"Is there a particular reason you're in a rush for them?" he asks.

"I need"—I try to think of the right word—"closure." Closure and proof are basically the same thing, right? "I don't remember much from that night. One minute I was pregnant and excited to see my baby, and the next I'm told he's gone... and it doesn't feel real."

He nods and rubs his chin. "She," he corrects me. "I can see how there would be a disconnect for you."

Disconnect? That's what he's calling it?

"How would you feel if you were told your child was gone?" The words leap from my tongue, my burst of anger a surprise to both of us. His eyes widen, then he blinks rapidly, over and over, like he's stuck in processing mode.

"I'm sorry," I say with a sigh.

With a quick shake of his head, he stands and fiddles with his watch. "It's all right. I am very sorry for your loss. I would really like it if you spoke with that therapist," he says. "In fact, I'll set it up and make sure that Mr. Eaton knows."

I slowly rise. "I'll take care of it," I assure him. "There's no need to involve the Eatons."

"No, no," he insists, "I'll take care of it."

"But I—" I stop because he's already at my door with it open. He casts me one long look, and there's so much in his gaze, but I can't read any of it.

When the door closes behind him, my heart sinks. I need to be more careful. The goal is to get back my son, first and foremost.

I take a look at the photo again, confident that it's Marcus on the screen. I need to be careful how I bring this up. The last time I asked Marcus about that party, he told me he was tired of the silent accusations.

This time, they won't be so silent.

SIXTEEN

ROSALIND

The door to my husband's study is open and I hear my name. It's not until I'm at the door that I realize I wasn't being called; I am being spoken about once again.

"My wife... You can't be serious about this," Trent says.

I edge closer, more curious than ever now.

"You heard what the doctor said," Marcus says, obviously trying to convince Trent of something. "You have to think of the girls."

"The girls are fine."

"Are they? You can't seriously believe what's happening with Rosie isn't affecting them."

Affecting Riley and Addison? My stomach plummets at the idea, at the possibility that I've somehow hurt them.

"I said my girls are fine." I hear the emphasis on *my*.

"What about last week? Were they fine then? Was Jack?"

"I... I can't answer that." There is a softness to Trent's voice, a surrender. "We agreed not to talk about that."

"But it happened. It happened, and it could happen again. You saw how she was."

What are they talking about?

I try to breathe, to control the pace of my heart.

"We need to think long term here," Marcus says, his tone authoritative and controlling. "What if she goes back to the way she was last week? She can't be trusted to be alone with Jack, and you know it."

"She just needs time and support," Trent says, but there's no strength to his voice. There rarely is when it comes to standing up to Marcus.

"Time?" The incredulity in Marcus's voice surprises me.

"And support," Trent repeats, softer than before.

"From who? You? You're running from one business meeting to another, meetings that don't need to be face-to-face, no matter how much you insist they do."

He's what? I thought that was all because of Marcus?

"You're forgetting which one of us is her husband," Trent says, a warning in his voice.

Marcus scoffs. "No, I think you are. You leave, assuming I'll handle things, like I handle everything else. When it comes to your family, it's not my place, though, is it?"

"So now you decide it's not your place? It's because of you we're even in this situation to begin with, aren't we?" There's a tinge of bitterness in Trent's voice.

For the longest time, nothing is said.

Marcus eventually responds with, "None of this is my fault, and you know it. All I've done is put our family first. If it wasn't for that damn clause in the will... Unless you're willing to lose it all? If that's what you want, say the word and we can come clean, here and now."

"Don't be an asshole," Trent mutters.

"We agreed to take this path, and we knew the consequences."

"We didn't agree on *this* path. You did. This is all on you."

I hear a smash. I imagine Trent's coffee cup being thrown across the room, coffee spilling in anger.

"I will not send her to the clinic, Marcus. I won't."

My breathing is shallow. My world is unsteady, crumbling.

"She is a risk to herself."

"You don't know that."

"I was there, Trent, or do you think I'm lying to you?" Marcus's words fill me with anxiety. "I saw it with my own eyes as she started to shake Jack, screaming he was just a doll. My God, she would have thrown him across the room if I hadn't grabbed him from her."

My stomach coils at his words, and I'm going to be sick. What is he talking about? That never happened. Why is he lying?

"What if it happens again?" Marcus continues. "Are you willing to take that chance?"

Trent's silence fills me with despair. "She's my wife."

"So how about you start acting like those children are yours, too?"

"You promised you wouldn't go there."

I agree with Trent. That was a low blow. Years ago, when we'd been trying to have a child and couldn't, after a lot of testing, we discovered Trent was sterile. Over drinks one night, the idea of Marcus being a donor came up. At first, I said no, putting my foot down. Then I found out about the clause in the will, how only the first male child from the firstborn son would inherit the company, and if there is no male to inherit, then the company's assets and income would be broken up to several different charities. It's a stupid clause, one that's been passed down for generations, and it's never been an issue until now. Trent is the firstborn son, so if he's sterile, then there is no one to inherit the family dynasty.

Marcus came up with the idea of us going to a clinic in Europe for the procedure, the Nova Clinic in Switzerland, which we all swore to keep hush-hush. The only people who know of our arrangement are the three of us. I've never even told Trina. The first visit gave me my twin daughters. Our last trip, under the guise of a family vacation that also included time in Italy and Greece, added another member to our family.

"She needs more than what you can give her right now," Marcus says.

I hate this man. It's been so hard to pretend otherwise all these years, and I'm not sure how much longer I can continue.

Finding out about Trent made me realize everything Trina had said about that night when we were teens was true. Until that point I never believed her.

It was Marcus who took advantage of me, a drunk seventeen-year-old. Marcus, the father of my first son.

In the years since finding that out, I've been playing the role of a lifetime, and so far, neither one of them has ever guessed a thing.

"No. This is not your call." Trent's voice is sharper than the knives in our kitchen, and for a moment, I would have sworn that was Marcus talking.

Again, nothing is said. Not verbally at least. The boys have this way of having silent conversations that say all too much.

My hands shake, and my whole body trembles.

"If what you are saying is true, then I'll think about it," Trent says. "Until then, we have Grace and Trina. Between them and us, we can make sure Rosalind isn't alone with Jack until we know she's one hundred percent better." Trent sounds tired, worn out.

Hearing the weary betrayal in my husband's voice is too much. My knees buckle, and I plant my hands on the wall for support, but everything tilts, spins, and nothing feels right, and suddenly, everything goes dark.

When I come to, I see duplicates of the same face hovering above me.

"Sweetheart, are you okay?"

I close my eyes and lean into the arms holding me.

"Rosie, honey, open your eyes, please," Trent whispers with a sense of urgency.

My lashes flutter. I feel so tired right now. "I'm okay," I say, or at least, I try to. The words come out garbled.

"Marcus called Dr. Harmon. We caught him before he was about to leave," Trent says as I struggle to get up.

I shake my head. The last thing I want is to see the doctor again.

"I'm okay," I say, "really."

By now, I'm sitting up, legs bent, and the crazy dizziness that hit me like a herd of trampling hooves is gone.

"I'd still feel better if he checks in," Trent says.

Trent helps me up, takes me into his office, and sits with me on the couch.

"Trent, I don't... I don't want to go to that clinic."

He pulls me in close, and I feel sheltered and secure in his arms. "I know you're scared. So am I. We're going to get through this, Rosie, I promise."

I want to believe him. I really do. But I don't.

He pulls me close again, and this hug is a warm blanket wrapped around my shoulders, comforting and everything I need.

"I love you," he whispers. "Nothing will change that," he tells me.

We sit together like this until my heartbeat slows and I feel more in control. "Should we go sit outside?" Trent asks. "Maybe some fresh air will help, and we can wait for the doctor on the porch."

He leads the way. It's not too long before Dr. Harmon appears. He mops at his forehead with a cloth he pulls from his pocket.

"I see you're on your feet," Dr. Harmon says as he sets his bag down. "Just a little fainting spell? How do we feel now?"

"Is that normal?" Trent asks.

The doctor gives a slight *maybe* type shrug. "It's a typical symptom with the medication she's on. I'm not overly worried," he says. "It's important that you eat and stay hydrated. And be sure to drink those smoothies."

"Smoothies?" Trent asks.

Dr. Harmon proceeds to tell Tent about the disgusting powder he's trying to force me to drink. All he wants to do is keep me drugged and that's the last thing I want to be right now.

Am I okay? No. Far from it. I feel off, not myself, and I have bouts of memory loss that don't feel normal. Other than blaming it on postpartum, the only other reason I can think of is because of the drugs and those damn smoothies.

"Perhaps it's time to discuss the clinic again?"

I inhale sharply; I can't help it. Trent shoots me a quick look before he leads the doctor away, out of earshot.

"Mrs. R? Your phone's been going off for the last few minutes." Mabel walks up to me and hands me my phone, along with a nice cold glass of tea.

I take a look at the screen and see a photo that Trina sent. Wow, talk about a time capsule. The girl I was then and the woman I am now, it's like we're two different people. I show Mabel the photo.

"Is that you two as babes? Look at you," Mabel says, holding her hand tight to her heart. "So young."

"But not so innocent," I tell her.

"Well, no one really is at that age, are they? Look at my Matty." Her eyes twinkle, but I hear the concern in her voice.

"How is he?" It's not often Mabel will bring up her grandson to me, so when she does, it makes me happy.

"Back in the barn, doing some light work. Mr. M promised

me he'll go easy on him after dislocating his shoulder like he did. The doctor said it was a good thing he didn't break it."

"It's been a while since I've been down there. Maybe I'll go check in on him." Matty is a good kid, with a good head on his shoulders.

"Oh, you don't have to do that."

"I know that."

There's a look on Mabel's face I can't read. "You've always been so good to him," she says softly, glancing out toward Marcus. "You have no idea how much that has meant over the years."

I lightly pat her hand. "He's family, Mabel. And family means everything to me, you know that."

I've learned the hard way what it means to fight for the family you not only have but also for the family you want.

The family I have means everything to me.

Everything.

SEVENTEEN

TRINA

My body feels like a million ants are running under my skin, and there's this foreboding feeling growing inside me that something is wrong.

I just don't know what.

There's not much action outside. The cowboys are off in one of the far fields with the cattle, which means things are quiet and calm here. I've been walking the grounds and haven't run into anyone for almost an hour.

Which is strange. Normally, this place hums with people and creatures.

I head toward the main house, and when I crest over a hill, I notice there are no vehicles in the driveway.

This is the opportunity I've been waiting for. My fingers wrap around the key in my pocket as I hurry toward the main house.

The back door is open, so I let myself in. There are two bottles of pills sitting on the counter, both for Rosalind.

I read the labels, my brows racing to my hairline as I learn which drugs the doctor has prescribed for her.

Risperidone and lorazepam. One is an antipsychotic, and

the other reduces anxiety and agitation. I know that last one fairly well. I was on Ativan while a teenager. One of the foster homes I was in put all the teenagers on them, whether we needed them or not. Apparently, it was intended to help us stay calm, perform well in school, and avoid trouble. Personally, I think the foster mother was just lazy and wanted zombie kids in her house.

Combining the two could explain Rosalind's mood swings.

I head toward the pantry, where I know there's a locked door hidden behind a shelving unit. Rosalind showed it to me years ago. It's where Mabel keeps all her prepping supplies, in case anything were ever to happen. I try the key, but it doesn't work.

I head upstairs. It's quiet, and I think I'm in the clear, but then I see Rosalind standing in the middle of Jack's nursery.

"Hush, little baby, don't you cry," she sings softly as she rocks Jack in her arms, slowly, back and forth.

She doesn't see me. She's solely focused on Jack.

I take a moment, almost not believing what I'm watching. This is the mother I remember, how she was with her girls, so soft and loving.

"That's it, little sweetie. You're okay." Rosalind paces back and forth, only looking at Jack and nothing else. "You are so loved, so loved."

I take a few steps backward, down the stairs. "Rosie?" I call out. I give her a few moments before I step back up.

This time, when I see her, she's holding Jack out at arm's length.

"Trina, can you... can you take him, please?" She stares at me, wide eyed.

"Rosie, what's wrong?" I ask, wondering what I just saw, why the sudden change.

"Please?" Her lips are slightly parted. She swallows hard. "I need help. I thought..."

I take him from her, cradling him in my arms. She covers her mouth as soon as her hands are free and stands there, her body shaking.

Something is wrong with her. Her emotions just switched on a dime and this isn't the first time I've noticed it.

The sleepy boy in my arms closes his eyes. Holding him is like heaven and putting him down is the last thing I want to do, but I do it anyway.

"Where is Grace?" I ask.

Rosalind only shakes her head. She watches me stand over the crib and there's a sadness that fills her, from the defeated slump of her shoulders to the sheen in her eyes.

"Where's the monitor?" I ask, looking around. I see it on the change table and grab hold of it. "Come on," I say, taking Rosalind's hand. "Let's go downstairs and let him sleep."

She follows me, and I'm trying to wrap my head around the woman I watched unaware compared to the woman holding my hand, and nothing makes sense.

We climb down the stairs, head to the back porch, and walk out onto the patio with the fire pit. She drops down into an Adirondack chair, pulling her knees up tight to her chest and burrowing her face into the crevice.

"What is going on?" I ask, hoping she'll tell me the truth.

She shakes her head. "That photo you sent me brought back a lot of memories. Where did you find it?"

"Do you remember Sarah Clemmens?"

"Who? Oh, wait... she was in our last foster home, wasn't she?"

"No... we went to school with her. I saw her tagged in a photo online," I tell her. "I reached out."

"Reached out? Why?" she asks, giving me a weird look.

She knows why.

"Are you still trying to dig up dirt on my husband?"

On Trent, no.

"On Marcus?" she asks, giving me a full-on eye roll. "Why? I thought we were past that."

I shrug.

"No, seriously, Trina. Why are you digging all that up again? Honestly, there's no need, not anymore." Her voice rises, her hands flatten against her thighs, but it's the heavy breathing that really connects it all for me.

"You're upset with me."

"Just annoyed," she says, shaking her head. "Why can't you leave the past in the past? I was the one who went through it. I was the one who lived with it. Me that—" Her voice breaks. "I love you, but you have no idea what I've had to go through."

The woman who ran the foster home when Rosalind got pregnant after that party was a mean SOB and wouldn't take Rosalind to the hospital, leaving her to give birth in a bathtub. Her son was stillborn, or so the foster mother said later. Rosalind doesn't remember because she'd fallen unconscious, and when she woke up, her baby was gone, taken from her, and she went crazy, believing someone had stolen him.

For all she knows, the woman sold her baby for profit, which I wouldn't put past her.

"It wasn't just you," I softly remind her. I was there for her through all of it. Holding her hand, stealing the prenatal vitamins from the drugstore, and helping her hide her pregnancy for as long as possible.

"It was me, though." She closes her eyes for a moment, but it's long enough for me to see how much this is eating at her. "Me who had my body violated. I was the one pregnant. I was the one who gave birth, alone, in a bathtub. Yes, you were there for me, you've always been there for me, but I'm still the one who had to live with it. Who still has to live with it. If I can leave it behind me, why can't you?"

"I thought I could." I honestly did.

She finally reaches out and takes hold of my hand. "I get it, I do. You need something to focus on right now. I, of all people, understand what it's like to give birth and not have a baby to hold after." Her words pierce my soul in ways she probably doesn't understand. "But this isn't something to get fixated on, not again, okay?"

"Do you understand what I'm going through?" I drop her hand and half turn toward her. "Because you don't act like it. I was willing to scorch the earth with you, Rosie, do you remember that?"

Eyes wide, shock reigns in her gaze.

"We made the person who took your baby pay the ultimate price, and we never looked back. Remember?" I tap my phoenix tattoo. "Someone is dead because of what we did. Why isn't that happening now?" I look out at the gardens, the view swimming in the pools gathering on my lashes. The anger that's been swirling inside me, constant, ever present, boils over and I want to lash out. I want to burn Rosie, I want to destroy the Eaton brothers, I want to torch this whole place and everyone in it, just to get my son back.

Rosalind sits up and takes my hands in her. "I've got you," she whispers. She gets out of her seat and wraps her arms around me as tears scald down my cheeks and sobs rip through me, shredding me to pieces, one tear at a time.

"You've got me?" I laugh, the sound ripping from my throat. "No. You've got Jack, that's what you have, and I have nothing. Nothing. Of all people, I thought you would understand, that you would have my back, but you're just as bad as them, aren't you? A true Eaton." I spit the words out while pushing her away. "I hope you're proud of yourself."

I push myself to my feet and stop myself from saying anything more. What I need to do is leave, run as fast as I can before I truly destroy all chances I have at getting my son back.

EIGHTEEN

"What the hell is going on with you two?"

Wyatt stands behind us, arms crossed over his chest, and the entire air compresses in deference to the weight he carries. He measures us, back and forth, his stare a silent referee's whistle.

"Anyone care to explain?" Wyatt's voice is a low rumble, not raised but more powerful for its restraint. The words hang, demanding honesty from both of us, a kind of justice. "I could hear you guys all the way from the house. Do you realize that?" The censorship in his voice is enough to make me realize I went too far.

"I don't know," Rosie says, looking from Wyatt to me and back again. "What have I done?" she asks me.

Her words hang like wet laundry, limp and heavy. This is on me, I know that. And yet, nothing I said was untrue, so how do I backtrack from that?

"Rosie, I'm sorry. I shouldn't have said that." My voice sounds unlike my own—thin, battered. I watch as the apology lands, see Rosalind's eyes flicker and dart, her face contorted with the kind of pain that only ever comes after a wound has been acknowledged but not cleaned.

"Do you hate me that much?" she asks, breathless, afraid of my answer.

I want to say no. I want to tell her I don't hate her at all. I want to confirm that we're okay, but I can't.

Wyatt is a sentry, unmoving, unwavering. He doesn't say anything, but then he rarely does. I expect him to pick a side, to mete out judgment and force us to apologize again, louder, as if volume could make atonement more real. But all he does is take a measured step forward, arms uncrossing as he crouches so his face is level with Rosalind's. His expression is unreadable, somewhere between a father and a prison guard.

Rosalind's hands twist in her lap, white-knuckled. Her gaze is fixed on her knees, and I can't tell if it's shame, anger, or just exhaustion that's draining the color from her skin. I want to reach out, to touch her shoulder or her back, but my own arms feel like they're encased in wet cement, heavy and unwieldy with the knowledge of my failure.

I've hurt her.

But she's hurt me, too.

Wyatt's voice is softer now, the edges dulled but not blunted: "Trina, sit." He doesn't say please, doesn't have to—Wyatt's authority is felt on the atomic level. I drop to my chair, feeling very much like a child caught with my hand in something it shouldn't be in.

"Trina is back to prove Marcus is evil," Rosalind says, leaning back in her chair and staring off into the distance.

Wyatt doesn't react.

"I have proof he was there, at that party."

Rosalind lurches forward, fingers clutching the edges of her chair. "You what? You didn't tell me that!"

I didn't?

"You have proof?" Wyatt is calm, but I know this man. Beneath the surface, there's a churning happening.

"It doesn't matter anymore," Rosalind says, pushing herself to her feet. "Why can't you just leave things alone? What does destroying him do?"

"I—"

"No," she interrupts me. "Destroying him destroys my family, don't you see that?"

"Rosie, he was there. He was the one who—"

"Stop." She stomps her foot. "Don't you think I know? I've known for a long time now."

It's like we're in a bubble with no air; everything is sucked out of me and I stand there in shock. She didn't just say what I think she said, right?

"Rosalind," Wyatt says, "think about what you're saying." There's caution in his voice, and the way he's watching her, it's like he's waiting for her to bolt.

"You don't think... I can't..." She chokes, and then she's gone, marching along the walkway until she hits the stairs for the back porch. For a second, I imagine Wyatt going after her, but he just stands there, examining the dust motes twisting through the patch of sunlight at his feet.

He sighs. Rubs the back of his neck. The gesture, so human and weary, nearly undoes me. When he turns to face me, the lines around his eyes are deeper than I remember, as if someone has taken a chisel to the soft places of his face.

"You need to go after her," Wyatt says finally, voice flat. "Make sure she's all right."

"You heard what she just said, right?" I'm still trying to process it.

Wyatt stands in front of me and takes my hands in his. For a moment, I smell horse sweat and cedar and the faintest metallic tang of blood—he must have come in directly from the barn, barely enough time to wash his hands. He looks tired, and older.

"Look, Trina. I don't know everything that's going on. But

you need to remember who we are. What we've all been through. What it took to get us to here, right now." The words are soft, but there's an iron bar of command under them. It's the same voice he used back in the group home, the one that could talk a bully down or keep me from breaking a window out of sheer frustration.

I want to argue. I want to list every single thing I have done for this family, every time I've put their needs above my own. I want to tell him about the note that says not to trust anyone; I want to tell him about what I saw back in the nursery. I want, no, I need him to understand that she has my son and is keeping him from me. But the words evaporate, sucked out by the vacuum of Wyatt's disappointment.

"I haven't forgotten anything," I whisper, not trusting myself to say more. "But we're not the same people anymore. She's not the same."

Wyatt's gaze hardens, but not cruelly. There's still affection there, somewhere beneath the exhaustion. "There's more happening than you know, Trina. Trust her. She's never betrayed you; deep down, you know that." He stands, and with a last glance—equal parts warning and plea—he turns and follows after Rosalind. Eventually I hear the slam of the screen door and I feel very alone in a yard that feels both too small and infinitely vast.

What is happening right now? The worst part is that Wyatt's words echo, and I can't silence them. *More happening than you know. Trust her.*

Wyatt is my tether, a steadying force I've always needed and hopefully never taken advantage of. If he's wavering, even for a moment, then I really might be alone here. But they took my son. What am I supposed to do with that? How am I supposed to trust Rosalind knowing she stole my baby as her own?

My legs tremble, unsteady. I squeeze my eyes shut and for a moment, just one, I let the bitterness seep out as tears. I don't have the luxury of breaking down.

Not now.

NINETEEN

Rosalind insinuated she's known about Marcus all along.

How is that possible? How could she continue living in this house, being part of this family, if she knows the truth?

If she could keep that a secret, what else is she hiding?

By the time I walk back toward the house, whether that's where I want to go or not, the first thing I see is Grace sitting on the back porch with Jack, rocking him in a chair, a light baby blanket wrapped around him, and I pause, instinctively turning toward him.

"He likes being outside," Grace says. She pats his back with small taps. "Is everything okay?" She looks toward the door. "Mrs. Eaton rushed in looking upset."

"Everything is fine." I can't tear my gaze away from Jack, from the tuft of hair peeking out from the blanket. "Don't you think it's too warm out here for him?"

Grace points toward the ceiling fan. "That's giving us a nice draft." She continues to rock, back and forth, back and forth, and I want to change places with her, to be the one holding my son.

"Can I have him?" The words come out on their own.

"He's just about to fall asleep," Grace says, but she sees the yearning in my eyes and a semi-smirk appears on her face. "Sorry."

She's watching me, with a knowing glance, as if she knows more than I do, as if she's privy to a secret I don't know.

Except I do.

"Your friend probably needs you." One brow lifts as if challenging me to choose. "Jack is safe with me."

The screen door opens and hits the side of the house with a thud. Wyatt steps out from the doorway. "She needs you upstairs." His voice is grave and I know right away something is wrong.

"Give me Jack," I tell Grace, my voice firm. I reach out and take him, and her arms drop. I hold him close, looking down, and see the flutter of his lashes as if I woke him and he's reorientating himself.

"Hey, sweetie," I whisper. "I've got you." My heart feels full with him in my arms and I never want to let him go.

"Trina?" Wyatt takes off his hat and wipes his forehead with the edge of his sleeve. "She needs you." There's something in his eyes, something that I haven't seen in a long time.

He's scared.

"She needs you," he repeats, his voice breaking.

Those three words have changed my life in so many ways over the years. We were first introduced in a car and told we had a lot in common. We were the same age, two foster kids trying to survive, both having lost our parents at a young age. *She needs you*, the social worker whispered as I stared at a scrawny girl clutching a teddy bear tight to her chest.

She needs you, a foster mom said, nudging me to go to her after she'd fled the dinner table because another kid ate her food.

She needs you, a random stranger at a party told me,

pointing me toward a bedroom door after I'd been searching for more than thirty minutes for her.

She needs you, another pissed foster mother told me when I came home from school, where I found Rosie in the bathtub, unconscious and having just given birth.

She's always needed me. But where was she when I needed her?

I head into the house, carrying Jack, my son, and make my way upstairs.

Marcus is there, standing in the doorway to Rosalind's room. I stop in my tracks, not expecting him to be here.

"What happened?" Marcus glances my way, concerned. "Why do you have Jack?" He moves toward me, as if he's going to take my son from me, but I hold Jack tighter to my chest.

"Wyatt says Rosalind needs me?" I look inside the bedroom and find her curled up in her chair, arms wrapped tight around her knees.

"Maybe Jack is all she needs," Marcus says.

I don't spare him a glance. "Rosie?" My voice is soft and full of questions.

She doesn't look up, glance my way, or say a word. She doesn't even show any expression. She's a blank slate and I get why Wyatt seemed shaken downstairs.

"What brought it on this time?" Marcus asks, his voice low, gravelly.

This time? "We..." How much do I tell him? "Argued."

"About what?"

"The past." My mouth thins. I want to be away from this man, from who he is, who he was, and what he represents.

"This is why she needs to go to the clinic. To get the help we can't get her."

Jack fusses as I readjust my hold and pat his back lightly. "She doesn't want to go to the clinic."

"I don't think the decision is hers to make."

"And it's yours?"

If he had a gun on him, I'd be dead. The glare in his eyes confirms this. "Do we have an issue?"

It's on the tip of my tongue to say yes, of course we have a problem. There are so many problems I don't even know where to start, but I bite my tongue.

"You don't need the baby nanny anymore." He won't listen, he won't agree, but it's the safest thing for me to say right now. "I can take care of him."

He scrubs at his face. "We've already been over this." He pulls out his phone.

"What are you doing?"

"Calling Grace. She's never where I need her to be lately and I'm getting tired of it."

"She's downstairs on the back porch." The resignation in my voice comes out louder than I'd anticipated.

He heads down the stairs, casting me a look over his shoulder. I hear him open the screen door and call her name.

I breathe in the scent of my son. I snuggle him a little closer and promise him this isn't the last time I'll hold him. The two minutes it takes for Grace to come inside and climb the stairs isn't long enough.

"Here, I can take him." Grace takes Jack from me, whether I want her to or not.

Left alone, I do the only thing I can, and I head into Rosalind's room, closing the door behind me.

I look around the room, on the shelves, bedside tables, even by the window.

"There are no cameras in here," she whispers. She unfolds her legs but doesn't look at me. "I mean, if that's what you're looking for."

That's exactly what I was looking for.

"What's going on with you?" I sit on the edge of the bed, my voice calm.

She leans forward and rests her elbows on her knees. "I don't... I don't feel right. Does that make sense?"

"Is that why you left like you did?"

She shrugs. "I didn't feel like there was much left to say, you know?"

I pull out my phone, bring up the photo of Marcus at the party, and show her.

She looks, then glances away.

"You knew?" I don't feel like I need to clarify my question. She knows exactly what I'm talking about. "Rosalind, did you know?"

"It doesn't matter anymore, does it?" She reaches for a throw and wraps it around her. "I'm freezing; how is that possible?"

"Don't change the subject, please. This matters."

"Why?" She finally stops her fussing. "Why does it matter when we already know who he is and what he's like? This is our lives now, Trina. Bringing up the past isn't going to change any of it."

"It changes everything."

"How? Trina, I have a beautiful family now. Destroying him destroys that, don't you understand?"

Yes, I understand that. But if she was willing to destroy everything because she lost her son all those years ago, why does she think I'm any different?

"When do I matter?"

"What? Of course you matter. What are you talking about?"

Knock-knock.

I answer the door and find Grace there.

"Is everything okay?" she asks.

"Everything is fine." I don't bother to hide my annoyance.

"It's just that I could hear everything," she says. "Not just now, but also outside."

"And?" I don't care if she heard everything. Nothing she heard can be construed to mean anything to someone who wasn't there and doesn't know us.

"Just be careful, that's all." She looks toward the office door that is partially open and shrugs. "If you want everyone knowing your secrets, have at it. Just thought I'd be nice."

I watch her as she walks away, and a shiver spreads over my skin. Something tells me I need to be careful around her, but I still don't know why.

The need to walk, to find some peace or sense of understanding of what just happened is strong, so rather than head back to my cottage, I take the long path around the property. I plug in my earbuds and listen to an audiobook, letting my feet take me wherever they want to go. I need some distance from the house, from the people, from everything that is going on.

I take a long circular path and am back close to the garden when I see her. Grace. Pushing the stroller along the pathway, head bent. I take out my earbuds, and I can hear her softly singing. She's good with him. She's done this before.

I stop at a bench and sit, not ready to announce myself, or make conversation, when I hear a voice carry across the lawn.

"Grace!"

It's Matty. He walks toward her, all legs, arm in a sling. His grin splits wide when she looks up.

"Matty," she says, like she's been waiting for him.

My skin prickles.

He leans over the stroller, grinning at Jack. "You always said babies do better when they're outside. Guess you were right." His voice carries on the wind and my breath catches.

Always said?

Grace laughs. "And you never believed me. But look at you now."

My heart hammers helplessly in my chest. They know each other? More than know each other. This isn't a chance meeting between the new nanny and Mabel's grandson. This is... history.

Maybe it was Mabel who recommended Grace for the job? But I thought she came from a staffing agency?

I should say something, make my presence known, but I don't. Instead I watch. I listen. I learn. The way Matty looks at Grace... and the way she looks back... My stomach turns. There's something here, something none of them are saying.

And I'm the only one who seems to see it.

TWENTY

I've been feeling antsy all day. Yesterday was a whirlwind of discovering secrets—Rosalind knew about Marcus, and the shared history between Grace, Matty, and Mabel. I struggled to process it all and barely slept.

I should be tired, but instead, I'm wired and need to do something.

That something is figuring out what this key I was given opens. I should have asked Rosalind yesterday and I don't know why I didn't.

I'm in the house and thankfully everything is quiet. Every door upstairs is closed, which gives me the freedom to explore.

I head toward the spare bedroom beside the office.

It's been a while since I've been in here. Marcus used this as his bedroom for a while after the girls were born, wanting to be close to help. It's basically a second master suite, with its own bathroom and walk-in closet.

It's the walk-in closet I'm interested in. There's a small storage cupboard in the corner of it. Last I recall, Rosalind uses it to store out-of-season clothing and Christmas gifts she doesn't want anyone to find.

The room is pristine, featuring a neutral color scheme. The closet isn't empty, which surprises me a little. It's stuffed with boxes, the racks full of suits and dress shoes. I wonder if Trent uses this closet now.

The small storage cupboard is locked, and—surprise, surprise—my key slides in easily. I'm about to turn it when someone clears their throat behind me.

"Anything I can help you with?"

It's Marcus. His hair is in disarray from running his fingers through it, his dress shirt has two buttons open, and his sleeves have been rolled to his elbows.

He looks completely different from before. Did something happen?

"Trina?"

I shake my hand and pull the key from the door.

"Just playing Nancy Drew, I guess." I give a half-laugh, like this whole thing is completely funny, and once he understands, he'll agree.

Except, I know he won't.

"And what mystery are we solving?" He holds out his hand but my grip tightens around the key.

Damn it.

"The case of the mysterious key." I pretend like it's nothing serious. "Just wondering what it unlocks."

He's still holding out his hand. "Where all have you tried? Can I see it?"

Reluctantly, I place it in the palm of his hand. "Every door in my cottage, even the garden sheds out back," I tell him, which is a lie. "I tried all the doors downstairs I could find and figured I might as well try up here. Didn't Rosie used to use this cupboard as storage for Christmas ornaments and gifts?" It takes everything in me to keep my voice relaxed.

"You'd probably know better than me." He looks the key over, then pockets it. "Where did you find it?"

One breath to calm the pitter-patter of my heart. Two breaths to squash the rising panic in my chest. Three breaths to place a somewhat convincing smile on my face.

"Honestly, I don't remember. It kind of just... appeared." Technically, that's not a lie.

My phone buzzes in my pocket just then, and without thought, I pull it out and see it's another message from Sarah Clemmens with another attachment.

"It's probably for an old lock or maybe something down at the bar. Either way, I'll take care of it. Why don't I walk you back to your cottage?"

While he doesn't say it, that's a clear *it's time for you to leave* kind of message.

He follows me as I leave the room and head down the stairs. For a moment, I falter. There's a memory... something that's just on the edge of clarity, but it has something to do with these stairs. My hand was on the railing, someone was beside me...

"Everything okay?" Marcus asks.

My foot slips and I fall back, my feet flying out from beneath me, but Marcus is there, catching me, just in time.

"Whoa, careful," he says. "Are you hurt?" His grip is strong and will probably leave bruises on my arms.

He helps me down the stairs, like I'm a frail woman, but I don't say anything, mainly because he's the only reason I'm still on my feet. A heavy sense of dread sits on me and I feel like I'm suffocating from the weight.

"Here, sit." He pulls out a chair from the island.

"Is everything okay?" Mabel stands opposite me, drying her hands on a dish towel.

"She almost fell down the stairs." Marcus rests his arm across my shoulders. "Are you hurt?"

I shake my head. "I'm fine, honestly. Thank you for catching me."

"I'll always be here for you, you know that." His words

should give me a sense of comfort, safety, but they don't. They feel more like a trap.

"Why don't I put on the kettle and we can have a cup of tea while you catch your breath." Mabel suggests.

"A cup of tea sounds good. Thank you." I attempt to give her a smile, but I doubt it comes across that way.

Marcus leaves my side and heads to the stove. The scent of garlic and onions fills the air as he lifts the lid off a large pot. "Whatever you're making, it smells delicious." He replaces the lid and smiles at Mabel. "I'll get out of your hair. Trina, are you okay to walk back to your cottage on your own?"

"Of course," I demur. When he leaves, there's a nice dose of silence in the room while Mabel picks up a knife and starts cutting vegetables.

"Can I help?" I point toward her cutting board.

"Not on your life. You just sit there and catch your breath. No doubt that fall brought back some bad memories. You poor thing." She takes a carrot and starts cutting it into pieces. "These past few weeks, they haven't been easy. Between you and Mrs. R... why, I'm just glad Grace is here, aren't you?" Her voice is casual but with an edge that makes me think she knows more than she lets on.

I'm curious why Mabel is bringing this up now. Mabel doesn't do casual conversations. When she asks questions, it's for a reason. I feel it across my ribs, a slash of uncertainty. "Why is that?"

"Pregnancy can do a number on some women, and they need extra... help. Lord knows I see it with my own daughter right now. I tell her she needs to hire a nanny, but she won't listen to me." There's a censorship in her tone that I catch, but only barely. "Maybe Mrs. R should go to that clinic, the one I heard the doctor mention. I worried something like this might happen." She says this last part beneath her breath.

"What do you mean?"

She shakes her head.

"Mabel? What do you mean?" I push. Mabel has been with the family since Marcus and Trent were little, and if there is one thing Mabel is, it's loyal to the Eatons.

"That night..." She glances at me, hesitating. "It was a hard night, for you, for Mrs. R, for everyone. That... that never goes away, you know?"

"No, actually, I don't, because I don't remember much about that night."

Her brows knit together, then she dips her head and returns her attention to the vegetables in front of her. Except, she doesn't continue chopping them, she just stares at them, knife held up, as if someone hit the pause button.

Then she sighs. "Maybe it's better that way."

"Better? No." One thousand percent no. "I'm living a nightmare, Mabel." I lean against the counter. "One minute I'm with Rosie, the next you're leading me down..." I stop, the memory hitting me with the weight of bricks. "You led me down the stairs." Was it her hand on my back? There's a silent accusation in my voice. Does she hear it?

She shakes her head.

"Everything was happening at once. We were coming down here for some tea when you tripped. Between you and Mrs. R, it was a night of chaos." Her lips tighten then. "I'm sorry."

I tripped or she tripped me? Did Mabel push me down the stairs? I don't want to believe it and yet... I feel the weight of a hand on my back, even now.

"You know, something has been bugging me, Mabel. Did you give me or Rosalind anything to eat or drink that night?" The words tumble out of their own accord, and from the widening of her eyes, I can't help but wonder if I struck a chord. All this time, I've believed someone poisoned me, that's why I fell down the stairs, but maybe I'm wrong.

Maybe I was pushed.

"Of course not. Mrs. R was in labor. She wasn't allowed anything other than ice chips, and you, you were so focused on her, we all were." She sets down the knife. "Why? You don't think..." She stops and slowly puts the knife down on the counter.

She heaves a long sigh, one that has her shoulders sagging forward. "All of us here, we all have the same goal. We want to love and protect this family. That's all I've done and will continue to do. You, Trina, are family. Why would I ever hurt you?"

She would if she were asked to. I don't say that, though.

I can't prove anything. I can't prove she pushed me down the stairs. I can't prove I tripped. I can't prove that I was poisoned, although I'm starting to doubt that myself.

I can't even prove that my own child is mine.

Mabel watches me, waiting for an answer. Do I believe her? Does it matter? What I do believe is the hurt I hear in her voice.

"I'm sorry, Mabel," I say. "I just..."

"You're living in a nightmare. It's okay." She parrots my words back to me.

There's a slam from a door at the front of the house. Mabel wipes her hands on her apron. "Better go check who that is," she says before leaving.

I hear the low sound of conversation from the front door. I can't make out who it is or what they're saying, but it's not my business and Mabel is taking care of it. The kettle screams, so I get up, turn off the stove, and pour the water into a waiting teapot.

I head to the stairs and pause, waiting to see if I can hear Mabel still. Despite Marcus having that key, I did manage to unlock the door and now is my chance to go look and see what's in there.

Quietly, I run up and head to that spare bedroom, but when I go to open the door in the closet, it's locked.

I try again. I know I unlocked it, but it won't open, not even if I pull. I didn't imagine that, did I?

"Trina?" Mabel is calling my name. Despite my frustration, I leave the room and return downstairs.

"Did you go upstairs?"

I nod. "Just to use the bathroom. Rosalind has a hand cream up there I like to use," I say as I rub my hands together, pretending I have cream on them.

"Ahh, I know the one. We actually have it down here now, too." She pours me a cup of tea. "Not that I'm trying to push you out of the kitchen, but why don't you go relax on one of the recliners on the porch? Put your feet up, listen to a podcast, and I'll bring out some fresh cut veggies for you?"

Once outside, I find the recliner and get comfy. I open up my phone, remembering the message from Sarah.

Me again. I found another photo and thought I'd send it. Wasn't she in the same foster house as you? I can't remember her name—Tammy, Theresa? I was scrolling through your profile and where you live looks dreamy. A scene right out of Yellowstone. Tell me... are the cowboys rugged and handsome too?

I pull up the attached photo and gape in shock.

Grace's face is staring back at me. A younger Grace, but her nonetheless.

Except, Sarah is right. Her name isn't Grace. It's Tammy Lee and she did live in the foster home with me and Rosalind. I knew she looked familiar. If memory serves me, we both hated her. She was the type of girl who'd smile to your face while plunging a knife in your back and we never trusted her.

What the hell is she doing here?

TWENTY-ONE

"Wyatt, where are you? I need to see you."

He's my first call. My first and only. He'll remember Tammy Lee, he'll confirm it's Grace, and he'll find out why she's here.

There has to be a reason. There's no such thing as coincidence.

"I'm at the main barn. What's going on?"

"I need to see you." Those are the only words that come out, the only things I'm able to say as I stare at the photo on my screen.

"I'll come by during my rounds." He sounds tired but I don't care in this moment.

He's not taking me seriously, I can tell. "Wyatt, please." I add urgency to my voice and pray he can hear it.

"Where are you?" He hears it, thank God.

"Back porch of the main house. Rosie is sleeping and I can't..." I can't leave her. I can't leave Jack. Not with Tammy Lee in the house with them.

"I'll be right there."

I can't sit still. I pace the porch, holding the mug of tea in one hand and my phone in the other, and wait for him to arrive.

He's driving a pickup and parks off to the side. I leave the porch and head his way. He's scruffy, smelly, and sweaty. He takes off his hat, pulls out a dirty rag from his back pocket, and wipes his forehead, leaving smudges that only add to the smudges already there.

"What's going on?" he asks. "Are you okay? Is Rosalind?" Real worry laces his voice.

"Look at this." I shove the phone in his face and hold it. My hand shakes and he reaches out, fingers wrapped around my wrist to steady me.

"Who is that?"

"Tammy Lee."

There's nothing. No recognition.

"Tammy Lee," I repeat. "From that last foster home."

"I don't see it." His uncertainty is a poison. It seeps through my skin, into my bloodstream, into my mind.

"Look again." This time, I'm begging.

"Okay...?"

"Don't you get it? Don't you see who that is?" I push the screen closer to his face but he moves it out of the way. "It's Grace."

"Grace? What the hell are you talking about?"

I grit my teeth in frustration. How does he not see it? That is her. I know it.

He takes the phone from my hand and stares at it. I give him the time, the space, to make the connection, and finally, I see it. His eyes at first light up, then narrow. He looks at the house, his lips pursing together, before he hands me the phone.

"What the hell is she doing here?"

"My question exactly." I stare at her photo again. "Was she there when...?"

He shakes his head. "The house was empty—well, except for..."

I nod. That's what I thought. "But she was there, right? Like, before? Before the fire and everything?"

He doesn't say anything and that's answer enough.

"It's not a coincidence. I know it's not. I've never liked her, never trusted her, and she's in there, right now, with my son."

His gaze flashes to me. "Trina." One word and it carries a rebuke more than anything.

"What? That is my son, whether you believe me or not, and I won't leave him with her. Not now, when I know the truth."

Wyatt gives me a slight nod, and that's all I need. "Does Rosie know?"

I shake my head. I doubt it. She'd be freaking out if she did.

"She's here for a reason," Wyatt says. "What all do you know about her?"

I lift my hands then drop them. "Nothing. I was under the impression that Marcus hired her from an agency but..."

"But?"

"Well, I saw something yesterday. Her with Matty."

He looks at me, one eyebrow raised. "And?"

"And they know each other." I twist my fingers together. "Not just polite hello-nice-to-meet-you know each other. Like *really* know each other. She was walking Jack outside and he came running up to her like he was happy to see her. He said something about how she'd always said babies like being outside. Like they'd talked about it before. And she, well, she ruffled his hair, Wyatt. Like what someone you know does."

Wyatt doesn't answer, not right away. "You're sure that's what you saw?"

"Yes!" My voice cracks. "I was right there. He lit up when he saw her. It doesn't make sense, right?"

Wyatt exhales, steady, calm in a way that makes me want to scream. "Is it possible you're seeing something that's not there?"

I shake my head. "I know what I saw. It's like when I walked in on Mabel and Grace in the kitchen, talking over tea. You remember how long it took for Mabel to warm up to me, right? Why would she be so friendly with a temp nanny?"

Wyatt steps closer. "So what do you want to do about this?"

I sigh. "I don't know." I honestly don't. "Do we tell Rosalind?"

He shakes his head. "No. Rosie is hanging on by threads as it is. If we tell her this, that Grace is really Tammy Lee... She doesn't need that right now."

"She deserves to know the enemy is sleeping under her roof."

"She needs us to take care of this for her." His voice hardens. He squeezes my shoulder, gentler now. "We stay quiet. We watch and we sure as hell protect Rosie as much as we can. I'll do some digging, okay? Let me handle this."

I nod, but my chest aches. Silence feels like betrayal, but shouting the truth feels like suicide.

"Her file, if there is one, is probably in the upstairs office," I suggest. "I'll see if I can sneak in and find it."

Wyatt pulls out his phone and looks at something. "They're both away tonight," he tells me. "I need to drive them into the city for a meeting."

"Then I'll look when the house is quiet." Which is perfect, because I'll look for proof about Jack at the same time. "If I can get Tammy Lee out of her room for a bit, I'll go through and see if I can find anything. There's got to be something in there to prove who she is."

Wyatt stares out toward the barn. "She asked if she could do some riding today," he says, rubbing the back of his neck. "I can keep her occupied for an hour or so, if that's enough time."

That's perfect.

The screen door slaps against the frame and we both turn.

"I had a feeling that was your voice I heard," Mabel says,

wiping her hands on a towel. "I need some help getting a container down, if you have a moment."

"For you, I have all the time in the world, Ms. Mabel." Wyatt gives me a look before following Mabel inside. "Happen to know if Grace is around? She was asking for some more riding lessons." The screen door closes behind him and I retake my seat. I'm not heading back to my cottage now, that's for sure.

I can't stop staring at the photo.

Tammy Lee. We never got along, always butted heads, and she always came across as if she was better than anyone else, even as a foster kid. She'd always be in our room stealing our things, specifically Rosalind's things—hair ties, makeup, perfume, clothes. I once caught her burning an essay Rosie had stayed up all night working on.

Why is she here? What's her endgame? Her being here, that's not a coincidence; that much I know for sure.

It doesn't take long before I hear voices coming from the kitchen. A few minutes later, Wyatt and Grace join me on the porch.

"Gonna take Grace here out on a riding lesson," Wyatt says, as if I didn't already know.

Grace smiles. "Being a city kid, I never thought I'd ever get to ride a horse. Jack is down for his nap, but Mabel will listen in for him."

"She's busy making dinner," I say, keeping my voice light and friendly. "I'll go grab the monitor and keep it out here with me."

"Oh, don't you worry about that. Jack will be fine. His belly is full, he has a fresh diaper on, and he'll sleep right through, I'm sure. Besides, I won't be long." She lifts a hand in a wave and I catch a shining glint from a bracelet.

My bracelet. The one I'm missing.

My mind whirls and I remember her being in my house the one time, when she'd brought the girls down for that visit. She must have taken it then.

My lips thin with anger and I'm about to say something when Wyatt gives me a hard look. I know what he's thinking—take advantage of this time, and I fully plan on it.

I wait about fifteen minutes before I head into the house with my empty cup. I don't see Mabel anywhere, so I leave it on the counter and head up the stairs as quietly as I can.

The first thing I do is sneak a peek at my baby. He looks so peaceful right now. Content and safe. I stand there, staring at him for the longest time, unable to pull myself away from his side, but then I hear a noise downstairs, a door closing, and that's all it takes to make me move.

I half expect the door to her bedroom to be locked, so I'm surprised when it opens after twisting the knob. I glance over my shoulder, looking directly at the camera, and then walk into her room.

Not much has changed. The room still has the girly vibe Rosalind was going for when I slept in this room.

The same white bedspread covers the queen bed; the same soft green and pink hand-braided round rug, an item Rosalind and I picked up from a store in Calgary during one of our shopping trips, is beneath the bed. On the dresser is a two-tier tray made from recycled china plates, which Rosalind and I found at a shop in Brooklyn called the Brooklyn Teacup during a girls' trip. In the basement of a cute brownstone was a slew of china settings, from cups to plates to soup bowls and even teacup candle holders. We both fell in love with the idea. I have a few similar pieces in my cottage, and there are several around the main house as well. All of my pieces have a blue and white china look, while Rosalind used various color schemes to fit each of the rooms in the main house. This one has soft pink roses on the pieces.

The room itself is spotless. There's nothing on the floor, no clothes tossed on the corner chair, and other than a few toiletries on a small table, the room looks like no one is staying here.

There is one item on that table that stands out, though. A bottle of perfume that looks just like the one Rosalind brought home from Paris. I notice some gold etching on the back, and without thinking about it, I pick up the bottle.

My love. My heart. My life.

That's the same wording Trent used on Rosalind's bottle when they bought it. This is Rosalind's. Why would Grace have it? I highly doubt Rosalind freely gave it to her; in fact, I know she wouldn't have.

I start to open a drawer when I hear someone behind me.

"Is there something you're looking for?" The voice is gentle, calm. Grace stands in the doorway, head tilted, honey-blonde hair falling from her bun.

Marcus stands behind her.

I hate her. Hate that honey-blonde hair. Hate that sweet, innocent smile. Hate the way she looks at Marcus like he's her dessert she's about to devour.

"Trina, why are you in Grace's room, going through her things?" Marcus asks. His lips are stretched tight, his eyes narrowed, his shoulders slumped.

He's upset.

I slowly withdraw my hand and stand to my feet.

Grace smiles, soft and serene, and I'm sure it's meant to mock. It digs deep inside me.

"Do you need something for Jack?" Her eyes are wide, sympathetic but now that I know who she is, I see the mockery behind the shield.

"Trina?" Marcus's voice is firmer now, more insistent. "I need an answer."

"You're right, I was looking for something." There's a boldness in my tone that surprises me. "I saw Rosalind's perfume on the table and started wondering what else Grace might have taken."

"Taken?" Marcus cocks his head, looking at the perfume I'm pointing to.

"She's wearing my bracelet. I've been missing it for a while now."

Grace gives me a strange look as she lifts her arm. "This one?"

I nod. "I bought it in Santorini. There should be a little S on the back of the cross."

Marcus eyes Grace. Maybe he believes me now.

Grace twists the bracelet to show the S but she shakes her head despite my triumphant smile. "This is from the last family I was with. They had a little girl named Sarah and added her initial to it."

"No, it's the one I bought while in Santorini."

"I'm sorry, Trina. I really am," Grace says.

"What about the perfume?"

Grace steps past me. "Mrs. Eaton gave this to me to spray on a sweater. Jack seems to like it and we thought it might help comfort him when I hold him. I totally got sidetracked this morning, otherwise I would have returned it right away," she says, her voice soft, her eyes gentle, but I catch the glare in them. "I would never keep something like this," she says. "Mrs. Eaton told me it was a gift from her husband."

"Sorry, Grace," Marcus says. "Obviously, there has been a mistake. This won't happen again, will it, Trina?"

I know he wants me to agree. I know he expects me to apologize and to leave, but I do none of those things. I watch her while she watches me. The way her lips curve into a condescending, sneering smile is all it takes for my fists to clench and my nose to flare. "I know—"

"Trina? It's time you returned to your cottage." Marcus is rather firm now. He steps out into the hallway.

"It's okay, Mr. Eaton, honestly," Grace says, her voice sickeningly sweet. "We've gotten off on the wrong foot, that's what you were going to say, right?" She directs this my way. "I know, I felt that too. Wyatt got called away, which is why I'm back so early. Maybe we could grab a coffee and chat while Jack is still sleeping?" The way her cheeks blush a soft pink as she flutters her eyes, I want to strangle her.

"I know what you're doing."

There's a brief hesitation in her smile; it falters slightly before she checks herself.

She knows I know the truth.

"Trina?" Marcus calls again, and this time, there is no doubt of his anger.

"I have no idea what you're talking about," Grace says, her voice soft enough that only I can hear.

"Really?" I reach out and tear the bracelet off her arm. It's broken now, but I can get it fixed.

There's a flare in her eyes, a growing look of panic that gives me a jolt of satisfaction. I leave and follow Marcus out into the hallway, stuffing the bracelet into my pocket.

"She's not who you think she is," I tell Marcus, who's standing at the top of the stairs.

"I'm going to walk you back to your cottage," Marcus says.

"I'm serious, Marcus."

"So am I."

The walk back to my place is silent.

Marcus opens the front door for me and watches me with those intense, focused eyes, like I'm a wild horse to be tamed, or perhaps I'm too broken and he's not sure what to do with me.

"You have no idea who you've let into your house," I tell him.

"No, I don't think I do."

"I'm talking about Grace. She's not who you think she is." I don't like the look on his face, the coldness in his gaze. Fear snakes through me as he says nothing.

"Marcus, I need to show you something." I pull out my phone and unlock it.

"No. Trina, sit down."

I shake my head and show him the photo of the woman calling herself Grace but he won't look at it.

"I don't want to talk about Grace. We need to talk about you, about what you're going through, about how you've been acting lately. Honestly, I'm worried about you." Whisper-soft words spoken with pain that I wasn't expecting. He's worried about me?

"You lost a baby. We... we lost a baby. And I haven't been there for you like you need. I blame myself." The grief and concern that radiate from him catch me off guard.

We had a one-night stand in Santorini while on a family vacation. It was late, I'd gone for a swim in the outdoor pool, and he couldn't sleep. Add in some wine and, well, things happened. But that was the only time. I was angry at myself the following day, disgusted that I'd let something like that happen. The following morning, he even apologized, which surprised me. Life went on as normal, me focused on the girls and him being him.

Until I found out I was pregnant.

We'd agreed to co-parent, so our child would always know the love of both parents. I was going to move in with him, not to live as a couple but as a family unit. While I was packing up my things, he was setting up a nursery and a bedroom for me in his ranch house. Life wasn't going to be perfect, and it sure as hell was going to be messy and complicated, but we were going to make it work for the sake of our child.

All that changed the night I went into labor.

While I lay in bed, broken by grief, Mabel came in and unpacked my things.

While I dozed outside, body needing to recover, Marcus visited me every day, making sure I ate, making sure I took care of myself. Making sure I knew I wasn't alone.

The grief in his voice right now—is it real? I don't want to believe it. I can't. I want to say that I haven't lost anything. My son was taken from me, by him... but I stop myself. His grief stops me. It sounds honest, gut-wrenching, but how can that be?

"I'm fine, Marcus. This isn't about me. This is about Jack and—"

"You are the only one I'm concerned about. Jack is fine. You're not. You can't be going into other people's rooms, Trina. That wasn't your place."

I shrug. I'd do it again and again if I had to. In fact, I will.

I want to know why she's here. Her. Us. After so many years.

He slowly twists his neck until the *pop-pop-pop* of his joints is loud enough to make me wince. "I need to make time to see the chiropractor, but Dr. Ron is away on holiday." He makes an obvious change in the conversation and my jaw hurts from gritting my teeth. "He's in South America or something," he says.

"Paris," I correct. "It's Ursula's birthday gift." I have to look away. The fury building in me is so fresh, I know he'd be able to see it in my eyes.

"It's been a while since you've had an appointment with him, hasn't it? I'll have one scheduled for you. In fact, I should schedule you a full spa day. I also think Dr. Harmon should see you next time he's here."

"I don't need to see him."

"Yes, I believe you do. You need to take care of yourself, Trina," Marcus says. "And if you don't, I will." His voice is smooth and low, wrapping me in concern I do not want. "I mean that."

"The one you should be concerned about is your baby nanny. Did you do a background search on her? Her real name is Tammy Lee. I don't remember her last name, but both Rosalind and I know her from our foster home days."

"You've talked to Rosalind about this?"

I shake my head. "Not yet, but I will."

"No, you won't. You'll leave this with me. Do you understand?"

I don't answer because there's no point. Instead, I grit my teeth hard enough a headache forms.

"I mean it, Trina. You won't like the consequences if you keep going like this. This isn't like you and I'm worried."

He's worried about me? He should be more worried about the snake he's let into his home.

And if he won't do something about it, I will.

In fact, I'll do it tonight when Marcus and Trent are gone and Rosalind is asleep.

TWENTY-TWO
ROSALIND

The phone in my hand shakes as I fumble to find Trina's phone number.

It's midnight and Jack has been screaming now for a solid thirty minutes. He's only four weeks old—a little baby like him shouldn't be crying with so much pain. Nothing I do seems to help him either. Why don't I know what he needs?

The volume of his cries ebbs and flows as I stand in my bedroom, the monitor turned down low so that I can call Trina and beg her for help. I swipe at the tears on my face, sniffling hard, and as soon as I find her number, I hit call.

Her voice crackles on the other end, a lifeline I'm desperate to grab onto. I need help. I shouldn't, but I do, and for some reason, I'm all alone in this house.

"Hello? Rosie? What's wrong?"

I don't say anything. I can't. Jack's screams surround me.

"I'm coming." There's a soft click when the call ends.

Back in the nursery, little Jack's fists flail about as his legs scrunch up so that he looks like a potato bug.

I pick him up, but it has no effect. He just looks at me with tears on his cheeks, mouth open wide as he screams. Is he in pain? Is there something wrong with him? Why won't he stop?

I need him to stop. I'm doing everything I can, using up all the reserves I have within me to help him, but all he does is take, take, take when I have absolutely nothing left to give.

As horrible as it sounds, I could walk away. Walk away from it all. From him. From this house. From this life. The only things stopping me are the girls. At least to them, I mean something.

I hate that I feel this way. I hate that when I look at him, at this baby in my arms, I feel nothing.

I'm an empty vase, full of spider cracks, sure that one day it will be too much and I'll buckle and break.

I'm almost there. I can feel it. I can see it.

I know this isn't normal, that this is an extreme case of post-partum depression, but knowing it and having that make a difference in how I'm feeling right now are two very different things. The medication I'm on should be helping. Or maybe it is, and if I weren't on it, I'd be much worse.

I would never harm Jack. My chest tightens, my heart spasms, and shudders run down my skin at the thought. No matter what Marcus says, I know I wouldn't do that.

Why does this always happen when I'm alone? Trent lately seems to leave when I need him the most, flying off to meetings, enjoying life while I drown in Jack's relentless cries. It's like it happens on purpose, like he doesn't want to be here. Not even Grace is here. I bet she's down at the ranch house hooking up with one of the cowboys.

She better keep her hands off of Wyatt.

I grip the wooden railing of the crib. My skin crawls, my hair itches, my bones ache.

Jack's cries stab through me. I watch him as he squirms, tiny hands balled into angry fists. How can someone so small make so much noise? I pull in a ragged breath. Maybe he's hungry. Or maybe he needs changing. Maybe he's sick. Or maybe he just hates me, hates me like I hate myself. I squeeze my eyes shut. Can't he feel how much I want to love him? I really do.

My legs wobble as exhaustion drags me down until all I want to do is curl up in a ball and sleep. The thick carpet softens my steps as I walk in circles with Jack in my arms. Jack, who won't stop crying, who never stops crying, who should be comforted by the simple fact that I'm here, holding him. I stop and stare at him, shushing sounds leaving my lips with each breath. I'm so tired. So freaking tired.

Jack's face is red, scrunched, wet with tears and snot. The words I whispered over and over again when I first held him echo in my mind. *I'm sorry. I'm sorry. I'm sorry.* Sorry for what? The reason doesn't matter, not really.

His pale blue eyes search my face, seeking something I'm obviously not giving him. He needs me, he needs something from me, and whatever I'm doing, it's not enough.

It shouldn't be like this. It wasn't like this with the girls. They were so easy, even with them being twins. They loved being held. They loved being with me, unlike Jack, who never seems to feel safe or happy in my arms.

When Trina arrives, she appears like a ghost, and it takes me a moment to realize she's calling my name.

"Rosalind," she says softly, her arms reaching out for Jack, who's twisting in my arms, his tiny body a bundle of screams and flailing limbs. "Rosie, give him to me. It's okay. I'm here."

My fingers uncurl around Jack's body and then drop away the moment he's safe in Trina's arms.

His screams soften. His hair is damp, sweaty, sticking up in red-gold tufts. Trina bounces him gently, turning him back and forth as she pats his bottom. He's still crying but already it's softer, softer. "Shh, baby boy. Shh. It's okay. You're okay. You're loved, sweet pea, no need to cry." She whispers sweet nothings that mean all the things to him because it seems to be working.

My stomach twists into a tight knot as she does what I couldn't do.

I watch as she slowly checks him over, each movement careful and loving. She feels his forehead, checks his diaper, and runs her hands over his tiny limbs.

"I already changed him." My voice is weak, uncertain. "I even tried to feed him, but nothing would work. What did you do? Why does he calm with you but screams with me?"

I see the pity in Trina's eyes as she gives me a soft smile. "He's okay," she says. "Really, Rosalind. He's okay."

He's not okay. Not when he's with me. He's fine with everyone else. He seems to hate being held by only one person —me. I sit on the edge of the rocker, elbows on knees, fingers pressed against my eyes, desperate to erase the look of utter love and peace on Trina's face as she sways from side to side, her gentle motion easing Jack's cries. He hiccups as Trina fills the quiet with soothing words.

"I'm here now. I told you I would be, didn't I?"

Is she saying this to me or to Jack?

"Thank you for coming," I say, my voice hoarse, so hoarse. "I don't know what I'd do without you." I mean that, I truly do.

"I'm not going anywhere."

She holds Jack closer, humming softly as he slips toward sleep, giving one last little hiccup before settling into Trina's arms, his eyelids fluttering closed. She tucks him in tight against her shoulder, kisses his tiny head, her rocking motion smooth and easy. "There we go," she murmurs. "See? He's fine. He just needed..." She stops herself, but I know what she was about to say. Just needed a little love. Just needed a little attention. Just needed her. "He just needed a little extra tonight."

"Trent should be here," I say, accusation filling my voice as I wrap my arms tight around my body.

"Where is he?"

I shrug. "Some emergency came up that requires both him and Marcus to be somewhere early."

"Marcus couldn't handle it?"

He could. For sure. That's supposed to be the plan, isn't it? "Whatever crisis is happening, they both need to be there." I'm so tired.

My voice crumbles as my eyes struggle to remain open. "I tried. I really did," I tell her, pointing toward Jack. "I fed him, changed him, bounced him, walked with him, even gave him a warm bath. He's been crying for hours, Trina. Hours. Nothing I did worked. She's not even here, either," I say, nodding my head toward the door at the back of the room.

Trina frowns and I swear she's about to say something, but whatever it is, she keeps it to herself.

"I can't do this." I'm never one to be a defeatist, but here I am, admitting it.

"Can't do what?" Her voice is low but full of worry.

"This. Him. Like this, I just... can't." It's a simple statement—simple words—but admitting it out loud crushes me in ways I didn't expect, leaving me breathless and aching. I try to hide the shudder, but it rips through me.

"I..." My heart and mind battle for the right words to say. I'm holding on by the tiniest thread. "I can't. I'm sorry." My voice is hollow.

When I stand, I notice Trina is holding Jack tight to her chest. She's all he has right now. He quiets in her arms. Soothes in her arms. Loves her arms more than mine. I'm not even going to pretend that doesn't hurt.

Trina settles into the rocker I just left. Her heart is so full while mine is so broken. "It's okay," she says softly. "He has me."

TWENTY-THREE

TRINA

My heart hurts for the pain Rosalind is feeling, but sitting here, holding little Jack, I don't let myself get lost in her need.

I can't. My son needs me.

"Why don't you go rest?" I take in the circles under her eyes, the paleness of her skin.

She glances at Jack. "If you don't mind? When he falls asleep, be sure to put him back in his crib, okay?"

Like she needs to tell me how to take care of my child?

The sound of quick footsteps and the nudging of the door stops me from saying anything in response. The girls stand there, crazy bedhead and all.

"Momma," says Addison. "Is Jack okay?"

Rosalind wraps her arms around the girls. "What are you doing out of bed?" she asks, bending down so she's at their eye level. The way she is with them compared to how she is with Jack is so different, it's mind-boggling.

"Did Jack wake you up, too?" she asks softly, brushing her lips against both their foreheads, one at a time.

Addison nods.

Riley peeks over toward me and Jack. "I don't like when he's so sad." Her eyes are brimming with worry.

"I don't either, but you know what? It seems like Trina has the magic touch because, look, he's falling asleep," Rosalind says, her voice hushed. "And you should be too."

"Will you read to us, Mommy?" Riley whispers, placing her hand within Rosalind's and leading her down the hallway back to their room.

Addison lingers in the doorway before she makes her way over and places a soft kiss on Jack's head. "I love you so much," she says before skipping out of the room to follow her mom and sister.

I adjust Jack's blanket and look back to where Rosalind and the girls disappeared. They didn't even say goodnight. Jack sighs in his sleep, his warm breath on my neck. "They don't get it, do they?" I murmur. "They don't know how lucky they are."

When I was younger, I was alone. No one to fight for me. No one to stand up for me. No one to comfort me in the still of the night when I was scared of every noise. I would have given anything to have a sister back then.

I squeeze him closer, pressing my cheek against his head. It's me and Jack. It's just Jack and me.

I'm not so alone when I'm here, with him. But back at the cottage, I'm more alone than I've ever felt. That's when all of this sucks me under like it's a tidal wave and I'm its helpless victim. But here, in this room, with my baby in my arms, I don't feel so alone anymore.

"Why did they take you from me?"

Jack snuggles closer, like he knows my voice, my heartbeat. Of course he does. It's home to him.

His little legs kick, and his eyes are barely open, but they are just enough to see me, to see me seeing him. I give him the sweetest smile I can, one that makes my heart feel full, so full that tears gather on my lashes. "You get some rest, sweet baby," I say, rubbing his back.

I tenderly lift him to my shoulder, careful not to jostle him more than necessary. "Shh." My lips touch his ear, and he turns his head into my shoulder.

I wrap a soft blanket around him, and my eyes sting as I breathe him in. "Shh, Jack. I've got you. I've got you." The weight of his small body is almost too much to bear.

He's so warm. So soft.

Burying my face into the crook of Jack's neck, it's hard not to let all the feels overwhelm me. "I will always be there for you," I promise him. "Life may try to keep us apart, but we know the truth, don't we?" I rock him, closing my eyes for just a moment.

A sudden poof sounds, with his little bottom lifting in my arms, and all of a sudden I feel a warmth against my skin. "Well, I bet you feel better now, don't you?" I say as the smell of his dirty diaper hits me. I make my way over to the change table and realize the explosion went up his back. I quickly undress him, cleaning him up as best I can, before I take him into the bathroom to give him a bath.

A soft coo leaves Jack's mouth, and my fingers brush against his delicate cheek, unable to stop the tears from forming in my eyes. "Hey there, little man."

He looks at me with a smile that matches his father's. He looks at me with eyes that match my own.

Jack fusses more when I put him down, so I keep a steady hand on him while preparing the bath. "I know, I know." My voice is soft, gentle. It's tender, nurturing, and full of love. He needs to be in my arms all the time. "You don't like being alone, do you? Neither do I."

Jack's eyes don't leave my face, and the more I hold him, the more I want to. The more I can't let him go.

Once he's in the bath, I gently rub the soap on his skin and hum a soft lullaby, the sound filling the room.

He's such a small thing. His delicate skin slides under my touch as I lift him from the bath and onto a small towel. I wrap the towel around him and rub him gently, drying his small body with tender, loving motions.

A flash of pain courses through my heart. These people I call family, they've stolen these moments from me. I don't know if I'll ever be able to forgive them.

I lift him up and hold him close, and when I look in the mirror, I realize one part of the towel has slipped. It has slipped and revealed something I never thought to check.

The mark.

My mark.

A tiny, star-shaped birthmark below his shoulder blade. The exact same birthmark on my back, the one I've had since birth. The one my mother had as well. Birthmarks aren't generally genetic, but in my family, they are passed down from the mother to her children.

My hands tremble as I trace the star with my fingers, and the reality of what I'm seeing sinks in.

This is proof. This mark, along with my light hair with red undertones and the blue eyes... they are what I've been looking for. Proof.

My heart thumps so hard I feel the pain ripple through my chest. My lungs fight for freedom from the ropes wrapping around them, and there's a bubble of air stuck in my throat that won't let me breathe. I grip the edge of the counter as I continue to stare in the mirror, at Jack.

At a baby that I know now beyond a shadow of a doubt is mine.

TWENTY-FOUR

I've been back in my cottage for five minutes before the desperation for answers sets in.

Fifteen minutes ago, Grace walked into the bathroom, coming from nowhere, holding out a phone. Not a single word was said between the two of us. I took the phone; she took the baby, my baby, and walked away.

All I remember is Marcus's voice on the other end of the phone telling me that it was late and Jack needed to sleep. He told me to let Grace take care of the baby. He then hung up before I could say a single word.

I don't even know what I would have said, though, if he'd given me the chance.

I'd forgotten about the cameras. Forgotten I was being watched. Am being watched. I can't believe he called Grace just to take Jack from me. Why would he do that?

I'm not imagining the birthmark, the same birthmark that is like my own. The light hair. The blue eyes. I'm not imagining any of this.

I know I'm not.

Disbelief has set in, and on its heels are anger and determination. I pace around my cottage, my mind scrambling with revelations. The people I call family tore my family from me. Rage takes over with a frenzy. This is the proof I've been looking for, proof that Jack is mine, but I know it's not enough. Not when it comes to the Eatons, the family who gets away with anything and everything. So I tear my cottage apart, emptying drawers, rifling through cabinets, dumping file folders. There's no order to the madness. No sense, either. Any proof I need won't be here—it's going to be there, in the main house, in Trent's office.

My hands shake as I fight for breath, remembering the outline of that tiny birthmark on Jack's shoulder.

I bury my tears with gritted teeth. Jack is mine.

Jack. Is. Mine.

I. Hate. Them. Rosalind's betrayal hurts most. I haven't wanted to believe, not deep down, that she would do this, but she's seen his birthmark. She knows it's identical to mine. I know she does.

I slam my hand against the drawer and spit back a curse at the pain in my finger as it gets jammed.

My knees hit the floor with the weight of it all. I think about Marcus, how he's been so attentive and was always there after I gave birth. Marcus, who has played me time and time again. Does he know? He has to. If he didn't put Rosalind up to it, then she convinced him to do it.

Just like she's always been able to convince both me and Wyatt to take care of things for her.

It all makes sense. The one person I've trusted with everything is the one person who has destroyed me.

Anger swells up inside me, digging deep and taking root. I've always known my baby was alive, that I heard two cries.

This is why Rosalind can't bond with Jack. From guilt. This

is why they don't want me taking care of Jack, because I'll find out the truth. This is why Trent is always gone, because he can't bear the guilt of being around a child that isn't his.

Are they all in on this? I don't want to believe it. I can't.

And where does Grace—or, rather, Tammy Lee—fit into all this? Why is she here?

I can't breathe. There is no more air in the room. I turn in circles, hopeless, knowing there must be proof somewhere. My eyes fall on my phone, and my heart beats wildly at the thought. It's late. Too late for anyone to answer, but I can leave a message. I can beg for someone to call me first thing. I find the clinic's number and hit the call button.

"You've reached Dr. Harmon's office during after-hours service, and it is a non-emergency line. If this is an emergency, please hang up and dial 9-1-1. Otherwise, please leave a message."

The line beeps, and for a split second, I freeze. I have to do this right. I can't sound paranoid or hysterical. "This is Trina Emmet," I say in a voice that doesn't sound familiar. Telling them Jack is mine won't do anything. I need proof. "I know Dr. Harmon said it could take some time, but I want a copy of my baby's birth certificate." My voice cracks. "I can come in and pick it up but can you—" I swallow back the tears. "Can you email me a copy so I have proof? I really need to—" I catch a sob in my throat. "I want to do a DNA test, because the Eaton family stole my baby."

The phone slips from my hands and hits the ground with a crack. I hadn't meant to say that part. But it's too late now.

I bend to grab the phone when I hear a faint click—so soft, I almost miss it.

I freeze. Did I imagine that? Then I hear it again: a subtle crackle, the sound of air being swallowed by something hidden.

I stay where I am and slowly move my head, looking at

everything around me. I'm eye level with a bookshelf. I slowly look over the titles, check to make sure everything is in its place, the framed photos, the little figurines I picked up with the girls in Greece last year, and then I see it. It's a small circular device resting beside a frame, partially hidden by a lone piece of paper, something one of the girls had drawn me, half bent.

Without making a sound, I pick up my phone, take a photograph of the device, and do a reverse image search.

It's a listening device. Someone has bugged my home, listening in to my conversations.

Someone just heard me admit that I believe the Eatons stole my baby.

I can't take it. I head outside, my footfalls crunching against gravel, each step more like a death march, every thought a noose around my heart as I walk in circles out in my front yard. It was too claustrophobic in my cottage.

Anger still fuels me, but the rage and desperation are gone. Now, all I feel is numb. My best friend took my baby from me. Someone has bugged my home. I can't process either idea right now.

I almost don't see the shadow in the darkness that blocks my path as I find myself heading toward the main house. All I'm thinking about is proof. I need proof and the only place to get it is in that house.

Wyatt stops me. He's as tall and serious as ever. There's comfort in the way he moves, in the way he stands. Firm. Unwavering. Quiet. I've always appreciated that about him.

"What are you doing out so late?" We both speak at once, two sides of the same desperate coin.

He shrugs and shoves his hands in his pockets. "I was asked to do some rounds," he says. He doesn't look surprised to see me. "What's got you walking the grounds at this time of night?"

I chew my lip, unsure if I should tell him.

"What's going round that pretty little head of yours, sweetheart?" he asks in a drawl normally reserved for the twins.

I decide on honesty. "I'm about to do something really stupid or really life-changing."

He lifts a brow. "How about none of the above, and you head back home to climb into bed instead? Nothing good happens at this hour, and you know it."

"You don't understand, Wyatt. They..." I reach out and grab hold of him, needing him to understand me, to understand how serious this is and just how much I need his help. "They bugged my home and have been listening to my conversations."

"What do you mean?"

"I found a listening device. I just called the doctor's office, saying I need that birth certificate and I want to do a DNA test."

"You what?"

"They stole my baby. Jack has my birthmark. I saw it."

He runs his hands around the nape of his neck. "I can't... This family is crazy," he mutters. "Leave the device there so they—whoever it was who planted it—have no idea you know about it, but just watch what you say from now on. Okay?"

I nod. "Fine, whatever. But what about what I found out? The birthmark? I want my son back, Wyatt. I need proof, real physical proof that they stole him, before it's too late."

"Trina, that's..." His voice trails off, and I wait for him to tell me I'm crazy. Wyatt's voice is measured when he finally does speak. "That's a big accusation."

"You think I don't know that?" I think of all the signs I've convinced myself are true. "Think about it, Wyatt. When the twins were born, they both had dark hair and eyes, right? And the way Rosalind instantly bonded to them? Now think about Jack. His light hair." I touch mine. "His light eyes." I point to mine. "And my birthmark?" I pull down the shoulder of my top to bare my mark. "Jack has this in the same spot. The same mark. That means something."

Wyatt crosses his arms and watches me like he's trying to figure out a complicated equation, something that doesn't add up. "Are you sure?"

"What do you think I've been trying to tell you? I've known from the very beginning. I heard two baby cries, Wyatt. They're gaslighting me, saying I had a daughter, but I know the truth. They stole my baby." The truth spews forth, pulled straight from my heart.

He shakes his head, not in disagreement but something else. Disbelief. "Do you really think Rosalind would do that to you?"

Rosalind. A barbed hook stuck deep in my heart pulls, ripping me apart.

"Trina?"

I hesitate, and I don't need to answer. He sees it all over my face.

"Someone did," I finally say, because I know if I outright accuse her, he'll turn on me. "She has to know in her heart that something is wrong; she must."

"She would never do that and you know it."

"Then it's him. Marcus. Maybe he is the monster we've always believed him to be. He's probably the one who bugged my house."

I hold Wyatt's gaze. I need him to believe me. "It's something he would do. You know that. You know how he is."

I wait for him to agree with me, to tell me I'm not insane.

"But this? I don't see it," he says instead. "It doesn't make sense, Trina. None of it."

He sounds like Marcus. He sounds like Rosalind. He sounds like everyone who keeps trying to tell me my baby is dead and that I'm grieving.

I press my hand to my forehead. It's burning. Everything is. "I know. But that doesn't change anything."

His voice is too loud. "Trina—"

"Think about it," I say. "It makes me sick to my stomach, to think, to believe even for one second, that she could do this. I don't want to. I want to believe she's innocent... but what if? Wyatt, what if all the issues she's having are because she knows?"

His jaw clenches. "Don't."

"Wyatt—"

"Don't go there." He paces in front of me, hands out of his pockets now, clenched into tight fists. I see anger on his face, the same kind of anger he used to have whenever something bad was said about Rosalind. That anger was always directed to someone else, though, never to me.

I was stupid to think he'd see my side in this.

"She wouldn't," he says with a firm belief in his voice. "You know her better than that. Think of all she's done for you. How could you accuse her of something like this? You're just... you're grieving. And seeing Jack, holding him, taking care of him, you've hit your breaking point."

I reel back, the punch of his words leaving their mark.

"Were you there that night? I heard them, Wyatt. I heard my son. I heard Rosalind's baby. They were both alive." The words are barely audible, but they're there, out in the open, and I know he heard me.

He shakes his head. "Then what happened to Rosalind's baby? You don't honestly believe they would steal yours and give him to her? A baby died, Trina. I'm so sorry it was yours, but that's the truth."

My knees wobble at his words, and he reaches out to steady me. I'm wrecked beyond what I thought I could handle. I thought he would be on my side, that he would believe me, if I could prove it.

That's all I can do now. Prove that Jack is mine.

"Someone's baby died," I say, agreeing with him. "But it wasn't mine. And I'm going to prove it."

For the longest time, Wyatt just stares at me. His hands finally drop. Why do I feel like I've lost him?

"Be careful." I don't know if he's giving me permission to find out or if I should take it as a warning. He looks at me with hard eyes and says nothing else. There was a time he'd follow me anywhere. A time he'd never question me. That time is gone now.

TWENTY-FIVE

I sneak up to the main house, footsteps swallowed by the thick, heavy night air.

Wyatt left me, and I almost turned back, but the need to know is stronger than the need for self-preservation and I'm desperate for the truth.

There's no alarm on the door, which means someone forgot to turn it on, which is strange since Wyatt is doing his rounds. While we're relatively safe out here, in the middle of ranch land, when Trent is away, Rosalind is religious about setting the alarm.

One can never be too careful.

I keep my footsteps light as I walk up the stairs, careful to avoid the squeaking areas. The nursery door is closed, Rosalind's door is closed, and the girls' door is also closed. It's just me, alone in the hallway, where every noise I make is louder than when the girls were young and loved to bang on pots and pans for fun.

The office is just ahead, and that door has been left cracked open. I stop. What am I doing? This is... crazy... I know it, I know it in my head, but it's what's in my heart that propels me forward.

The first thing I do is reach up and move the camera lens so it's pointing toward the wall. I'm tired of being watched.

Then, I begin with the desk. Every time I open a drawer, I cringe, the squeak sounding loud in my ears.

I search for minutes that feel like hours. I go through the desk, the closet. I pull open drawers and rifle through Post-its, stamps, pens, and the odd disregarded paper. I find receipts and everything but what I'm looking for. My nerves are on edge. I'm convinced even the smallest noise will alert Rosalind. I know I'm being recorded, sure that they can hear me even if they can't see me, but it's late. Unless Marcus has his notifications on. I listen for the sound of a door opening and footsteps on the carpet outside this room, sure that once again, Grace will stand at the door and hand me her phone, with Marcus on the other end.

A part of me doesn't care. Let him see me. Let him call. I will scream at him until he gives me the proof I need, the proof that my baby is alive.

The filing cabinet is locked, but that doesn't stop me. I know where the key is hidden, in a "best dad in the world" mug that sits on the bookshelf beside it. I open each drawer, one at a time, and look through the files. Most of it doesn't mean anything to me, having to do with the ranch and their company. A few do and they have my fingers pausing as they dance from one file to another.

Staff files. Mine. Grace's. Mabel's. Wyatt's. And everyone else employed on this property. I grab mine and pull it out, thinking that maybe what I'm looking for will be in there, but it's not. All it contains is my employment record, the letters from HR confirming any bonuses and raises, a list of keys that I have in my possession, a copy of my driver's license, and a photograph of me and Rosalind. That is all.

Glancing at the door again, I then pull out Grace's file. It's very thin, with only a few references, her résumé, and her employment letter. Basically nothing. There's almost nothing on her résumé too, which would have been an instant red flag for me.

There are no files for the children, not in here, and I end up closing the drawer in frustration.

I know the birth certificates have to be here somewhere. The question is where?

The safe. Of course. I go to yank open a drawer on the bottom of the bookshelf, but it's locked. I think about the times I've seen Trent open the closet door and reach up, and I head there.

In the top left corner, as soon as you open the closet door, is a box. Inside the box is a hunting knife and a key. My hand shakes a little as I hold the box, questions running through my head about the knife and why he would need one here when he also has a locked gun safe behind his desk. I pull out the key and return the box.

I clutch the key like it's my lifeline. I slowly insert it into the lock and let out a breath when it turns. There's a loud click, almost as loud as my sigh of relief, as I open the drawer.

There are two things inside. The first is the key Rosalind had thrown at me and Marcus took from me. The other is a single envelope with the word "Private" stamped on the front. I pocket the key and pull out sheets of paper. Sheets that hold all the answers, sheets that tell me what happened the night Rosalind and I gave birth.

Two birth certificates. One death certificate.

My fingers tremble. I'm not ready. What if this tells me my baby is dead? That Jack isn't mine? What if it tells me that Jack is mine and Rosalind's baby is the one that died? Am I ready for the answers? For the truth?

The office door swings open, and I freeze.

Rosalind stands there, wild and dark, hair to her shoulders, an untied robe, white and heavy, hanging off her narrow frame. She sees me with the envelope, and her eyes widen.

"What are you doing?"

I open my mouth to say something, to say everything, but no words come out. Only air.

"Trina," she says, a little louder now. "What are you doing in here?"

I blink back whatever madness is in me. "I'm sorry." I slide the papers back into the envelope and set it down on the desk, not wanting to let it go, not wanting her to grab it. "I didn't mean—"

"You didn't mean to... what? Break into my husband's office and go through his things?" Her voice isn't accusing. It isn't angry. I don't know what it is.

I shift on my feet. "I'm sorry if I woke you."

She crosses her arms. "You didn't. I have a headache and was up getting water. I saw the light on in here and thought Trent was home." She looks over her shoulder, then back at me. "I didn't expect to find you in here."

She looks as horrible as I feel right now. There are bags under her eyes, shadows of doubt, shades of uncertainty. Does she know why I'm in here? Does she know what I found?

She takes a step into the office, the door still open, the truth still between us. "What are you doing in here, Trina?"

Her words are not a demand. They're a question, and that's the worst thing she could ask me.

I slump into Trent's chair, the envelope still on the desk, still between us. "I need to know."

"Know what?"

"What happened that night."

"Trina—"

"I need proof," I interrupt her, unwilling to listen to the excuses, the reasons, the lies she will tell me.

"Proof? Of what?"

I don't say anything at first; instead, I stare in the direction of the nursery. "I need proof that my baby is..." I pause, letting the words trail off, wondering if she'll answer for me instead.

This is the perfect time for her to come clean.

"If your baby is...?" She waits for me to finish.

"Asleep in that crib." I stare down at the envelope, my chest aching as I say the words.

"Why would you think that?" There's no accusation in her voice. No fear or concern. In fact, there's no emotion in her voice at all.

"He looks like me, don't you think?" I ask her. "Light hair with a bit of red in it, blue eyes, my birthmark."

She holds her robe closed with trembling hands. The door remains open. "Trina..."

"You've seen it, haven't you? The birthmark?" I ask. "You know the story. How it's hereditary. How it's the exact replica of mine?" I pull down the shoulder of my shirt and show her my mark. There's a need inside me for her to confirm it, to say that yes, she's wondered, that yes, it's why she can't bond with Jack, why she doesn't like holding him. I need her to tell me the truth for the first time.

If she does, I'll forgive her. We can move past this.

The silence is so loud and so long that I can't stand it.

Rosalind looks at me.

Rosalind looks at the envelope. "What's in there?"

"Proof of our children's birth. And proof that one of them died."

She firms up her lips and pulls her robe tighter. Then she closes the door and locks it behind her.

TWENTY-SIX

ROSALIND

New mornings mean new beginnings, something I've always believed in, something I tell the girls all the time.

New beginnings mean new choices, new decisions, new attitudes.

I guess it's time I listen to my own advice.

I wasn't able to sleep after I found Trina in Trent's office. I tossed and turned all night and my brain will not stop.

My heart thuds to a frantic beat as I watch the sun slowly rise over the land, the pale hues slowly sun-kissing the wildflowers. The view should calm me, but calm is the last thing I'm feeling. My head and my heart are being pulled in so many directions, I don't even know what to do.

No, that's a lie. I know what I can do. I can find out the truth.

My cell phone sits in my lap like a ticking time bomb. A bomb called Trent. A bomb called Marcus. A bomb called Jack. I'm the trigger.

My fingers hesitate over the screen, a dance of uncertainty. Trina's accusations batter my mind, breaking down the walls I'd put up. Everything is a disaster now.

She had so many questions for me last night. Did I do this? Did I know? Does Trent know? I might have uttered the words that this has Marcus's fingerprints all over it, but I don't think she believes me.

What are you doing in here?

I hear myself asking the question again. The pain in Trina's eyes, in her voice, in her hands as they trembled around the envelope—it's all I see. It plays over and over in my head, me asking the question, her looking up at me with so much pain.

Are you sure?

Why did I ask her that? Why would I doubt her? I know why.

It doesn't make sense, Trina.

Trina is so sure Marcus is responsible. She's been on a witch hunt for years regarding him and she's been right. She's always been right; unfortunately, I didn't realize the truth of it until it was too late. I wish I'd known sooner, then I wouldn't have fallen in love with Trent and I wouldn't have married into the family of the man who raped me, an underage, wasted, teenager.

The light of the sun rises and rises, spilling into every dark corner, refusing to let anything stay hidden, refusing to let me stay blind. I am exposed, raw, and uncovered. I'm also caught in a truth deep down I've been too afraid to admit.

I stare at the phone, at Trent's missed call from last night, at the messages he sent me but I haven't answered, at the texts from Marcus asking how Jack is doing.

I didn't answer any of them yesterday because I knew anything I said would have been a lie. Trent would have known right away I wasn't okay. Marcus would have called in the cavalry and had the doctor back out here to "check on me," and I didn't need more hovering.

The phone in my hand is heavy. I close my eyes, but there is no shutting out the truth. No shutting out what comes next.

Trina knows.

As if I could fall asleep after finding Trina in the office. My world has shattered. My universe has collapsed. My sanctuary is gone. I'm being buried alive with the weight of the truth, and there's nothing I can do.

All I want is for our life to go back to normal.

Except, I know that will never happen, not anymore.

Normal would mean being the mother my children need me to be.

Normal would mean being able to trust my husband, leaning on him, but then that would mean he'd actually have to be here instead of traveling for work, something he promised me he wouldn't do.

My legs feel as heavy as the rest of me as I force myself to stand, to move. I pace the room, letting the air close in on me until it wraps around me like a straitjacket.

What are you doing?

My words play on a loop. The voice is mine, but it doesn't feel familiar. I think about the way Trina's eyes widened as she dropped the envelope, the way she looked at me, desperate and knowing.

Knowing.

The light is harsh and unforgiving, and all I want to do is climb into bed, hide under the covers, and pretend I don't have to face any of this.

It may be what I want to do, but I won't. I can't.

My fingers start to dance on the screen, and I send my husband a message.

I found the death certificate.

Five complicated words. There are numerous answers he could give me, but I'm only searching for one. The truth.

Three dots appear.

I can explain.

The phone rings moments later. When I answer, my voice is shaky, my resolve weak.

"Please do," I say to Trent. The words fall from my lips, a plea, a command, a desperate need to hear him tell me everything's fine, that everything's okay, that everything is as it should be.

What I don't want is for him to lie to me. I can't do any more lies. The weight of the ones I'm already carrying are too heavy for me to bear; they're burying me to the point I'm not sure I'll survive.

"The doctor filled out the wrong forms." Trent's voice is strong, unworried. It is as confident as it is apologetic, both firm and soft. "He mixed up the names, along with who the parents are, but now it's a process, and it's taking a long time for our lawyers to fix." He sounds so incredibly sure of himself. I want to throw up.

I expected him to question why I was in his office in the first place. I expected defensiveness, even him lashing out in anger. I expected more, but instead, I got this.

Lies.

"And the death certificate for Josie?" I need him to answer this one.

Nothing. No stuttering over words he wants to say. Just simple silence.

"That was a mistake too."

I snort. "To clarify, the doctor wrote the wrong baby names on each certificate as well as forgot to list you as the father of our child, correct?"

"All mistakes that we're in the middle of fixing. I swear."

I know he wants me to believe him. I know he wants me to accept his answer, but I know he's lying.

Our whole marriage, all he's done is lie to me.

"Rosie, please tell me you believe me?"

"Which part? What was the mistake, Trent? The names? The death certificate that lists our little girl as deceased? Our baby girl according to the ultrasound, right?"

"Another colossal mistake on Harmon's part. The technician was new and should have waited to share those results." This time, the words come too easily and are too smooth.

And yet, I still want to give him the opportunity to make it right. I want to believe him. "So it's not true?" My voice is barely a whisper. I've been coiled tighter than a rattlesnake since walking in on Trina and his words do nothing to release that tension.

Last night, I told her I needed to think, that I needed time to digest what she had told me and come up with a plan, if it's all true.

She was disappointed that I didn't believe her outright. I don't blame her. I hope she'll forgive me, eventually.

"Oh, love, no, it's not true. I should have told you, but I didn't want to add more stress."

Trent's belief that he is right is so complete that he doesn't even see how wrong he's been.

He doesn't understand that I know he's lying to me.

TWENTY-SEVEN

With no more distractions, my gaze drifts to the window. There's movement outside, and I see a lone figure walking toward the house. It's like I've been waiting for him.

Wyatt. If there's anyone who can help me make sense of all the thoughts in my head, it's him. He's always been the one with a clearer head than my own.

I grab a light sweater, slip my feet into sandals, and head downstairs. I step onto the wide wooden porch at the front of the house and watch him approach, dust swirling around his boots, his eyes lifting to the weathered clapboard house.

He's almost to the porch by the time I step off the top stair.

We stand under the broad eaves, the summer sun already warm on our skin. Somewhere, a horse whinnies; the cows drift slowly toward the water trough. My chest heaves so fast I feel dizzy. I look at Wyatt and see a reflection of myself—tired, worn thin by worry.

"You doing okay?" he asks.

I sit in one of the chairs and pull my legs up, hugging my knees close to my chest.

"Rosie?"

"I'm sorry," I blurt. "I haven't thanked you for always being here. I haven't appreciated you like I should." Our eyes lock, and his quiet smile tells me all is okay. If only he knew.

"Rosie—"

"I'm serious." The words tumble out, like the dam's burst open and the flood is finally breaking free. "I don't know how to say this," I add, stumbling over each syllable.

"Do I need to be worried?"

I watch the dust drift over the pasture, gold motes in the glare of morning light. I study Wyatt as he waits for me—broad-shouldered, steady. "Something happened last night."

He nods, slow and certain, but doesn't say anything, giving me space to continue.

"I found Trina in Trent's office last night," I admit. "She… she believes Jack is hers," I say, bracing for his reaction.

Wyatt takes his time answering. He rubs the back of his neck and frowns. "What makes her think that?" There's something in his voice, something that tells me he knows more than he's saying.

"She went snooping and found the birth certificates as well as…" I struggle to say the name, but I know I have to. "And Josie's death certificate. Trent had them locked in his safe." I try to keep my voice steady. "Guess Dr. Harmon messed up with the certificates and put the wrong names on them." I hold my breath and wait for his reaction. "At least, that's what Trent said when I asked him."

He simply stands there, steady, reliable as the rising sun.

I sigh. I wish I could read him, read what he's thinking. "Trent said he's taking care of it. He didn't tell me because he didn't want to add to my stress."

"Do you believe him?"

It should be a simple question, but I hesitate like it's the toughest I've ever faced. "No."

Wyatt watches me, patient, thoughtful.

My voice wobbles as I finally say the words that have been eating at me. "This family, they live within the lies. I thought I could rise above and not let it touch me, but..."

He nods, and I see the gears turning behind his eyes. "What do you need me to do?"

I shake my head. "Everything is a mess, Wyatt."

He kicks a stone pebble off the porch. "Do you have a plan?"

"A plan?" My voice cracks like old peeling paint. "Only you would ask me that."

His gaze doesn't waver.

"I know something is wrong with me, but I'm not crazy, I swear. I just... I'm struggling. And Grace... I don't trust her. And Jack... well, it's all a mess, isn't it?"

"Did Trina talk to you about Grace?"

"What? No. Why, what do I need to know?"

"Do you remember Tammy Lee?"

It's like he's dropped a bomb and is waiting for the scorching wave to blast us away.

"Tammy Lee? No, why?"

He rubs at his face and frowns. "From the foster home."

That's all it takes. Memories of her face, of her laugh, of her meanness all come flooding back and my knees give out.

"Whoa," Wyatt says as he grabs me. "Are you okay?"

Am I okay? "That can't... she can't..." I struggle around the words, fear enveloping me as the past, my past, our past, collides with my present. "Why, Wyatt? Why is she here? What if... she doesn't know what we did, does she?" I'm shaking; I've lived with this fear that my nightmares would become my reality, that someone knew of what we'd done and I'd lose everything.

That can't happen. It can't.

He pulls me close. "It's going to be okay, Rosie. I promise. I'm looking into her and I'll take care of it, okay?"

"I can't... what does she know? Why is she here?" I'm repeating myself but I can't wrap my head around the fact she is here. Tammy Lee. This isn't good.

Wyatt pulls back, hands on my shoulders, face severe. "Rosie, it could be nothing. It could be a coincidence, but regardless, I've got this. You've got this. Say nothing, not yet, just... be careful, okay?"

Tears prick my eyes, hot and sudden. I can't hold them back.

"Of all the women I've known, you are one of those able to figured out how to turn lemon into candy. You are strong, Rosie. Regardless of what is going on, you can't let it bury you, do you hear me? They don't get to tell you who you are; only you do."

If only it were that simple.

"It is." He takes my hands and holds tight. I must have said that last part out loud.

"There's no simplicity to this, Wyatt. It's a mess, full of tangles, and there's no way to walk out of this clean." Everything about this is too complicated. I died while giving birth and something happened to me that changed me in ways I still don't understand, and to be honest, I'm not even sure I really trust myself.

"Depends on your definition of clean."

And just like that, I know I'll be okay, that he'll have my back, no matter what. He has more belief in me than I do.

I breathe in deep and a plan takes place. It's not a good plan, but it's a start and in this moment, the woman I used to be, the woman I remember, I can feel her again.

"It's going to get messy," I warn him.

He nods but I see the beginning of a smile play on his lips. "We've done messy before."

"Trina is going to hate me."

He shrugs. "Then give her a heads-up."

"I don't know." I barely whisper the words, but I know he hears me.

"Yes, you do."

He's right. I do. "But Trina..."

"You two are the strongest women I know. What do you believe you should do?"

I close my eyes and wait for the answer to pop into my head. "Has she said anything to you?" I ask him. "About believing Jack is her child?"

A faint smile tugs at the corner of his mouth, like sunlight breaking through scattered clouds. "Since when do you answer a question with a question?"

"When the answer is too hard for me to accept."

He gives a slow nod and I know he understands. "Life doesn't play fair. And the Eaton brothers, well, all they do is play games they know they can win. If this is a road you're going down, you'll need proof."

He's right. Proof. Proof like what Trina found, but something so undeniable that my husband won't be able to come up with another lie.

"Will you help me?"

"Whatever you need."

What I need is for him to get a DNA test done without my husband or Marcus finding out. I tell him as much.

"You get the cheek swab; I'll take care of the rest," he tells me. He flicks at my chin. "There she is," he says, pressing a hand to my shoulder, giving it a gentle squeeze. "Strong. Fierce. Loyal. The woman who will do anything for her family."

Family. I think of the twins, of my husband, of all the certainties slipping through my fingers. I think of the child I lost, the child I wasn't given the ability to grieve.

I think of the ones I made into my family, the ones I survived life with. The ones I'd do anything for. The ones I will always make sure are okay.

"What if I'm wrong?"

"What if you're right?" he says, answering my question with a question.

I bite my lip as I think about all the things I can do, should do, will do. Whatever decision I make, it will affect all of those around me, everyone I love. There is no right or wrong, no clear path. There's only the right path. But right for whom? For me? For my children? For my husband? For Trina?

Whatever I do, someone I love will consider me a monster. Am I prepared for that?

"Will you take care of Matty? Make sure he's okay if... well, if I'm not here?"

His face is a stone. He knows the truth about Matty, about who he is. He's the only one who knows that I know. I figured it out years ago after overhearing Marcus call Matthew his son during a call with his mother. Wyatt was the one who suggested we do the DNA test and worked out how to do it. One day I'll confront Trent and Marcus about this, but until then, I'll bide my time and wait to play this card.

Finally, he nods.

"Family first," I whisper.

"Always." He wraps his arms around me. "And family never apologizes."

His words snare a hook so deep inside me that I'll never be free.

He's telling me no matter what I decide, he'll support me. He won't judge me. He won't condemn or challenge me, either.

"I love you," he whispers into my ear. "Always have, always will, no matter what. You know that, right?"

"You're just as bad as them, you know," I whisper back moments before I pull away.

"How's that?" His brows crease as deeply as his frown.

"You don't play fair either."

"Ahh, but here's the thing, Rosie. When it comes to you, I

never do. Win or lose, it doesn't matter as long as you're involved," Wyatt says, stepping away from me and off the porch.

As I watch him walk away, there's a sense of clarity that washes over me, and I realize I know exactly what I'm going to do.

TWENTY-EIGHT

TRINA

I'm on my way out for a walk when I hear the sound of an engine approaching. Wyatt pulls up and rolls down the window, watching me with those eyes that know too much, those eyes that read my thoughts before I can voice them. I move closer to the vehicle, unable to hide a yawn.

"Not sleeping too good?" His voice is light, but the tone is heavy with concern.

"I tossed and turned all last night," I say, not explaining why. All I could think about was Jack, how he's my baby, and how he was stolen from me.

There's a question in his gaze as he stares at me with an intensity that makes me slightly uncomfortable. Does he know? Has Rosalind said anything to him?

"Headed anywhere in particular?" He glances at the basket in my hands.

"Up to the house to see the girls. I miss spending time with them."

He frowns. "Didn't you hear?" He opens the door and gets out, walking to the back of his truck to pull down the tailgate.

I follow and watch as he grabs a toolkit and a bag. I shake my head. "Hear what?"

"The girls are leaving this morning."

I step back in surprise. "What? Since when?"

He shrugs. "Guess the big Mrs. E is flying in for an appointment and will take them home with her."

Regina Eaton, the matriarch of the family, retired to Vancouver Island after her husband passed away and rarely leaves it unless necessary. I knew there was talk of them going but since I hadn't heard much since then, I was kind of hoping they'd changed their minds.

Is Rosalind going with them? Taking Jack with her?

Wyatt watches me, his gaze deep. I swear he can see into my soul. "You didn't know."

I shake my head and my tears well up. "Why?"

"No clue. Just got a text from Marcus with the instructions. You know me, do as I'm told and don't ask why." He starts heading toward my cottage. "Bet they didn't tell you I'd be coming here this morning either, did they?"

I'm so confused. "Why *are* you here?"

He drops the bag on a chair by my front door and pulls out a box. "Need to put up some cameras outside your place. Security upgrade and all. With Marcus and Trent traveling more, we just need to keep things safe, or so I'm told."

Cameras around my place? There are cameras around the main house, around the barn, but I've always had my privacy at the cottage—well, until lately.

"This won't take me too long," he says. "I'll let you know when I'm done, okay? I'll also take out the recording device from inside, if you'd like?"

I feel the exhale all throughout my body as I nod. Having that in my house, knowing everything I'm saying is being heard... I haven't liked it.

I leave Wyatt and head to the main house, trying to understand what is going on. Why are the girls leaving now? It's not because of me, is it?

On the back porch, I pause just outside the screen door when I hear my name being spoken.

"It's the only way." Rosalind sounds exasperated, but why?

"But now?"

Rosalind is on a phone call with the speaker turned up loud.

"Marcus originally suggested it, so don't blame me," Rosalind says. There's a clinking of cups, water being run, and a drawer closing.

"No one is blaming you, love. I just don't understand the sudden urgency to have them gone, that's all."

"We did talk about it, though."

"It was a passing comment, one you vetoed."

"Plans change." There's something in Rosalind's voice that doesn't sound right. "Your mom is flying in for some appointment so it works out perfectly."

My heart twists in pain at the thought of everyone leaving me.

"You're going to miss them," Trent says.

I take that to mean she's not going, which loosens the pit of fear that was growing in my chest at not being close to Jack.

"I know, and it kills me to have them leave, but this is the right thing to do. Their safety is all that matters."

Their safety? What is going on?

Wait, so this *is* because of me?

"I just can't believe it, that's all. Marcus said she's been acting weird, but do you honestly think she would hurt our family like that?" Trent says.

What is he talking about? What has she told him?

"I don't want to argue about this, okay? Please? Mabel is running late and I need to get the girls ready before Wyatt is ready to go. He'll pick you and Marcus up first, so you can see the girls off."

"You're not coming?"

"I would, but"—Rosalind sighs heavily—"that's too long a drive for Jack, and—"

"So leave him behind. Grace is there."

Rosalind snorts. "About that. I want her fired, Trent, and I'm serious. We don't need her anymore."

"I'll talk to Marcus."

"No. This isn't his call. It's ours, and I'm telling you I want her gone. Please don't fight me on this."

"I won't fight you, but we'll talk about this more when I'm home. I can't just fire her. Love you."

There's a tightness in my neck that crawls its way up and lodges in my head. A tension headache is the last thing I need to deal with. I hear Rosalind say goodbye, and then I clear my throat loud enough to be heard and open the screen door, forcing a smile on my face.

"Good morning," I say. Do I tell her I overheard the conversation, or wait to see if she'll drop the truth bomb on me?

"Hey?"

This feels awkward. "I thought I'd surprise the girls and have breakfast with them, if that's okay? I miss them."

Rosalind blinks and casually glances at the table. "Um, didn't you get my message? I sent it earlier this morning." Rosalind frowns as she pulls out her phone.

She sent me a message? I too take out my phone, but there's no message. Not from her, not from anyone.

"Well, crap, I didn't. Hmm, this will be fun," she says with a forced brightness. "The girls are headed to their grandma's this morning."

I try desperately to mask any thought I have.

"All summer?"

She nods. "All summer long. I'm going to miss them." Her voice is a little off, like she's been crying.

"Are you going with them?" The girls are only four years

old, too young to be away from their parents all summer, in my opinion.

"Not at first... maybe later," she says with a shrug.

"Would you like me to go with them? Help keep them occupied?" A big part of me hopes she'll say no because I don't want to be away from Jack for that long.

"That's kind of you to offer," Rosalind says, "but not necessary." She won't look at me. "I know it's sudden, but the girls will love it, even if I hate every moment they're away from me."

"Rosalind, is everything okay? Is this... because of me? Because of what I found last night?" I step close to her and keep my voice low.

She looks away and tidies up an already tidy counter.

"I need you to trust me, okay? I know it's sudden, but it's for the best. We'll talk later. Right now, I need to get the girls ready and Mabel—" She stops as Mabel rushes into the kitchen.

"I'm sorry, Mrs. R," Mabel says, one hand on her chest as she tries to catch her breath. "My daughter's little one isn't feeling well and—"

"What's wrong with her? Do you need the doctor?" Rosalind asks, cutting her off.

Mabel shakes her head. "He was just there—Mr. T took care of it."

"Trent? Why on earth did you call him?" Rosalind shakes her head. "Never mind that now—listen, the girls are going to their grandmother's for the summer, and I haven't had time to grab them breakfast. Can you make them some waffles real quick? They leave in an hour. Trina, come help me pack, will you?" She then leaves the kitchen, coffee mug in hand, but I just stand there, still in shock.

This has to be because of what I found in Trent's office last night. That's the only reason any of this makes sense. Rosalind said it was Marcus's idea; he must have seen me in the office. Why else would he have the girls leave?

I suddenly feel afraid, and I'm not sure why.

TWENTY-NINE

The three of us stand here, Rosalind, Grace, and myself, silent sentries as a plume of summer heat follows the vehicle down the dusty lane, taking the girls' laughter with it as they wave goodbye. My arm remains lifted, knowing Riley is probably twisted in her seat to watch us until the very last possible moment. I let one single tear drop as I think about how much I'm going to miss those girls while they're gone.

Despite Wyatt turning down my offer to join him on the drive, I suggested it to Marcus as well. Unfortunately, Marcus was very on point with his rather strict request that I not leave Rosalind alone.

The minute we can no longer see the vehicle, Rosalind turns and heads into the main house, announcing she will have a bath and then climb into bed for a nice, long nap. She asks me to join her after so that we can talk.

I nod silently, mystified at how she's acting. I get it, she's sad to see the girls go, but what about last night? What about the information I showed her, proving Jack is my child? She's acting like none of that happened.

"Why don't we chat now?" I suggest, stopping her as she climbs the porch steps.

Grace stands off to the side, tucking Jack into his stroller before heading on their daily walk around the ranch, not saying a word to either of us.

"I'm tired, Trina. I need some time, please?"

She's tired? She needs some time?

After finding that birth certificate which listed myself and Marcus as Jack's parents, there's nothing I want more than to be with my son, and I said as much to Marcus via text earlier, but not in those exact words.

Last night, Rosalind asked for patience, to give her time to find out what was going on, and I promised her I would. But giving her time and staying away from my son are two different things. In my text to Marcus, I told him that with the girls gone, there was no need for Grace, and that I was more than capable of taking care of Jack.

He didn't agree. He sent me a simple five-word reply, in his condescending, abrupt, and heartless way he gets, that is forever burned into my retinas.

You are not ready, sorry.

At least he had the decency to apologize, or that's how I'm taking that "sorry" part.

As I close the door to my empty cottage, everything drops away, and I'm wrapped in the isolation within these four walls like a weighted blanket. But instead of feeling comfort, I feel claustrophobic. My cheeks feel raw from the forced smile I held while saying goodbye to the girls. The tears that I've held back fall, one by one, trickling down my face, leaving scalding marks in their path.

I don't want to be alone. My heart cries for comfort and company, and that one sentence plays on repeat in my head, over and over.

I don't want to be alone. I don't want to be alone.

I want to be with my son.

I have all the proof that I need. Not just the instant connection, the birthmark, the light hair and blue eyes, all the coincidences I was trying to brush off when I shouldn't have, but the actual birth certificate.

Jack is mine; I am his.

When I hold him, it's like every broken piece of me fuses back together.

A churning of something I'm not ready to acknowledge yet sizzles in my belly. Anger. Rage. It swells, its sweltering heat of righteousness resounding through me as I realize every emotion, every feeling, every moment of grief I've been drowning in has been for nothing.

Last night, I believed Rosalind when she said she didn't know. I trust her to find out and that together we'll figure out what to do. If she's telling me the truth, if she had nothing to do with any of this, then all of this will be settled sooner than later.

But I'm not sure how much longer I can stay away from my son.

There isn't much I remember about that night, but what I do remember haunts me in jagged pieces. The images are broken and foggy. I keep trying to stitch them together, but they slip from my grasp, fading back into unanswered questions.

I have no idea what is right or wrong, what is truth or fiction. My mind catches like a scratch on vinyl.

The silence in the cottage magnifies everything inside me. I curl up on my couch as flashes of memory close in, like dark shapes moving in my periphery. My arms ache to hold my baby. My breasts feel heavy, leaking, and useless.

In the shards of my memory, did I imagine being handed a cup of tea? It felt real, and yet... everything beyond that moment is fuzzy. Pain and shouting, a woman's voice, angry and frightened. Screams. Mine or Rosalind's? And above the screaming, I remember hushed voices. "Now is the time." And, "Not yet." Is that when it all happened? When someone stole my baby, switched them, giving Rosalind the only child who survived while gaslighting me into believing mine had died?

I sit up, planting my feet on the floor, and I remember something else. The burn of the carpet as I fell down the stairs, each step branding my body with bruises. Someone's hand on my back.

I was pushed.

That's the only answer. My breath catches, ragged and quick, and for one brief moment, it feels like I'm still falling, falling, falling. I remember the pain. The bright light. The faces as they hovered.

I suck in a lungful of air and steady myself. I press my palms to my eyes. My body feels bruised, achy, and heavy, like I just delivered all over again. I shouldn't dwell on this. It isn't healthy. I'm only torturing myself. Babies being stolen and switched only happens in the movies, never in real life, so why is it happening to me?

My thoughts are tangled like fishing line. No matter which way I pull, the knots only tighten. My arms ache from emptiness; my hands itch to reach for Jack and run.

Run? No. I promised myself I'd stop running.

And just like that, the *tick-tick-tick* of my racing heart slows down. There's a bond between Rosalind and me that can never be broken no matter what life throws at us. We will figure this out. She'll come up with a plan to right this wrong, I know it. She always has in the past.

I will get my son back. One way or another.

Hours later, my phone dings with a message. It's from Rosalind:

I'm out by the pool. Let's talk.

Finally.

THIRTY

By the time I make it out to the pool, Rosalind, in her bathing suit, sits on a lounger, large sun hat covering her face and a book set off to the side. She's rubbing sunscreen on her arms, and hands me the bottle in case I need it.

"Isn't it gorgeous out today?"

I approach with caution because I'm not quite sure of her mood. This doesn't look like a mother who recently said goodbye to her daughters, or one who recently discovered her deceased child has been switched with mine.

"It's beautiful," I say, sitting in the chair beside her, stretching out my feet and pulling my sundress up slightly so my legs can get sun-kissed. I slathered on sunscreen earlier since my fair skin tends to burn easily, but my legs are pasty white, so a little sun won't hurt. "I'm glad you texted. I've been wanting to talk about last night."

She gives me a quick side look and raises her hands above her head to stretch. "Let's just enjoy the moment, okay? A summer of sun, pool, and some good books sounds like paradise, don't you think? Maybe add in some road trips and puttering in the garden, and it's just about perfect." Her voice is a little singsongy, her words too dreamy for the woman who normally likes to fill her days with activities.

Something's wrong. Something's off.

"Rosalind? What's going on?" I look around, assuming maybe she's being coy because someone is close by, but I don't see anyone. "Is everything okay?"

"Okay? No, it's not okay. My daughters are gone for the summer and instead of wallowing, I'm trying to find the good in that. I thought you'd be happy? I mean, it is a good thing, right?" She inhales. "They'll have fun with Trent's mother, and she's so excited—you should see the list of activities she sent over already. The girls are going to love it." Her voice is hyped up, and I'm not sure if it's genuine or forced.

All things they could have done here, but I don't say that, as much as I want to. I feel like I'm tiptoeing on broken glass, unsure of a safe path through the chaos.

What is going on?

"And the downtime will be good for you too," she says, pointing a finger my way. "Our bodies deserve some time to heal, don't you think?"

I don't answer.

"Seriously. I know it's not ideal, but it's the cards we've been dealt, so we'll have to figure it out day by day, I guess. Right?" Rosalind twists in her chair so she's looking at me.

Day by day? Why is she ignoring the obvious? I want to talk about last night. Actually, there are a lot of things we need to discuss—the documents I found, the photograph I received, the note, the hidden microphone—but she just keeps going on about the girls.

She sighs before relaxing back in her seat. "If you're upset that the girls are gone and you're going to have a boring summer, you can blame Marcus."

"I'll just add it to the list," I say softly.

"Play nice, Trina."

Play nice? Did she really just say that? "Is Marcus behind those documents we found last night, too?" I ask.

"What? No. There is a simple answer to that. Trent said he'd call you. Hasn't he?"

I glance at my phone but no, there are no missed phone calls or even messages from him.

She leans my way. "I have an idea. Since it's just us, why don't we fly off to Europe for a few weeks? It'll be sweltering no doubt, but staying on the Amalfi Coast sounds perfect, don't you think? Plus, I never did get that tattoo in Italy like I wanted to last year." She rubs the small trail of rosebuds she has on her arms from when she was a teenager. Like me, her tattoos cover burn marks.

Europe?

"Don't you look at me like that," she says, her voice far less chipper than a moment ago.

"I'm not looking at you in any way," I mutter, although we both know I was. "I'm just trying to imagine Europe with a baby, that's all."

She doesn't reply, and I'm left wondering if she's thought about Jack at all. He's all I can think about.

"Where is Jack?" I try to keep my voice neutral.

"He's with Grace," she says with an air of indifference. "Probably having a nap or something. Marcus told her that she's only to take orders from him or Trent, so I wipe my hands of her."

Wipes her hands of her? "What do you mean by that?"

Rosalind rubs her hands over her thighs. "Oh, you know," she says with a distinct don't-care attitude. "She's here for a reason, so I'll stay out of her way and let her take care of the baby."

My brows knit together as I try to figure out the meaning behind her words. "I don't trust her."

She gives me a side eye. "Yeah, I know. Wyatt mentioned

that." Rosalind swings her legs over the side of the chair and stands.

"Wyatt did?"

She nods. "He's going to take care of it, okay? He's doing some digging, and when he gets to the bottom of why she's here, he'll... well, he'll do what he does best."

"Why wait?"

"Marcus." She says his name on a sigh. "I've tried to get rid of her, I really have, but it's out of my hands, okay?"

Okay? No, it's not okay. But apparently she's done with the topic and I'll need to discuss this with Wyatt instead.

"What is Trent supposed to tell me?"

She quirks her lips. "About that..."

Finally. "Yes, about that." I shield my eyes with the palm of my hand as I stare up at her towering over me.

She eyes me like she's unsure if she should say what she really feels or just choke back the words.

"Don't hide from me now," I tell her. "Say what you want to say. We will figure this out together."

She rubs the back of her neck as she sighs. "This is all giving me a headache. It was a mistake," she says, reaching for her tie skirt, which she wraps around her waist. "Dr. Harmon wrote the wrong names down on the certificates and filed them before noticing. Trent has his team of lawyers trying to fix it, but it's a mess, I guess. He never said anything to us because he didn't want to cause any undue stress, which is also why they haven't given you the birth or the death certificate yet."

Why is she lying to me?

My heart splinters into little pieces as I stare at her, as I realize that whatever we had, it's broken.

"I'm sorry, Trina," she says, bending down to my level and taking my hands. "I know this isn't what you were wanting to hear, but I believe Trent."

She thinks I'm devastated because of the lie?

"I don't." The words drop from my mouth instinctively.

"I need you to trust me," Rosalind says. "I've always had your back, haven't I? Just like you've always had mine. If you can't trust Trent, then trust me, please."

The pounding in my heart is so hard and fast that it's going to burst its way right out of my chest.

She wants me to trust her? Like hell I will.

"I know you believe Jack is your son—"

"Because he is," I interrupt. "He has my birthmark, my hair..."

She shakes her head. "I'm so sorry." She stares at me with remorse in her eyes. "I'm going to head inside and make a smoothie. I sent Mabel home so she can help her daughter take care of her new baby." She barely pauses for breath as she slides her feet into her sandals. "Are you coming?"

I came here today thinking we'd come up with a plan for me to get my son back, to make the Eaton men pay for what they did and instead... instead, I'm leaving with a broken heart because the woman I once called a sister has betrayed me for the last time.

And I can't do anything about it.

When she's close to the house, I hear her calling down to me. "Trina?" She sounds annoyed that I haven't followed her.

I follow. Not because I'm being told to, but because if I want any chance at getting my son, I have to play nice and hide my true feelings.

There's a very fine line between love and hate and in this moment, I have to pretend like I don't hate Rosalind. Like I don't want to kill them all for what they've done to me.

I'm living in the twilight zone.

I'm back in my prison cell, the shackles around my feet and wrists tighter than before. The only difference from four weeks ago to now is that I one hundred percent know the truth, and back then, I'd only guessed at it.

I have only one option and I don't like it.

If I were to do what I want to do, what everything inside me screams for me to do, it would be to take Jack and run as fast as I can from here, but I know they'd find me.

They'd find me and take Jack from me, forever.

I have no other options. I have to pretend like nothing has changed, like I love Rosalind as a sister and trust her like she's asking me to. I have to play a game I have no chance of winning and pretend like it's the only thing I want to do.

I hate myself right now.

My whole life has been about protecting Rosalind. She's always been the one who needs protection, needs someone to lean on, and I've always had to be strong for her. She had a hard life until she met Trent when we were in college. He is her knight in shining armor, the prince in love with the pauper, sweeping her off her feet and offering her a life of luxury—I only wonder if she views that luxury as a life sentence now. Does she have any idea of everything she's lost?

I doubt it.

I push myself to my feet, gathering all the dishes left behind outside. In the house, I hear the sound of running water. Rosalind must be having a bath, which will probably help with her headache.

I clean up our dishes and wipe the counters, trying to show respect to Mabel's area, when I hear a noise from upstairs. It sounds like a muffled scream.

I rush up to her room. She's not in there. The bathroom door is closed. I listen for the sound again, but I don't hear anything.

What was that noise?

I knock on the door. "Rosalind? Do you need anything?"

The water stops. "Trina? What are you...? Um, yeah, I'm okay."

From the tone of her voice, questioning and annoyed, I feel rather silly standing outside the door now.

"I thought I heard you scream."

"Just me getting in the water. All good. Thanks for checking in, though." And like that, I'm dismissed.

A small noise sounds from the room down the hall, a soft cry that catches my attention, and my heart leads the way to Jack, who's lying in his crib, fussy and restless. The way he looks up at me, his small features wrinkling into something like recognition, brings a warmth that wraps around the jagged edges of my heart. I lift him from his crib and press him close to my chest. A full bottle sits waiting on the side table, abandoned.

Where is Grace? The door to her room is closed, and I don't hear any sounds when I go to stand in front of it. That just makes what I'm about to do that much easier.

I settle into the rocking chair with Jack, and everything

fades except the softness of his skin, the way his small body curls against me as he feeds. There are no doubts, just pure contentment. Just him and me, and for the moment, nothing else matters. I study his hair, a light reddish tuft, and the birthmark on his tiny shoulder, and trace its outline, so familiar to me.

The door swings open, and I clutch Jack tighter. Grace stands there with her soft-soled shoes and pastel sundress. Her steps are quick, panicky. I continue rocking, holding the bottle at the right angle to eliminate air bubbles.

"Trina." Just my name, and yet there's so much warning in those two syllables that it takes everything in me not to sigh with frustration.

"Let me guess. Marcus?" I don't look at her, focusing instead on this little bundle in my arms. The way he looks at me with wide eyes, nothing could make me look away.

"I'm sorry, but he gave me specific instructions."

Of course he did. I should have realized he'd see me in here. I keep rocking, defiant. Jack keeps feeding, hungry. My chest burns, the need to pump strong. It feels ridiculous to be using a bottle when my body is producing what he needs and I could feed him myself.

"He's almost done," I say, my voice as calm as I can manage. But my arms tighten around him, protective, unwilling to let go.

Grace stands firm, her posture stiff. "Don't take it personally." Her voice is soothing, almost too gentle, the gentle you know is a dagger in disguise. "My only job is to keep Jack safe."

Jack answers for me. He lets out a long, determined wail, and I know just how he feels.

"I'm sorry, keep him safe?" She did not just insinuate that I'm a danger to my own child, did she? "Care to elaborate on that? I don't see Jack in any danger right now, do you?" I want to confront her, tell her I know who she is, but Wyatt is taking care of this, apparently.

I don't want to screw that up.

For a moment, I think she's going to refuse to answer me. She holds herself like she's ready for a fight, but then she lets out a soft sigh. "Fine," she says, pulling up a chair. But she keeps a careful distance, her gaze constantly darting to the camera. She gets up to angle it more toward the crib, and she hits a button on the top of the camera system.

"There's a mute button. Marcus doesn't want to hear Jack cry; he just wants to make sure he's being taken care of. And to answer your question, I'm only repeating what Marcus has told me."

Her eyes don't smile. Her face does, but her gaze remains cool, watchful, the way Marcus's always does.

I need to be smart and careful with my words.

"How about you tell me about yourself?" I give her an opening to be honest with me, to make things easier for herself.

"There's nothing much to tell," she says, keeping her attention focused on the door. "I'm a city girl who's always wanted to live on a ranch. It's like a fairy tale around here. Exactly like what you see on those shows—well, except for all the killing." She leans forward and gives me a conspiratorial grin. "Although, I wouldn't be surprised if this ranch has its own 'train station' if you get my drift."

It takes everything in me not to roll my eyes. She's talking about the television show *Yellowstone* and the fictional area that was created where the wealthy family got rid of their enemies.

"The Eatons are not murderers, if that's what you're insinuating."

She leans back. "Not them, no. They'd never dirty their hands like that, I'm sure."

But others would? Is that what she's hinting at?

Does she know? She can't. She wasn't there.

"The politics in places like this always amaze me," she continues. "Take Wyatt, for instance. No formal education behind him, and yet he's like the second-in-command out here, after the Eaton brothers. Who would have thought, right?"

Her words and tone border on familiarity, almost like she's goading me.

"What about you?" she asks me.

I readjust the blanket around Jack as I think about my response. "What about me?"

She shrugs. "Oh, I don't know. Where are you from?"

"I'm a city girl too," I tell her, not that she doesn't already know that, "but this is home now. The Eatons are my family."

She cocks her head to the side and narrows her eyes a little. "I forgot, you've known Rosalind for a long time, haven't you? You grew up together, isn't that right?"

I don't respond because she already knows the answer. I hate having to play this game, pretending I don't know exactly who she is.

"You know, I feel sorry for him," she says, staring at Jack. "Babies deserve unconditional love and acceptance."

"And he's getting exactly that." My tone is a little sharp at her suggestion that he's getting less than what he deserves.

"Is he, though? Mrs. Eaton—"

"Be careful." The warning in my voice fills the room with ice.

"Oh, come now, Trina, surely you see it, don't you? The mood swings? How unhinged she can get? There's a reason she's not allowed to be left alone with him, you know."

"Excuse me?" What is she talking about?

I lean forward, the chair creaking softly, Jack a weight and comfort against me. "You have no idea what you're talking about."

"Really? I thought you were in the loop. I guess they really don't trust you, do they? You didn't know that she was shaking Jack like he was a doll? That she's gone to yank him out of my arms numerous times to throw him across the room? Sadly, she's gone a little..." Grace raises her finger and makes a circle in the air.

"Stop it." The words explode from within me. I don't know what she's talking about, but she had better not be spreading these rumors. Rosalind would never treat Jack like that. Never.

"I'm only telling the truth, as hard as it might be to hear. She really should go somewhere where she can get the help she needs. I mean, she's been through so much in her life. Honestly, I'm surprised she hasn't gone psycho before now."

I want to smack her. I want to see a red imprint from my hand on her face as I yell at her. I want to tell her she has no idea what she's talking about, that she's stupid and I'm onto her game, but I don't do or say any of the things running through my head right now. Instead, I shush the fidgeting baby in my arms, adjusting him and rubbing his back.

"I'm sorry, I shouldn't have said that," she continues, as if she's truly apologetic, but she's already shown her true colors. "I'm here to help, to make sure Jack gets the best care possible. I have some experience raising boys," she says, giving me a smile I wish I could make her eat.

"Where is the doll?" Of all the things I want to say, of all the things I want to accuse her of, that was the very last thing on my mind, and yet, there it is, front and center now.

She sighs. "I have no idea what you're talking about," she says.

"Rosalind told me you'll often put a doll in the crib and pretend it's Jack. If anyone has gone psycho, it's you."

She laughs. "Really? That's what she's said?" Standing to her feet, she walks forward and takes Jack from my arms. "I'm sorry, Trina, but this has gone on for far too long," she says. "It's Marcus's wish that you rest and heal for now, and I have to ask that you respect that. Plus"—she glances at my chest, which is now soaked through from my leakage—"you probably need to go deal with that."

A voice from downstairs interrupts anything I'm about to say. "Hello? Anyone here?" It's Dr. Harmon. His steps are heavy as he climbs the stairs.

Grace and I look at each other. She shrugs. "I didn't call him," she says before taking Jack to the change table.

"I received a text and thought I'd come out to check in on my two favorite patients. Trina, I'm assuming you're up there?" He huffs and puffs as he continues the climb and pauses as he makes it to the top. "Ahh, there you are. I did check your cottage first."

"Who sent you the text?" I leave Jack's room and meet the doctor in the hallway.

"The boys." Rosalind's voice carries through her closed door. "Trina, I'm sure the doctor would enjoy some of Mabel's homemade iced tea out on the porch. Maybe you can keep him company while I make myself presentable?"

"Ahh, yes, that would be lovely. I should have waited down-stairs instead of trudging all the way up." He sighs. "Did I see you come out of the nursery? Marcus did mention he was a little concerned..." He gives a quick glance toward my chest, and his lips press together. "Perhaps you should go take care of that, yes?"

I cross my arms to hide the wetness and follow him down the stairs.

I'm surprised when I find Mabel in the kitchen, and she's already in the middle of preparing a tray. She, too, notes my wet shirt.

"Mabel, I thought you had the rest of the day off?"

She gives me a tight smile. "Dr. Harmon, would you like a piece of coffee cake? I made it fresh this morning," she tells him while shooing me out the door. "Mr. M asked me to be here," she tells me. "Don't worry about the doctor, I'll keep him occu-pied till Mrs. R comes down, don't you worry." She offers a sympathetic smile before closing the screen door behind me. "I can't tell you how thankful I was that you came out to look at the baby this morning," I hear her saying as she walks away, "and I know how much you love my coffee cake."

It doesn't surprise me that the boys are micromanaging things. This is probably all Marcus. Dr. Harmon's words play in my head. *Marcus did mention he was a little concerned...* He didn't say that about Rosalind. He was referring to me.

Why would Marcus send him out to check in on me?

THIRTY-TWO

ROSALIND

The sun is high, the warm air from the breeze brushing against my skin as I sit on the porch and let Mabel finish setting large glasses of homemade iced tea on the table between us. Dr. Harmon is polishing off another slice of her cinnamon coffee cake while sweating through his woven shirt, and I'm waiting not so patiently for him to finish.

My heart hurts that I had to send the girls away the way I did, so sudden, but it's the only way I know to make this work. I need to protect them from what's to come. Thankfully, all I had to do was say the right thing to Marcus to remind him of the idea and let him do the rest.

"I'll turn up the fans," Mabel whispers as she passes by. I give her a smile of gratitude. Installing the ceiling fans on the porch was one of Trent's smartest ideas, especially given our hot summer country breezes.

When the doctor is finally done, he sets the fork down on the plate and turns to me, a practiced smile on his face, his body language saying more than I want to hear. His attention makes my skin prickle, and I feel more vulnerable than ever. I cross my arms tightly, hoping to ward off the inevitable conversation.

"Rosalind," he finally prompts, leaning toward me. "Tell me what's on your mind."

What's on my mind? So many things, but I know I have to be careful with whatever I confess.

"You know you can tell me anything," he prods, his voice very gentle, very grandfatherly. "Mr. Eaton mentioned you'd found out about my mistake," he says, clearing his throat.

I nod. "Trina did, actually," I admit.

His caterpillar eyebrows rise.

"She... I found her in Trent's office, going through his things. She believes..." I hesitate. Should I say anything? My head pounds with the growing headache that hit me earlier. The first thing I did when I got to my room was scream into a pillow, then I sobbed in the bathtub, which only made things worse.

I've been getting so many headaches lately, I don't know if I should be worried or not.

"Go on." His voice is calm, inviting, like we're chatting over coffee instead of dissecting my sanity.

I breathe, trying to hold onto my thoughts before they slip away. "It's about Jack. She was in Trent's office looking for proof that Jack is hers, which I get. I mean, he looks like her, plus that birthmark, and how he calms when he's in her arms." I stare down at my hands. "A mother knows her baby," I whisper to myself.

"What's that?"

"Trent told me what happened, though," I say instead of repeating myself.

The doctor nods slowly, pulling out a pen and small notepad from his front shirt pocket. His pen scratches against the paper. "Ahh, yes. A slight mistake on my part that has become a nightmare." He shakes his head and actually looks embarrassed. "So you are worried that this just opens fresh wounds, then?"

I nod and blink, but I can't stomach this, all the lies.

"I can't apologize enough. Why, this is the first time in all my years of being a doctor. I... I have no excuse. Mr. Eaton did mention to me that he, too, is concerned about Ms. Emmet and her attachment to Jack."

"Trent or Marcus?" My brows furrow. It matters.

"Marcus." He clears his throat again.

"Well, of course she's attached. That's normal, isn't it?" It's easy to come to Trina's defense. "Any woman would be in her shoes," I say, choosing my words carefully.

He cocks his head to the side. "Normal isn't how I would describe it. Expected, perhaps, considering everything. Most grieving mothers would not be in this situation, however, having given birth at the same time as you, living on the same property, caring for your children." I realize he's judging me. Judging us. "I'm afraid I agree with Mr. Eaton that the situation is unhealthy for her. I did suggest that maybe she needs to be somewhere other than here, even for a little time, to be around those who could help her work through all this."

Shivers cover my skin at his words. I will not let them send her away.

The doctor watches me carefully. "How are you, Mrs. Eaton? How did you feel when she found those documents, and before your husband could explain things?"

"I felt like it explained so much," I admit, the rawness in my voice exposing me more than I want it to.

"Ahh, yes, I imagine you would feel relieved at that? That perhaps it explains the bonding issues you've been having with your son?"

I nod. The truth of the matter is that I was more than relieved, but now waves of sadness drown me with the realization that it's my baby that has died, my little girl, and I don't know how to process that.

"But now that you know the truth? Does that change anything? Do you think that perhaps your history has anything to do with it?"

A simple question, but it hits me like a punch to the stomach. My hand goes to cover the tattoos on my arm, which cover the burn marks from the aftermath of that awful day.

Should I be honest? Something in his voice warns me to be careful. Whatever I admit to next could change everything. I falter, glancing at the doorway for an escape. Instead, I see Grace passing by, her honey-blonde hair catching the sun.

"Grace!" My voice is sharp, too loud. "Can you bring Jack down?"

She stops, turns, and smiles with that gentle, unreadable expression. "Of course," she says, and the sound of her soft-soled shoes fades down the hall.

I twist my wedding ring, the metal cool against my clammy skin. "Marcus says that I..." I pause, struggling to even say the words, horrified if any of this is true. "That I shook my baby like he was a doll," I whisper when Grace is out of earshot. I stare at the floorboards, at the sky, anywhere but at him.

The doctor sets his notes aside, leans back, his expression thoughtful. "Yes, that is very concerning and can be harmful for the baby. It's a good thing Mr. Eaton was there to stop you."

"Am I a danger to him?" I say these words as mouse-quiet as I can.

"I'm afraid you've always been a danger to him," Dr. Harmon says, his gravelly voice piercing my soul.

I'm horrified.

"This is why I've been insisting you go to that clinic. It's best, you understand."

"I can't... I can't believe I would do that." My voice breaks with real emotion. I don't believe that is something I would do. It has to be another one of Marcus's lies.

His words throw me into a void filled with edges lined in sharp broken mirror pieces, reflecting my ugliness back to me. Maybe it's a good thing the girls are away. I don't want them to see me fall apart more than they already have.

I know and understand I'm not well, that something has splintered in my mind. I blame this man. I blame my husband. I blame Marcus.

Dr. Harmon studies me in silence, taking in my hunched shoulders and how my hands shake in my lap. He doesn't need to say anything; I already know what he's thinking. He's going to demand that I be sent away; I can see the resolution in his eyes.

I hear Grace's footsteps before I see her, and relief floods through me. She steps into the light, holding baby Jack like a prize she's not sure I deserve. I don't, but neither does she. He's swaddled in blue, tiny and peaceful, everything I'm not. The doctor doesn't speak; he just watches me, his beady little brown eyes behind his glasses taking in every move, every facial adjustment I make, and every word I say, cataloging it all.

My hands move toward Jack, the gesture mechanical, and at the doctor's nod, Grace hands him over.

The doctor's silence needles me more than any words, his eyes measuring every inch of failure I can't hide.

"And how does that feel? Holding your son?" the doctor finally asks, cutting through the silence.

"Good," I say too quickly. "Like it should. He's an absolute angel," I say.

My words are empty and rehearsed, like lines from a script I now say by rote. I try to meet Dr. Harmon's gaze, to make him believe me, but he has this distinct skill of piercing through the facade, seeing the hollow truth beneath.

Am I doing enough to sell this?

I look down at Jack, at his tiny, trusting face. I will make this up to him, right a wrong that is everyone else's fault but mine. The large outdoor clock's slow and relentless tick is louder than my own heartbeat.

Jack makes a small sound, a soft cry. My arms tense, holding him at an awkward angle. I'm supposed to feel maternal, supposed to feel love. And I do. Now that I know the truth, I can fall in love with this little boy that I'll consider family. But for now, I need to sell the image that I'm still struggling.

I turn my attention toward the doctor, pleading for rescue. He stands and takes Jack from me. He does it gently, naturally, like he's done it a thousand times before.

"He's a healthy, growing baby," the doctor says, cradling Jack effortlessly. "Holding babies is probably my favorite part of this job." He cocks his head as he watches me. "I'll check in on Trina before I leave."

I nod, thankful.

"Thanks for the smoothie recipe," I say. "I actually got Trina to drink one today, if you can believe it. Maybe you can convince her I'm not trying to drug her every time I offer her one?"

"Drug her? Why on earth would she believe that?"

"I wish I knew."

He smiles, the practiced one again, and I wonder what he's thinking.

Grace holds out her arms, and the doctor hands Jack back over like he's passing a file. My stomach twists with a mixture of relief and shame as I sit here, the air still hot against my skin, wishing I could shed my doubts as easily as I shed my discomfort. This whole conversation will get back to Marcus. I wonder what will happen then?

Grace lingers a moment, and I can't read her intentions. I don't know if she's here to help or if she's just another one of Marcus's spies or maybe something else.

They leave together, Grace with Jack in her arms and the doctor with his judgments. I'm alone with my thoughts, and the weight of everything presses down harder than the heat.

I sit on the porch, the air warm and suffocating, wrapping around me like the silence I can't escape. I need this to work.

THIRTY-THREE

TRINA

The knock on the door is expected, yet I still run my clammy hands down my dress.

Even before I can yell, *Come in*, Dr. Harmon's face peeks around the corner as he lets himself in.

"Oh, there you are." He looks almost shocked to see me. "Sorry for walking right in," he says as he does just that. "I figured you would be outside." His cotton shirt is slightly crumpled, and a hint of sweat is visible on his brow. "I would have been here sooner, but I wanted to check in with Mrs. Eaton and the baby." He glances at the bags of pumped milk I left sitting on the counter, and I notice the slight bob of his head.

"My milk has actually increased this past week," I say, my mouth a little dry.

"Hmm. If you've been spending more time with the Eaton baby, that might be why." He sets his worn leather medical bag on the table and clears his throat.

"Rosalind mentioned you haven't been drinking the smoothie mixture I provided." I hear the question in his statement.

"I didn't realize, until today, that you expected me to drink them."

He pulls at his shirt. "Not expect, per se, but it was a suggestion."

"Not one I was told." There's a curtness to my tone that I don't bother to hide.

He cocks his head to the side. "Perhaps you just don't remember." He glances around my kitchen area. "I left you some when I came to see you... oh, probably during that first week."

He did? I head to my small kitchen area and think about where the jar of his smoothie mixture would be. Did I put it away somewhere? Maybe Marcus set it in a cupboard on a day he came by? I start opening doors, one by one, and sure enough, right in my pantry cupboard, there is a glass jar with the label *Restorative Drink*, just like the one Rosalind has.

"Ahh, see, I knew I'd left it. It's all natural, nothing dangerous. Simply use a scoop of it in your smoothies every day. Full of vitamins and such." He gives me a bland smile. "Mrs. Eaton drinks one every day, but now with some added supplements." He says this like it should make all the difference to me, but it doesn't.

"What exactly does it do, what's in it, and where do you buy the mixture from?" The way he's eyeing me, I'm on guard. He makes me feel like I've said something wrong, but it's the exact opposite. I'm only asking very simple questions.

"Mrs. Eaton mentioned something that caught my attention," he says, not answering me.

"And what was that?" I cross my arms over my chest, feeling very defensive and unsure why. Is he here to admit to his mistake about the paperwork?

"Do you believe I might be poisoning you?"

He catches me off guard. Do I believe he is trying to poison me? The answer should be no. He's a doctor. He's legally and morally bound to do all he can to help me heal. Do no harm and all that.

Dr. Harmon sighs, like he's disappointed, and pulls out a chair from my kitchen table, sitting down with a heavy thump.

"How long have you been feeling this way?"

"I'm concerned about what Rosalind is taking," I say instead. "I think, perhaps, it's all a little too much and the side effects are what is causing her to..." I think about the words I want to use, words that paint her in a good light. "Well, I just wonder if her medication and whatever it is that she's drinking could be not mixing well?"

One brow lifts and his lips thin as Dr. Harmon looks me in the eye. There's no hiding from his intense gaze. "I assure you, Trina. They are perfectly safe."

Something in the way he speaks those words makes me doubt them. "It's my own blend. Perfectly routine. Both you and Mrs. Eaton had difficult pregnancies. They are nothing more than herbal supplements to help with your postpartum recovery, and I do wish you were taking them."

I shake my head. "Her mood swings, the tiredness, lack of energy..." My voice grows bolder, even though I realize how insane it is for me to question a doctor on the medication he's prescribed to his patient. That voice that was shouting in my head now becomes a whisper.

"There are always side effects, yes, but there's more to what is happening with Mrs. Eaton than I feel comfortable sharing with you."

My cheeks turn red at his rebuke.

"I am here, though, for you," he says, "to see how you are doing."

I shrug and stand awkwardly at the counter.

"Please, come sit," he encourages. "Talk to me. I can only imagine how difficult all of this must be." He smiles as I take a seat opposite him.

"All of this?" I ask.

"Well, yes, all of this. Losing your child and being so close to the Eatons, their children, and, of course, their baby. All of it must be so difficult for you. That's why the insistence on the certificates and the DNA request."

I don't reply. I look at him and work my hands together, stuffing down the anger, resentment, and frustration at yet another person telling me how I should be feeling. Why do I have to explain myself? Why do I have to defend my emotions when I'm the one feeling them? When I'm the one living every single second without my child in my arms?

"The night the babies were born..." I keep my voice level, though my insides twist. "I need to know what happened. I heard two babies crying, I know I did."

The silence in the room stretches longer than it should. "Ah, yes. I suppose we should discuss that as well. I owe you an apology. I would have told you sooner, when you first asked for the birth and death certificates, but I was ashamed, to be honest. Additionally, I was waiting for Mr. Eaton's lawyers to resolve the issues. It's generally a simple solution, but because I made so many errors on both documents, Mr. Eaton felt it would be better to let his team correct things."

My lips thin. I don't hear an apology; I just hear excuses.

"I understand you thought Jack was your child, and I am very sorry at the trauma I have caused from that."

I don't hide my sigh. I'm disappointed.

"My delivery was a difficult one, wasn't it?" I insist, knowing I can't lose this chance to learn more. Knowing I have to get answers.

Dr. Harmon seems genuinely taken aback, and I'm unsure if it's my forwardness or his memory of that night. "Your delivery"—he pauses—"well, nothing went as expected that night." His lips purse together as he stares down at his hands.

"Falling down the stairs, did that have anything to do with...?"

He shrugs. "It could have been a factor, yes. Or no. It's hard to say. The cord was wrapped around your baby's neck, and there was nothing we could have done at that point."

Wrapped around his neck? "So that's why you did the caesarean?"

"I'm worried about you," Dr. Harmon says instead of answering. "Maybe all of this has been too much for you. I'm afraid, as your doctor, I'm going to have to insist that you stay away from the Eaton house for now. Specifically, away from their baby."

I let out a small cry of pain. I will not be separated from my son.

"I'm sorry, Trina," he says, leaning forward and taking my hand, his hold strong and unrelenting. "I'm sorry it has to be this way."

"No," I say, shaking my head. "You can't do this." His words are more painful than he realizes. They echo in the empty chambers of my heart, taking up too much room and leaving no space for anything else. I manage to pull my hand from his hold. "You don't understand what you're doing."

The way he watches me, with pity and sadness, it's too much. I look away.

"We weren't expecting it to affect you this much," he says. "You're tougher than this. I didn't know it was going to take such a toll." His words are meant to be comforting, but they aren't. They sting.

"So what now?" My question hits the air, barely audible. But loud enough that he knows the pain I feel.

"Do you have any family you could go stay with?"

The question causes me to laugh. "Rosalind is my family."

He tuts, and I see the sympathy, or pity, he feels for me.

"You don't understand."

He sighs again. "You can't replace the child you lost with Jack."

His words cut deep, deeper than he knows. "I'm not replacing my baby." I say it with as much force as I can, but it's barely more than a whisper.

Dr. Harmon studies me, likes he's trying to determine if what I said is true. "Being this close to Jack is not healthy."

"I'm fine." I push the words from my mouth, knowing they're a lie. "It's fine." My voice betrays me.

He's my baby. Those are the words I want to say, but instead, I cover my mouth with my hand, stuffing them back in before I say anything that will cause him more concern. I remember the fear in Rosalind's eyes when she begged me to help her, that she didn't want to go away, and now I get it.

"I don't think you understand what's happening in that house."

"Then explain it to me."

So I do. Without telling him the whole truth about Grace, I instead say that I don't trust her, and explain about the doll. About the way both Rosalind and I are being gaslighted, but he only shakes his head, pursing his lips together tightly.

"I'm afraid it's already too late, isn't it?" he says softly. "I have to insist, Trina, that you go somewhere, for at least a month, and give yourself time to heal. If there's no family you can visit, I'll talk with Mr. Eaton and see if they will cover the cost and send you to a retreat center I highly recommend."

I shake my head. "No, please," I beg, hating myself for the weakness in my voice. "I don't want to leave," I say.

His crow's feet appear as he frowns. "I have to ask you to respect my request and stay away from the main house."

As he talks, he pulls out his phone and begins typing. He looks up and waits for me to answer. I'm helpless, left with no options, and so I do the one thing I don't want to do.

I nod.

He places his phone back in his pocket. "I just sent Mr. Eaton my recommendation and I'm sure he'll be in touch. I won't confine you to your home; you can walk around the property and visit the horses, but please stay away from the main house. I want you to start drinking the smoothies once a day, and I'm going to send a new prescription over that I'd like you to start taking as well." He pauses and eyes me carefully. "Can I trust you to take this medication and drink the smoothie, or do you need to be supervised?"

His question leaves me reeling. What is happening right now? Can he really do this?

"In the meantime, I'd like you to take this." He rummages in his bag and pulls out a small bottle. "One every six hours." He glances at his watch. "Do you need to program this into your phone, or will you remember to take them?"

"What is this?" I eye the package with suspicion. Of course I'm not going to take it. Why would I? I'll flush it down the toilet like all the others.

"Actually, let's have you take one now," Dr. Harmon says, as if reading my thoughts, "and I'll have Mabel come down to ensure you take the next one before bed and then at breakfast. I'll come by tomorrow and discuss things with the Eatons on what our next steps should be." Everything he says, he says it without an air of concern for me. He's clinical, with an expectation for his orders to be followed.

When I don't move, he heads into the kitchen and fills me a glass of water. Returning to the table, he places the cup in one of my hands and the pill in my other and waits for me to take it.

We have a staring contest and I lose. I place it in my mouth, hiding the pill beneath my tongue as I take a sip of water.

"Show me," he says.

I open my mouth, feeling like a child.

"Lift up that tongue for me." When I do, he tsks. He doesn't say anything more, just waits for me to take another drink, swallow, and then prove I didn't hide it again.

"Good girl." I don't think he hears the condescending tone, or perhaps it's intentional. "Now, you'll feel drowsy, and that's okay. This will help you relax and get the rest your body needs to heal properly. Don't fight it. I'll have Mabel prepare you a light dinner, one that I expect you to eat, you hear me?"

He returns to his seat and leans back in his chair, a move very unexpected because I thought he would be leaving now that I've taken his stupid pill, one that I intend to throw up as soon as he leaves.

I don't know what he gave me but I know I don't want it.

"I know the past few weeks have been hard for you, and I apologize that I haven't given you as much attention as I have to Mrs. Eaton, but I promise you this, you're not alone, Trina. You have all the support you'll need to get through this, and get through this we will." He leans forward. "I'll take good care of you."

His statement feels more like a threat, and from the smile on his face, I know there is nothing I can do about it.

THIRTY-FOUR

My head is heavy, my eyes are sore, and my body doesn't want to move.

How long have I been drifting? The memory of the doctor being here, of telling me I can't see Jack, is fading, like it belongs to another time, another place. Maybe it does. Maybe I imagined it.

But then there are moments of clarity, of the doctor sitting on the chair, watching me as I sank into a deep sleep on the couch. I half remember Mabel coming in, and zombie-like walking to the table to eat the reheated homemade soup I had in my freezer. I even recall how gentle she was when helping me into bed.

I roll to my side, and the room rolls with me. It tilts and turns, spins and dips, until my stomach revolts and I force my eyes closed. I take one breath, then another, waiting for this sensation to pass, but it doesn't, not for a long, long time.

I roll again, this time slower. The room doesn't move as much. I push myself upright, bracing against the dizziness, willing the floor to stay where it should be. My arm sweeps the nightstand, searching for an anchor. Instead, I find a glass of water, cold and full, with a drip on its surface. I reach for the glass, but it slips from my fingers, shatters across the floor. I watch it spread and pool.

Jack. My baby.

The effort of his name makes my head spin again. I lie back, willing the ceiling to stop swirling, knowing it won't, knowing nothing will. I stare at the pill bottle on the nightstand. Small, white, innocent. Dangerous. It stares back at me, a relentless reminder, a constant accusation.

My thoughts swim through the confusion, through the weight of doubt. Why do I have to take these? Why did the doctor have them in his bag to begin with?

I clutch the pill bottle, try to focus on the tiny label. I can't make it out. I can't make anything out.

I blink, slow and careful, the motion tugging at the edges of sleep. Something flashes, a movement outside my door, then another. I wait, unsure if I'm imagining this too, and then it opens.

"Oh good, you're awake. And just in time for breakfast." Mabel's voice is cheerful and unexpected. "How are you feeling? Okay?"

I nod. Or I think I do. It doesn't feel like my head is moving. "What time is it?"

"It's after nine. And it's Sunday. Thought you could use the rest."

Sunday. Nine. The words are numbers, the numbers are words, and they have no meaning to me. She pulls up a chair.

"Mr. M asked me to check on you. He says you need to take it easy and he'll come by shortly." She watches me with careful eyes, waiting for my reaction, seeing more than I want her to see.

Once we're out in the kitchen, I notice a tray on the counter. Mabel lifts the lid and I see a stack of pancakes. My stomach growls. There's a glass of water along with a tumbler, I assume, full of a freshly mixed smoothie.

"I tried something new to see if it tastes better," she says, handing me the drink. "Chocolate milk as well as a bit of that cocoa Mrs. R brought back from Paris. There's also a handful of fresh raspberries mixed in as well." Mabel's eyes are on me, patient and kind, waiting. Watching.

I take a sip, and my nose wrinkles at the funny aftertaste.

"Oh, dear, I was hoping you'd like this one."

"I didn't like the others?" I ask.

She shakes her head. "Yesterday, I did a pineapple-strawberry mixture, but you wouldn't drink it. You said it tasted funny."

"What else is in it?" I know I should know this, but the brain fog hasn't lifted.

"Just the usual."

"The usual?" I echo. "Then why am I so tired and foggy?"

She puts her hand on my knee. Her fingers are warm. "No, dear, that's the pills. Mr. M asks that you don't take any more till he comes down. As for the smoothie, it's what the doctor brought, Trina, nothing added, I promise."

The chair scrapes against the floor as she stands. "I'll let Mr. M know you're up. He's worried, you know."

I hold the smoothie, its cold surface sweating like the glass of water, like the tears I can no longer find. The urge to dump it out is overwhelming, but I don't. I instead tip the glass back, feel the thick, cloying liquid slide down my throat, and try not to grimace. When it's done, I'm done. "I don't want to drink that ever again," I tell her.

Mabel lingers at the door. "Is there anything else I can help you with?"

I want to say yes. I want to say no.

"Is Jack...?" The words slip and tangle, slurring together. What was in that smoothie?

"He's fine. Don't worry. Rosalind is, too."

"Did you...?"

But Mabel is gone, closing the door behind her. I slump back against my seat. My mind swims with the currents of doubt and sadness, with thoughts I can't hold onto, with words I can't remember how to say. I reach for them, but they're out of my grasp and I watch them slip away. I want to let them go but then something stirs in me, telling me to fight, to push against the flow, to do something rather than nothing. So I do.

It's hard, but I get up. I force myself to vomit, sure that I've been drugged, and then I make myself some oatmeal.

By the time Marcus finally arrives, I'm on the porch swing, forcing my eyes to stay open, to not give in to the sleep that wants to steal my clarity.

"Trina," he says, a mixture of surprise and relief in his voice. "I didn't expect to see you out here." He sits beside me, the wood creaking under the weight of his presence. "How are you feeling?" His hand covers mine, solid and warm.

I withdraw my hand and hide it beneath the blanket covering me. I swallow against the dryness in my throat, try to form words, to make them mean something. "Something's wrong," I manage, but the sound is fragile, like it's breaking apart before it reaches him.

His eyes narrow with concern, with focus. "What's wrong?" he presses.

"I think I've been drugged."

"Drugged? How?"

"The smoothie. The pills. Mabel... the doctor." I can't wrap my tongue around the words, but I hope he understands.

Marcus frowns, staring at me with an intensity that has me looking away before he heads into the house. When he comes back, he's holding the bottle of pills, studying it in a way that I find unnerving. "This dosage seems excessive," he says. I can't tell if he's agreeing with me or accusing me of something.

"The doctor..." I try to explain, try to put the pieces together. They keep slipping, just like my thoughts. "The pills..."

He pockets the pills in his suit jacket as he takes a seat. "He went too far," he growls beneath his breath. I notice his hands clenching before he rubs them on his jeans. "We'll get this sorted out." His voice is smooth, commanding. He takes charge the way he always does, and I let him. "You don't have to worry, Trina. I'll fix everything."

I want to believe him. I focus on his face, try to anchor myself in his certainty. It's hard to do. His features blur, shift, come in and out of focus.

"I can't..." I stop. What can't I do? Can't think? Can't breathe? Can't take it anymore?

"You're going to be okay," he says, a promise wrapped in authority, in control. "Trust me."

Trust. It's such a simple word. So small and full of everything I'm not. I do know this—I will never trust this man, no matter what he says or does.

"Jack," I say, and the desperation in my voice surprises me. I clutch the arm of the swing, try to steady the world, try to steady myself. "He needs—"

Marcus stands, and his shadow stretches over me, larger than life, larger than everything. He looks down, his eyes filled with intent. "You and Jack will be taken care of," he insists.

I watch him as he leaves, his back straight, his stride purposeful. He's already on the phone, already talking to someone, already fixing things the way he says he will. I lean back against the swing, the creak of wood fading into the distance as I close my eyes and stop fighting.

THIRTY-FIVE

It's been two days. Two days since Marcus took the pills and told Mabel to throw out the powder the doctor gave us. Two days of slowly feeling like myself again.

Two very lonely days, too.

Banned from the house and hating every second of it, I feel the walls of my cottage bearing down on me. I need to be outside. I walk anywhere and everywhere, taking familiar paths, my mind wandering toward Jack, his cries, the tiny beautiful life everyone is telling me isn't mine. I toss and turn between believing them too. My heart and my brain are at war. My heart screams that he belongs to me and I belong to him; my head says that it's just grief talking.

I find myself headed toward the main barn, toward Wyatt, wanting to talk this over with him. He's out in the pen with the others. The horses move in circles, wide and graceful, and as scared as I am to ride a horse, just watching them calms me. My hand finds its way to my stomach, and I find myself rubbing the wound that's there.

A sleek company car pulls up and a woman in a tailored suit steps out, her expression as precise as her clothing. I tense, unsure why Jessica, the Eaton family lawyer, is here, until her formality melts into something warmer. "Trina," she says, and it's like a balm. "Just the person I needed to see."

"You look good," I say, waving my hand at her suit. She's all dressed up in a pencil skirt, fitted jacket, and pale blue blouse. "Everything okay? Staying busy?"

"The boys are in a bit of a mess, and it's been meeting after meeting." A grimace covers her face. "But enough about that. I'm actually here to see you. Mind if we head to your cottage?" Her voice is inviting, her tone more an assumption than a question.

"Me?"

She points toward the passenger door. "Hop in." This time, the expectation is very clear.

I get in the car, and there's an awkwardness between us that is strange. While Jessica is the Eatons' lawyer, she and I have developed a bit of a friendship and we tend to go out for drinks every few months or so. "So, how are things?" Jessica's question is soft and gentle, and it means more than it asks.

"Oh, you know." I keep my words and tone vague. "A little curious about the visit, to be honest. Is something going on?"

"Just need to go over a bit of paperwork." She gives me a smile before focusing back on the short drive to my place. We pull up beside a work truck parked in front of the cottage. One of the ranch hands stands at my front door, his back to us.

"Can I help you?" I call out.

He turns, and I recognize him but can't place his name. He looks up, his expression curious. "Oh, hey, Ms. Emmet. Just updating the locks is all."

"Why?" No one told me this was happening, not even Wyatt. What's going on?

First it was the lock on the back door of the main house, the cameras, and now I'm getting new locks? I don't like this.

"Got this new system that gives out personal codes. It's been on back order for a while but finally arrived."

I vaguely remember being told about this.

"Do you know what my code is?" I ask. I notice he's setting a few codes into the lock.

Once he's done, he opens his notebook, writes down a five-digit code, and tears the page, handing it to me. "Here you go," he says.

"What were those other codes you put in?"

"Codes for others to have access. This new system will register each person who uses the codes so we can monitor who goes in and out. It's important you don't share yours with anyone." He pockets the notebook with all those codes written down.

"Can I have a list of that, so I know who has access to my place?" I'm a little miffed at the sudden lack of privacy.

"Sorry, you'll have to ask Mr. Eaton for that." He gathers his stuff and leaves.

"Can they do that?" I turn to Jessica before entering my code to unlock my door.

She nods. "It's in your contract, actually. We'll go through all that."

My phone pings with a message. It's Trent apologizing for not notifying me about the lock change. I glance up at the cameras Wyatt installed. I don't like being watched like this, where my every move is seen and documented.

Jessica and I sit down at my kitchen table, and she pulls out my employment contract. It's been four years since I last signed it, and it needs some updating, she informs me. A few new clauses have been added, and she shows me where I agreed four years ago to the stipulation that while my housing is provided, it is not considered private, something that now irritates me more than I will admit.

When we're done, there's no time for chitchat, and I wave

goodbye to Jessica as she drives off, letting out a very long breath and feeling antsy. I need to get out of here. Go for a drive. Head into town for ice cream. Stop by an antique store or bookshop, go watch a movie. I might even book a room for the night and not come back until tomorrow.

It doesn't matter what I do; I just need to get away.

I quickly change and putter around, tidying up an already tidy home before I leave, but something feels off, and I'm not sure what it is.

I know Wyatt said he'd take care of removing the listening device, but still I check where I found it earlier. Gone.

I move a stack of books from the end table and breathe in the scent of flowers from the vase. One of the cleaners must have brought it. Earlier this year, Rosalind decided to have fresh flowers delivered to the house and always made sure to include a bouquet for my place. As I look at it more closely, my stomach drops as I notice something that doesn't belong.

A camera.

I hold my breath and stand back, staring directly into the tiny, unblinking eye. Why is there a camera on this vase? My heart patters with an intensity that wasn't there before, and I look around, my eyes wide, frantic, searching for more. There, on the side table, a little sheep flower container, another camera.

Someone has been in my house. Someone has been in my house, and there's nothing I can do about it because, apparently, it's a clause in my contract.

My hands shake as I tear my place apart, from lamps to books to plant pots high up on shelves to searching beneath coffee tables, end tables, and even my kitchen table. I feel like I'm going crazy. In the end, I find only two different cameras in the living room of my home. But why are they even here? My breath is ragged, a jagged gasp of disbelief. Is this Rosalind's doing? Marcus's? Trent's? Who approved this, and why?

They don't trust me. That much is clear.

I can't take it. This feeling of being watched, of not being trusted, it's too much. I need to get out of here.

I grab my purse. The cottage seems smaller now, less mine than before. I reach for the car keys in their usual spot, but they're not there. My pulse skips, and I search the counter, the drawers, every place I might have put them. Nothing. The keys are gone.

I freeze and try to remember the last time I saw them. It's been a while. I haven't left the property in what feels like forever, if I'm being honest. Normally, I keep them either hanging beside the front door or in my purse.

I dump my purse out, its contents spilling onto the kitchen counter, but they're not there. Everything else is there: my wallet, odd receipts, lipstick, lip balm, hand lotion, hand sanitizer, a new soother still in its package with a cute Winnie the Pooh sticker on it, loose change, and gum. But no keys.

No keys. But there is a folded note with my name written on the front.

You are being watched.

A little too late for the warning.

Who placed this in here? I haven't used my purse in forever since I haven't had reason to. How long has this been here?

It doesn't make sense. But the need to get away is even stronger now.

I send Wyatt a quick text.

Lost my car keys and need to run into town. Any available vehicle I can borrow for a few hours?

Borrowing a truck in the past if I ever needed one has never been an issue before.

I'm fully expecting him to say sure, to tell me to come down to the barn.

Nothing available. You'll need to talk to the brothers. Sorry.

This gives me a little pause, but I try not to think too much on it. I take my purse and head to the main house, even though I'm not supposed to, and see one of the brothers up ahead.

"Trina," Trent says, his head tilting in the way it does when he's got something on his mind. "Everything okay?"

I inhale, filling my lungs and forcing myself to appear relaxed and calm. "I seem to have misplaced my keys, and I need to run into town. Is there any way I can borrow a ranch truck?" Why do I feel so uncomfortable asking this?

Trent frowns as he looks back toward the house. It feels like he's taking forever to answer. "We consider you part of the family, Trina," he says. "And as family, you get your own driver."

My own what? "What? No, no, I don't need someone to drive me into town. I just need a truck for a few—"

"Of course you do. Don't worry about it," he interrupts, his voice warm, like a blanket. "I'll get one of the drivers, hang tight." He pulls out his phone and starts to type something, but I stop him with a touch.

"No, honestly, Trent. I can drive myself."

"I know you can, but you don't need to."

"I just misplaced my keys."

He shrugs, like that's a moot point. I can't even begin to describe the unease I feel at the thought of having someone drive me places. "It's not an issue. Actually, it would make me feel better. With everything going on, at least I wouldn't have to worry about where you are and if you're okay."

"Why would you worry about me?"

"More like Rosalind would."

That's all he has to say. It deflates all the anxiety building inside me. "Okay... if it helps so that Rosalind doesn't stress," I say, "then thank you. One more thing if you don't mind?"

"Go for it," he says.

"Why is my contract being changed?" I keep my voice light, casual, like it's not the end of everything, like it's the most common thing to be discussing.

Trent looks confused. "I didn't know anything about that," he says, and I can't tell if he's lying or not.

"Jessica was just here going over it with me," I say, watching him, searching for a crack, for a slip, for anything.

His expression is believable. "I had no idea, honestly. Do you have a copy of the changes?"

I shake my head. "She's going to send over a finalized copy for me to sign by tomorrow."

"Don't worry, Trina." His voice is smooth. "Marcus probably forgot to mention this to me, or Jessica is just being proactive. Things have been a little crazy lately, and no doubt this is a ball we've dropped. Like me telling you about the lock change."

I nod, but the motion feels stiff. The majority of the contract changes are in my favor, so I'm not going to stress about it too much. I force a smile to show that everything is fine even though I feel the exact opposite right now. I don't feel fine at all.

He goes to turn but I stop him. "Trent, one more thing. Um" —I hesitate, not sure how to bring this up—"is there a reason why there are cameras in my cottage?"

He stops, a quick, sudden halt. "What?" he asks, genuinely surprised.

I smile, wanting to appear like it's not a big deal, and that smile feels like a stranger on my face. "Yeah. There are two cameras in my living room. I mean, I get why there are cameras on the outside of the cottage, but then my lock was changed, the new code to the main house... have I done something wrong?"

Trent frowns, a deep, thoughtful crease. "Rosalind did

mention she didn't feel safe with me gone so much," he says, each word careful, measured. "But I didn't realize that would include cameras inside your cottage as well." He sighs, jamming his hands in his jean pockets and stares at the main house, his features morphing into a very tired, very overwhelmed man. "I honestly don't know what to tell you about Rosalind right now. I thought she was getting better, but if this is true, I'm afraid it's the opposite. Sending the girls away was the right call." He says this so softly, it's almost like he's talking more to himself than to me. He purses his lips and looks like he's about to say more when his phone rings. "Sorry, I need to take this."

"This is Eaton," he says. I go to leave but stop. *This is Eaton* is something Marcus always says, but I've never heard Trent say it. I swear, if I didn't know better, I'd almost think that was Marcus answering the phone. I watch him as he walks away, studying his slight movements until I'm sure it's Trent; it has to be. But why would he pretend to be Marcus on the phone?

THIRTY-SIX

I watch the surface of the pool, tiny waves made by the splashing of my feet, and feel like for the first time in what has been a very long week, I can actually breathe.

Rosalind texted with a simple message:

Jailbreak at the pool.

No way was I saying no to that, no matter what the doctor ordered, especially if there's a chance she'll bring Jack. It's a beautiful day so I relax on a lounger, soaking in the warmth of the sun and wait.

"Trina."

When I twist to look behind me, she waves. She looks different. Her posture. The way she's walking toward me. The smile on her face. She looks happy—or happier, at least, than the last time I saw her, which feels like a lifetime ago.

She's alone, though. No Jack. It takes everything in me to force a smile on my face and not show my disappointment.

Rosalind pauses at the edge of the patio, light playing against her dark hair. She's a silhouette against the afternoon sun, a new shape, a new shadow. Her hesitation mirrors mine. She stops, a distance still between us, and I notice everything, including the slight falter of her smile.

We sit at one of the tables. She sets a baby monitor down and adjusts the volume.

"Is Jack asleep?" That can be the only reason she didn't bring him.

She nods.

Rosalind shifts in her seat, the uncertainty giving way to something more settled, more assured. "I can't believe they thought they could ban you from the house. I only found out this morning; otherwise, I would have acted sooner."

"What do you mean?"

"Marcus told me you wanted some time alone. That's why I thought you weren't coming around. I complained to Trent how much I missed you this morning, and he finally spilled the beans."

Why would Marcus tell her that when he not only knew the truth but he's been enforcing it as well?

"We can bring him down if he wakes up," Rosalind says as she adjusts the monitor volume.

I miss him more than I thought possible. "Where's Grace?"

She looks away. "In the kitchen with Mabel," she tells me. "She's like a cockroach. No matter what I do, she's always around," she mumbles. "How are you?"

The question catches me off guard. I take a moment, not sure how to answer. "Better." I pause, take a breath. "Where are the boys?"

"Another business meeting. They'll be back in a few hours," she says. "I've missed you." Rosalind glances down, studies her hands, and I watch for the slightest change in her expression.

"I've missed you too," I tell her, the honesty in my voice surprising me. The tightness in my chest eases a little, and the space between us fills with words, with relief. "Don't you find the closeness between Mabel and Grace weird?" I'm surprised, to be honest.

Rosalind notches a brow. "I don't think so—should I?"

"She never took to me that fast."

Rosalind snorts. "And that surprises you? Come on, Trina. Your spirit animal for the longest time was a porcupine."

I laugh, mainly because she's right. I've always had a guard up.

"I don't know why she's here but I'm not going to stress over it either. Wyatt's taking care of it, right? That's what he told me anyway."

"It doesn't bother you? That someone from our past is living in the room down the hall from yours?"

"Of course it bothers me. It scares me too. I mean, what does she know? There has to be a reason why she's here, but what? I don't get it, but there's nothing I can do about it until we know why."

I grit my teeth. How can she be so blasé about it?

Noise fills the monitor, and Jack's fussing grows louder, clearer as he wakes up. Rosalind rises, a small and powerful motion, but then she stops and sinks back in her seat. "Grace will get him."

Neither one of us says anything; we let the silence beat between us as we wait.

"Hush, sweet thing." Grace's voice fills the speaker. "I'm here; I've got you."

She starts to hum, and the second we recognize the song, Rosalind and I both jump to our feet.

"They have no idea, do they?" Grace whispers. It's not hard to hear the glee in her words. I picture her rocking my son, holding him up to her shoulder, and I clench my fists. "This wasn't the life I thought I'd have, raising her sons, and yet here I am, and she has no sweet clue."

Rosalind's eyes widen with shock.

"Rosie, what is she talking about?" Raising her sons? That couldn't be a slip of the tongue, right?

Rosalind drops back down onto her chair, her hand clasped tight against her mouth. Tears well in her eyes, but there's no sorrow in her gaze, only anger.

What is going on?

"Rosalind?"

She shakes her head but she's not looking at me. She's staring off into the distance, her chest rising and falling with rapid breaths.

"What a lucky little boy you are," Grace continues, her singsong voice grating on my nerves. "Let's go downstairs, shall we? Your mommy might not want to spend time with you, but you know who does? Mabel. You're lucky to have her here, you know that?" Grace's voice drifts as she leaves the room, but the power of her words sticks.

"I hate her." I grind the words between my teeth, my jaw clenching so tight, I feel it behind my eyes. "I hate..." There's a ball of fury and confusion and resentment tied together inside me.

"You hate me," Rosalind whispers.

I don't disagree.

When Rosalind finally turns her attention to me, the same fury I feel coursing through my body echoes in her gaze.

"None of this is right. None of it is fair, but..." She stops, biting her lips. "I wish things were different," she utters, her eyes closed, her body sagging.

"I'm sorry." I don't know why those are the words I say, and yet, there they are. But what am I sorry for? Sorry for what that horrific woman said? Sorry that we're in this situation? Sorry that I'm so angry, at her, at her family, at what they've done?

"Don't. Don't ever apologize to me, not for this. Nothing about any of this has been fair," she says. "As of right now, everything is back to normal, no matter what the men say. Deal? You. Me. Our lives and how they were."

Normal? What does that even look like anymore?

"I... need you to trust me, if you can." Her gaze burrows deep into my soul. "Sisters never apologize, remember?"

Sisters never apologize. Except, what have I done to need forgiveness for? Nothing. She's the one who should be apologizing.

THIRTY-SEVEN
ROSALIND

Moonlight spills through the curtains, tracing across my pillow, across my eyes. I jerk awake, my heart a frantic drum in my chest. Something's wrong.

It's too quiet.

My shaking hand fumbles for the baby monitor beside me. It shows an empty crib. There's a tightness in my chest, like someone has reached in with their fist and is trying to rip it apart. I stagger out of bed, urgency making my legs weak and my steps clumsy. My ragged breath barely keeps up with the pounding in my head as I rush down the hall.

The nursery door is open, and my fears flood in with the light.

Empty. The room. The crib. They're empty.

Panic seizes me, its grip iron-tight. I move through the room, a whirlwind of frantic energy. "Jack!" The sound of his name reverberates against the walls. My thoughts race faster than my body. Where is he? Where did he go? Where did I put him?

Did I even have him?

I shake my head, force myself to think, force my mind to obey. The room is blank. I'm blank. I grab my phone, hands trembling, barely able to dial. "Trent," I gasp, my voice breaking. "Trent, the baby's gone."

His voice is calm, too calm. It's infuriating. "Rosie, slow down. What do you mean?"

"My baby is gone!" The words come out as sobs.

"Honey, it's going to be okay. Trina has him. She probably has him in the spare room," he says, each word measured, deliberate. "Go look, okay?"

I look toward the closed door, and for a moment, I can't comprehend his words. Trina? Why would Trina have him? Grace should. Where is she?

"Grace is sick with a bad summer cold, honey. Marcus sent her down to one of the spare cottages and Trina agreed to sleep in the house and help with Jack. Don't you remember this?"

Remember this? What is he talking about? Why would Trina...? No. No. I don't remember. I don't remember any of this. I clutch at my head, at the pounding, and want to scream.

"Rosie, did you go check?"

I head to the door and open it. It's empty.

"Rosie? Rosie? Answer me." Trent's voice isn't so measured now, not so deliberate and calm. Good, he's as panicked as I am.

"Honey, I need you to calm down. Please. Please, honey, I need..." He stops, like he's trying to get a hold of himself. "Go check the room, okay? Trina will be in there. It's all going to be okay. Trina is staying the nights till I get home. Come on, sweetheart, you've got this."

Trina. Right. It's all coming back. Trina is here, helping with Jack until Trent comes home. Trent, who is away on another freaking business trip when he should be here with me.

"I'll go look."

"It's all going to be okay." The calmness in Trent's voice is back.

I head to the room on the other side of the nursery and open the door. "She's not here." The bed is a mess, the covers tossed like she got up in a hurry.

"Okay. Okay. Go get Marcus. He's sleeping in the spare room, right? I just texted him."

Marcus. Spare room. Right... while Trent is away, he's staying here to help me, but really I think he's here to keep an eye on me. Except, he's not here. It's just me. Alone.

In the nursery, I stare at the crib, at its emptiness, and it hits me that my baby is gone. My baby. My pulse roars in my ears, my heartbeat wild and untamed. I can't breathe. I can't think.

I pick up the phone again, the shaking worse this time, my fingers unsteady as I grip it. "Trent, where is our baby?"

"Marcus is on his way. He said he had to go down to the barn to check on one of the horses." The patience in his voice slips. "Rosie, he's going to be there soon. I need you to calm down."

But I can't. The tightness in my chest grows until it's unbearable, until I'm sure I'll explode from the pressure. I drop to my knees, sobs shaking me, each one a fresh wave of agony. Where is Marcus? Why isn't he here yet? Why isn't anyone here?

I grab the phone again, desperation raw and urgent. "Trent, please," I plead, a cry wrapped in tears. "What happened to our baby? Just tell me, okay? I need to know."

"You need to breathe, Rosie." His voice is firmer now, a slight edge cutting through the concern. "Marcus is almost there. You have to trust us."

But I don't trust them. I don't trust Trent and I certainly don't trust Marcus. Right now, I don't even trust myself. My mind latches onto the most horrifying scenarios, dragging me deeper into panic. What if my baby is gone forever? What if it's all a lie? What if I'm the lie?

The walls close in, too tight, as I stumble to my feet, search the room with wild eyes, my voice rising, breaking. "I can't do this, Trent. I can't. I can't lose another baby." The emptiness answers with silence. Silence and the soft, mocking hum of the monitor.

I pace, frantic, each step leaving a piece of myself behind. Marcus should be here by now. Shouldn't he? The waiting, the uncertainty, and the sheer terror grip me tighter than ever.

"This is my fault," I mutter, half to myself, half to the ghost of my past. "This is all my fault."

The panic claws at my throat, leaving me breathless, voiceless. I can't lose another baby. I can't. I see Trent in my mind, too far away, too unconcerned, and unwilling to share any of this with me. I see Marcus, too controlling, too hovering, and always very secretive. The pain of their betrayal stabs with every heartbeat, and with every wild thought.

"Rosie? Rosie? ROSIE!" Trent is shouting at me.

"I need help." My body is crawling with ants. Every inch is covered with fire. I'm on fire. I'm burning from the inside out and I don't know what to do. I want to collapse on myself, to let my body smolder into flames that torch this place, torch this haven of lies and deceit and emptiness.

"Trent," I choke out, barely able to form the words. "Help me, please."

"Marcus is almost there, Rosie. Just hang on." There's a desperation to his voice, a helplessness that he can't hide. Like the helplessness I've felt since the night I went into labor.

Hang on? Hang onto what? The sobs come harder now, each one like glass shattering inside me. I try to hold on like he's telling to, but my grip is weak.

I stumble to the bathroom, needing to douse the flames scorching me. The cold tiles sting against my feet, each step a shock. The water is frigid when I turn on the shower and I gasp.

My baby is gone. Forever.

My sobs fill the bathroom, the sound splintering in the cold, breaking me into pieces.

The water clings to me like grief, like guilt, like everything I've done wrong. I think of my baby, my other babies. I think of the cries I never heard. My fault. My fault. All my fault. The water pours down my face, mixes with my tears, with my memories, with my fear.

I try to block it all out, squeezing my eyes as hard as I can, but the images won't go away, the sounds pound against my ears, the thoughts keep coming, relentless, merciless. Where is Marcus? Why isn't he here? Why aren't any of them here?

The panic rises like a tide, swallowing me, drowning me.

I rock back and forth, clutching my knees. The water beats against my skin, a thousand tiny fists. I shiver, my nightgown like a second skin, and I don't know how long I've been here. I try to think, but the thoughts scatter, slip away. I try to feel, but the numbness is too strong, too fierce, too much. I try to remember, but everything blurs, everything fades.

Echoing footsteps cut through the darkness, and my name is called. The pounding water on my skin disappears, and I open my eyes and find Marcus standing there, larger than life. He wraps a towel around me, his touch a fusion of concern and control.

"Mmmmy bbbbabbbby..." I stutter trying to get the words out, my teeth chattering like I'm frozen in ice.

"Rosalind." He stops me, calm, measured, not a trace of doubt. "Trina has Jack at her cottage. You knew that. You must remember."

Marcus helps me up, guides me from the cold, wet, and dark to the chair in the bathroom. He wraps me in another towel, and I sit here, shivering, drowning in confusion.

"Why didn't you answer when I called?" His voice is soft but with an edge, as if he's scolding a child.

I stare at him, try to make sense of his words. My teeth chatter in my skull, a drumbeat of uncertainty. "I didn't hear," I manage, the words as fragile as I feel. "I thought... I thought..."

He reaches for a dry shirt, drapes it over my shoulders like a shield. "Trina didn't want Jack to wake you. You have that cold that Grace has, and Jack isn't feeling well either. And you"—he puts the back of his hand to my forehead—"are heating up like a furnace." He sighs. "We discussed this earlier. You were the one who suggested that if she thinks Jack's cries will wake you, she could take him to her cottage for the night while you sleep, and then you would take over while she slept."

"No," I say, my voice as shaken as I feel. "I don't... I don't remember."

The concern on his face deepens, shadows cutting across his features. "These memory lapses," he says, each word careful, precise, like a scalpel cutting into my sanity. "This isn't the first time, but I thought... Maybe it's just the fever."

I clutch the towel tighter. All I want to do is lie down, sleep, and maybe never wake up again. "I'm sorry," I whisper, but the words sound hollow even to me.

He watches me with those dark, all-seeing eyes, his focus unsettling, unnerving. "I am too," he says with a finality I don't like.

His presence is both a comfort and a challenge, both a lifeline and a chain. I can't look at him. I can't look away. "My body was on fire," I say, the words cracking, explaining why I was in the shower.

"I know," he says.

His voice pierces me, opening wounds I thought were healing, old scars, new doubts. I shiver, not from the cold, not from the wet, but from the fear, the fear that he's right, the fear that I'm not.

Marcus leans forward, and I brace for his words, brace for his control. "It's okay," he says. "We'll figure this out. Right now, you need to get out of that wet nightgown and climb into bed. I'll go make you a hot cup of honey and lemon while you get changed, okay? Can you do that for me?"

I wrap the towel tighter, tighter, until it's the only thing holding me together. "Okay," I whisper.

Marcus stands, looks down at me, a giant casting a long, dark shadow. "You're going to be fine," he says, a promise wrapped in certainty, in the control I wish I had. "We'll take care of everything. We'll take care of you."

The words sting. The truth stings more.

He heads into my bedroom and returns with a dry night-gown, handing it to me.

"Get changed, climb into bed, and I'll be right back," he says. Marcus pauses at the door. "I'll be right back, okay?"

"I want to see Jack." There's a strength to my voice that surprises us both. "I mean it, Marcus. I need to see him."

He pauses, like he's going to disagree, but then he just nods. "Join me when you're ready and we'll walk over together."

I nod, and then he's gone but not before I saw the look on his face, the questioning glance in his eyes. He may be a hard man to read, but in that moment, he was an open book.

And he's wondering if this is what crazy looks like.

THIRTY-EIGHT

TRINA

I stare down at the small bundle in my arms, whimpering as he fights against sleep while I walk with him around and around, trying to soothe him. Seeing him in distress and hearing his cries hurts my heart.

I remember when the girls had their first cold, around this age, and how helpless everyone felt at the time, including me. Rosalind and I would swap shifts, taking care of the girls. I'd take the night shift, giving her space to sleep, and she'd take over after breakfast, so that I could fall into a dreamless coma.

These past few days have been amazing. One minute I'm banned from the house by the doctor and the next I'm not only welcomed back with open arms, but being asked to take care of Jack, too. Being with him, holding him, rocking him to sleep, I feel complete.

Complete but exhausted. Summer colds on babies are no joke. I don't ever remember feeling this exhausted, though. My feet barely shuffle on the floor, my body wants to collapse in on itself, and if I stop moving, I'll do just that.

Jack's tiny face scrunches, his voice as fragile as I feel and as frantic as my heartbeat. We keep moving while I whisper to him, doing my best to push away the creeping sense of panic that I know I only feel because it's the middle of the night and I'm tired.

Summer colds are the worst, especially for little ones. For the longest time, the girls would get croup, and I'd walk outside with them, wrapped up against the cold, dark night, just to help them breathe a little easier.

"Shh, sweetheart, you're okay. Just close those eyes of yours, that's it. Your mommy has you," I croon in a whisper-soft voice. He doesn't feel as warm as before, which is good.

A series of loud and sharp *rap-rap-rap*s at the door snatches my attention. Jack, startled, screams.

"Shh." I barely make it to the door before it opens, revealing Marcus, with Rosalind at his back. She has a wild look in her eyes.

"Trina..." Marcus shakes his head, stopping me from saying anything else.

Rosalind lunges forward, hands reaching, then stops. Her arms fall to her sides. Her eyes burn with panic and disbelief. "You took my baby!"

My grip on Jack tightens. I am not letting go of my son. I look to Marcus for clarification.

"Rosalind woke up in a panic," he says with a little shrug.

I hold Jack tighter. "I didn't want to wake you," I tell her. "You said you were okay with me bringing him here if I couldn't get him to settle."

"I don't remember saying anything remotely like that. I wouldn't. I want him close, where I can see him, hear him. He's... he's my son." Rosalind's denial is weak, like her voice. She also looks horrible, like a wet mop.

He's my son. Like hell he is. He's mine. Not hers.

Rosalind bites her lip and casts a glance toward Marcus before leaning forward. "Sisters never apologize, remember?" She barely speaks loud enough for me to hear. "I just... Is he okay?" She lightly touches his brow. "Oh, he's warm. Poor thing. Should we call the doctor?"

What the... what is going on with her? "I already called for help," I tell her, watching her carefully. "They said to monitor his fever and keep him hydrated."

She lets out a small sigh of relief. "Of course you've got this; I wasn't doubting you. I guess I just..." She looks to Marcus as if searching for his help.

Marcus stands behind Rosalind, his presence calm and quiet, a strange contrast to Rosalind's vibe. He wraps his hands around her arms. "Now that you've seen Jack, are you ready to go back to bed?"

"I want my baby."

I feel like I've been gut punched by her words. Every time she calls Jack hers, I want to scream.

Marcus doesn't budge. "He's okay here, with Trina. You can trust her."

"I know I can trust her," Rosalind says, glancing my way. "It's not that," she says, as if to reassure me. "I just... I woke up and thought... I can't do that again, feel that again."

"Of course," I say, feeling a little off kilter now. Something obviously happened, something bad enough to bring her down here to make sure Jack is okay.

She wraps her arms around us. "You were right. I've kept it safe for your birthday," she whispers softly into my ear.

I place a hand on her back; the heat radiating from her body scalds my palm. Something is wrong with her.

"She's burning up," I say. "Has she taken anything to help bring it down?"

"I found her in a cold shower."

"Do you need to call the doctor?"

"Already done." Marcus is beside her, hand on her arm. "Come on, Rosalind, let's get you back to bed, okay?"

He leads her away, toward the door. "I'll be right back," he tells me.

They leave while I'm still holding Jack, and I don't know what to do.

Marcus is coming back. Why didn't he just take Jack with him? And then Rosie's words hit me. I was right. What does she mean? And she kept it safe for my birthday? That's months away. It must be the fever because she didn't make any sense. I glance down at the baby in my arms, and I hope she means I was right about Jack being mine, but something is off.

Actually, everything about tonight is off and it's because of the fevers. That's the only explanation.

When Marcus returns, I don't even wait for him to open the door. I meet him out on my front porch. "Is she okay?"

He shakes his head. I can't tell what he's thinking. His face is lined with weariness, and I know he's stressed; I can see it in his eyes.

"I don't think so," he says. He seems as surprised at his words as I am. "I have someone sitting with her now, and the doctor is almost here."

"Did she really think I stole Jack?"

He nods.

"But I only brought him here because—"

"I know," he interrupts, taking Jack from me, his motions sure, steady. Jack immediately calms. "You didn't do anything wrong," he continues while I stand there, taking in the sight. Father and son.

Of course I didn't do anything wrong. If anyone is in the wrong, it's him.

"She just had a nightmare," Marcus says, oblivious to my thoughts. "It has to be the fever."

The night presses in, a weight, a shadow, a constant

companion. We stand side by side, together, and I shudder as a chill wraps around my ankles.

"Marcus, we need to talk," I say, and the desperation in my voice is thick, tangled, wrapped around each syllable. There's a hint of curiosity behind Marcus's gaze.

"Can we talk in the morning?"

There will never be a time, not unless I force it.

"You know I found those certificates in Trent's office. You can't keep pushing this off," I say. I've been wanting, needing us to talk as parents about our child, but it's like he's forgotten about our connection to each other.

Marcus pauses. "You don't look well," he says. The words are cool, careful, meant to cut. "I'm going to take Jack up to the house. You need some sleep."

"What? No, I'm okay."

He shakes his head, his finger lightly stroking my cheek. "I'm going to need you tomorrow. Why don't you stay here and sleep? I've got Jack tonight—it's the least I can do for my..." He stops, a frown appearing on his face.

"For your...?" My words carry in the night breeze, and I'm not sure if he heard me but I definitely heard him.

He steps away, and if I don't say anything now, the moment will be gone.

"We need to talk about our baby," I call out. "The one you're holding." My breath catches as I let my words hang between us.

Marcus pivots, confusion etched into the features I thought I knew so well.

"What are you talking about?" he asks, as if he doesn't know, as if he doesn't know everything.

"I don't believe the lies about the birth certificates," I say. "Dr. Harmon wouldn't make a mistake like that. Not on three different documents. Documents where your name is on every single piece of paper as the father."

The pause stretches between us, thin and wide as I say the words I've been holding tight to my heart ever since I opened that envelope. I've wanted to discuss this with him to find out why, and every time he evaded me, it only made the questions more pronounced in my mind.

I take another step closer, my heart wild, a stampede of fear and hope and despair all jumbled together.

"Why are you listed as the father for both children, Marcus? Why isn't Trent's name on the birth certificate for their baby? The baby that died during childbirth?"

It's a wild accusation, I know that, but I still fling it out there and wait for his response, for the truth, for answers.

Marcus's face remains still and composed, but something slips, giving way beneath his cool exterior. "You weren't supposed to see those," he says, and there's an edge to his voice.

"And yet I did."

"The doctor signed the wrong forms, Trina." Marcus's words are deliberate, an attempt to control and confuse. "He mixed up the names."

"Did he? I really have a hard time believing that. He even said as much to me, that in all his years of experience being a doctor, he has never made this level of mistake. Never. So why now?" I look at Jack and my heart swells. "And don't blame it on his age. There's more going on. I want the truth, Marcus. I deserve that much."

His voice is smooth, too smooth, too rehearsed. "Why would I lie about something like this? You have no idea the mess that mistake has caused." Marcus shifts, Jack's small body cradled close, a wound too deep, too fresh. "Besides, what kind of monster do you think I am?"

Monster? His word, not mine, but it fits. His words always fit. They light a fire within my soul. "You stole my baby from me and gave him to Rosalind. What I don't understand is why." I gasp as I throw this accusation out, heavy and dense, deep and unforgivable. I finally say the words that have festered in my heart since the moment I knew Jack was mine.

Marcus's silence is an admission, an answer.

"You aren't going to deny it?" My arms cross over my chest as I wait for him to admit what my heart knows to be true.

"You need to listen to reason," Marcus insists, but his voice is different now, weaker, uncertain. He struggles and tries to regain control, and I see it on his face. Somehow, I've managed to unseat a man who never loses a fight.

He takes a step back, clutching Jack, clutching the lie, holding the truth. "Trina," he says, a question, a plea, a desperate attempt. "Don't do this."

I look at him, and everything slips away. All I see is the truth.

"Jack." His name is everything. His name is the past and the future, the end and the beginning. His name is mine. "Jack," I say again.

Marcus shakes his head, his hold on Jack tighter. He watches me with a look that I can't quite read, but I know there's fear in there somewhere. Why is he so afraid? What is going on?

I stare at him, unblinking, unmoving, waiting for him to crack, waiting for him to break.

He looks at Jack, looks at me. His eyes widen, and the certainty shatters. The world shatters.

"Don't you see it?" I ask, not giving up. "His hair. His birthmark."

Marcus takes another step back, then stops. His face is masked. His eyes, there's no emotion. None.

He didn't know? That's not possible. But then I remember who this is, what he does. He's a master manipulator, and I can't believe him.

The distance between us feels infinite, like an endless abyss.

I catch something in his gaze... It was lightning quick and I almost didn't see it.

"I want him back," I finally manage to utter. "I want my son."

Marcus's face softens, and I see pity, fear, and a small flicker of something else I can't quite name.

He doesn't respond. He only turns and walks away, and I let him.

My world tilts and spins as I watch the father of my child take him away from me.

THIRTY-NINE

ROSALIND

I'm waiting for Marcus in the downstairs living room. I took some pain medication and now I'm warming myself in front of the gas fireplace I've just turned on.

Did I do enough? Say enough? Did Trina understand my message to her?

I don't know how much more of this I can handle. I feel splintered and not in a good way.

"Why aren't you up in bed?" Marcus's voice fills the room, and suddenly I'm claustrophobic; the large expanse of the room is now closet-sized. "Rosalind, you have a fever; you're not well."

I wrap my arms around myself, like my strength is all I need to hold myself together when in reality I have no strength and I'm falling apart.

I know it. Marcus knows it. Trina suspects it.

I turn and see my brother-in-law standing in the doorway with Jack in his arms.

"I'll go put this guy to bed and be right back, okay? We need to talk about what just happened." He doesn't wait for my reply, doesn't even give me time to nod, before he climbs the stairs, holding Jack close to his chest.

The silence presses in tightly as I wait. I hear Marcus's heavy steps as he heads into the nursery. I listen for the thump on the stairs as he comes back down, but he only walks from Jack's room to the office. There's nothing for a bit, and then finally, he heads back down to me.

He pauses at the base of the stairs, phone to his ear. He's not speaking, just listening.

I haven't moved. I'm in the same spot, trying to warm my frozen soul.

He sees me and lowers the phone, holding it tight in his hand. "Rosalind," he says, his smooth voice calm, careful. He's treating me like a frenzied horse who needs soothing. "Why don't you sit?"

I shake my head, hugging my arms around myself. "I need to get warm."

He sighs, raking a hand through his hair. "You're overtired. You should be resting."

Marcus walks into the room, looks at something on his phone before setting it face down on the coffee table, and heads to the drink station. He pours and picks up two crystal glasses. They are new, having just arrived from Switzerland. They are a gift from the clinic we went to. I don't recall them sending a gift after the girls were born, though, but Trent told me not to think much about it, so I haven't.

His phone glows faintly with a new notification. While he's busy, my hand moves before my mind can stop it and I grab his phone.

And freeze.

A photograph fills the screen—either Marcus or Trent, smiling, a baby cradled against his chest.

The room vanishes. All I see is her face.

A big puff of dark hair. Big, beautiful, dark eyes, wide and steady. A mouth I know. A tilt of her chin that might as well be a mirror of my girls. She looks like them when they were so tiny.

She looks like me.

My throat closes. My hands tremble. I stare at the man on the screen and in my heart I know it's my husband. My husband holding this beautiful baby girl.

I swipe with my thumb, hungry, terrified.

Another image. Trent bent low, pressing a kiss to her temple, his expression softened into something instantly recognizable from when the girls were small—tenderness.

He's not like that with Jack. He barely gives Jack a second glance, now that I think about it.

I stagger, knees buckling. My breath is a gasp in the silence.

I recognize the background. Mabel's house. Grace's words slam back into me: *Mabel already has two things that belong to you.*

At the time, I didn't think much about it because I knew about Matty.

Now... Oh. My. God. Oh my God, she wasn't lying.

"Rosalind?"

Marcus's voice cleaves through my horror. He's there, in front of me, holding a glass of amber liquid. He sees the phone in my hand. His eyes flick to the screen, then to me.

For one heartbeat, something naked flashes in his expression. Then the mask drops back into place.

"Who is this?" My voice is raw, breaking. "Who is this?" I repeat, more insistent.

He sets the glass down slowly, deliberately, like a man setting aside a weapon. He takes the phone from my hand with that same precision, his jaw tightening.

"Keep your voice down," he says. "You'll wake Jack."

"Keep my voice—" My voice pitches high, ragged. "Marcus, she looks like the girls did when they were babies. She looks like—"

"Enough." The single word lands like a slap.

Tears sting my throat. My body shakes. "Is she mine?"

The silence stretches, taut and suffocating. He stares at me, his eyes flat, measuring.

Finally he exhales, slow, through his nose. "You've been under too much strain," he says softly. "You're not well."

The words gut me more than any confession could.

"You're lying," I whisper.

"You're exhausted." He takes my elbow, steering me gently toward the door. "You need rest, Rosalind. That's all. You're imagining things. Twisting them."

I wrench my arm back. "Don't you dare."

His voice sharpens. "I'm glad the girls are with my mom. I'd hate for them to see you like this."

"Like this?"

"Hysterical."

Shame floods me, hot and cold. He's always known where to strike.

I stumble back against a chair, gripping it to stay upright. "She's mine," I say, weaker now, almost to myself. "I know she is. Why? Why isn't she here? Why did you give her away?"

I already know the answer; I just need him to admit it.

Marcus's face doesn't change. "Go upstairs, Rosalind."

"I want an answer." I stand my ground, even if I'm shaking. Even if I know this could all go wrong.

Marcus looks like he's about to say something, something dangerous and life-changing, when his features soften and he looks at me with... pity.

"It's not your fault you're unwell," he says. "You've never been the same since that night."

That night. "The night I died, you mean? The night you gave my child to someone else? The night you handed me a child that isn't my own?"

He doesn't answer, and I wish he would.

He doesn't move, and for that I'm glad.

What he does, however, strikes fear in me and I know at this moment my life will never be the same again.

He smiles. Not a soft, brother-in-law type smile that says everything will be okay. Instead, his smile sends shivers coursing over my skin and destroys whatever hope I had left inside of me.

His smile screams, *You'll regret this.*

His smile whispers, *You have no clue how dangerous I am.*

The room tilts. My body obeys even as my mind shrieks. I walk out on shaking legs, up the stairs that suddenly feel steeper than mountains. In the hallway, the shadows press close, whispering Grace's words again and again: *Mabel already has two things that belong to you.*

In my room, I shut the door and collapse against it, pressing my hand to my mouth to smother the sound clawing its way out.

My. Daughter. Is. Alive. My daughter is alive.

And Trent has known all along.

FORTY

TRINA

There's a loud, demanding, and very heavy knocking at my door. A quick glance at the clock tells me it's barely eight in the morning. The *bang-bang-bang* continues as I wrap a robe around myself, tying the belt in a knot. The banging intensifies as I rub the sleep from my eyes and fiddle with the lock on the door.

Marcus is there, hand lifted as if to pound on the door once more. He looks a little frazzled, a little flustered, and very unlike the Marcus I know.

Actually, this looks very much like the Marcus I remember from that night in Santorini. I shake that image, the one of us in the pool, away. Now is not the time, and that will never happen again.

"Is Jack okay?" He's my first thought.

"I need you," he says. My heart hitches at the words, and intense dread fills me. He pauses and I hate the silence. "It's Rosalind. She's gone."

Gone? What does that even mean? "Where did she go?"

"We had a bit of a decline last night after seeing you," he

says, his shoulders dropping slightly. "Trent rushed home and finally agreed it was time to take her to a clinic on the coast. I'm surprised you didn't hear the helicopter early this morning?"

I did. In fact, I heard it come and then go several hours later, but I assumed it was one of them heading off to another meeting somewhere.

"She didn't want to be sent away." My heart sinks knowing how much she fought against the idea.

"We didn't have a choice," Marcus assures me, his voice almost broken. I've never heard him like this. "It was bad, Trina. Really... bad."

There's something in his voice he's trying to hide. "Is Jack okay?" A band of fear grabs hold of my heart and squeezes until I wince in pain. My son has to be okay.

He swallows and for a moment I don't think he's going to answer. My hand jumps to my chest, stifling a sob rising within me.

"Jack is fine, thank God," he finally says, but I see the haunting in his gaze. "But he almost wasn't." He glances away, back toward the house, and rubs at his face. "Rosalind... she could have hurt him."

I shake my head, not willing to read between the lines. "Rosalind would never."

"You weren't there."

"Marcus," I say, pleading with him. "You know she loves him. She would never hurt him."

He tightens his lips and doesn't respond, sending me reeling. This doesn't make sense. None of it does.

"We need you, Trina." I can tell it's the last thing he wants to admit. Not because he doesn't want to ask for my help but because he has to, because whatever happened actually happened despite everyone hoping Rosalind was getting better.

Something inside me rises up. I wish I'd been there for Rosie last night. I wish I'd been there to see her this morning, to offer her assurance, to let her know I have her back. I hate that she's going through any of this without me by her side.

"Of course," I say. "Anything."

"Would you mind moving back into the main house? At least until... Well, I don't know, honestly, especially with Grace sick. She probably won't come back, not if you are there. The girls will stay with my parents, of course, but Jack, well, he needs to be with you."

The world tilts, and I have to brace against the doorframe to stay upright. He needs to be with me? What does that even mean?

"Of course," I say. "Do we know how long she will be gone for? Will Trent stay with her or fly back and forth between the kids and her?"

"As long as it takes," Marcus says, his voice firm, his voice sure. "She'll get the help she needs. I promise. As for my brother, we'll figure it out as we go, I guess. For now, Jack will have us, so that's one less thing he'll have to worry about."

Jack will have us. He must believe me then.

"I'll move in too," Marcus says, "to help, be on hand."

I nod, not sure what to say, still trying to process everything. "What did Rosalind do?" I swallow hard, unsure if I really want to know the answer.

"She thought he was a doll again. It was really early, and I'd just gotten Jack to finally sleep and went to lie down. I guess I left the door to the spare bedroom open, and she thought Grace was back. She was going to throw Jack at her." He blinks, and something shutters across his face. "That's not the first time she almost did that. A few weeks ago, back before... she was shaking him, screaming that someone stole her baby and gave her a doll."

My hand goes to my mouth as I bite back a cry of shock. "Oh no," I say with barely a whisper. I can't believe she did that, that she was that far down in the whirlpool of her psychosis. My heart aches for her, for the fear she had to be living with.

How did I not see this?

"So you'll come? You won't be alone," he reminds me.

My mind spins with the suddenness of everything. "Who is Jack with now?" I ask.

"He's sleeping. Mabel is there to watch over him, but he'll probably wake up soon wanting to eat."

I nod. Of course Mabel is there. Ever constant. Always taking care of the family.

"Rosalind was fine," I find myself saying, trying to make sense of it, trying to wrap my head around all of this.

"She wanted to be, but I don't think she has been." He rubs the back of his neck. "I wish Trent had listened to me in the beginning, but thankfully, everyone is okay."

He needs to be with you.

My thoughts spin, round and round, trying to make sense of his words, to read behind them, to hear what he didn't say. Did he mean something else, or was it a slip of the tongue?

"Can you come now? I'll have someone pack your things so you don't need to be running back and forth." And there he is. The Marcus I know, with his overwhelming presence, a force of nature, a man with a plan.

He stands there, unmoving. He's so patient, waiting for me to wrap my head around things, to be the mother Jack needs right now.

Despite the swirling thoughts that collide and merge with the past, the present, and the unknown future, I know only one thing: Jack needs me. My son needs me. No matter what anyone else says, in my heart I know he's mine; I just have to prove it.

"Let me pack a bag really quick, okay? And then I'll make a list of things that someone can pack up for me." I go to move, but Marcus reaches out and pulls me to him, and for a moment,

I freeze, uncertain of what is happening. His grip around me tightens, his head drops to the top of mine, but I stand there frozen. I do not want him touching me. I don't want him anywhere near me, ever again, but I can't say that. I have to pretend that it's okay, that I'm okay.

His arms finally drop and he waits as I pack a quick bag of things.

When I'm done, he's on his phone and doesn't realize that I'm standing beside him, waiting.

"It's all taken care of. Now is not a good time. Just do your part and everything will be fine." He turns and blinks hard, pocketing his phone. My presence caught him off guard.

"Ready?"

"Everything okay?" I only heard the last part of that conversation but I find myself wary. What's been taken care of? Rosalind? Me? Did he find out what happened with our baby and why the switch?

"Everything's fine. That was just work-related." He places his hand on the small of my back and leads me to the door.

"Marcus, the locks and codes being changed, was that *because* of Rosalind or *for* her?"

He sighs. "A bit of both, to be honest. Paranoia is one of the symptoms of her psychosis," he says. "She thought someone would take Jack."

"Me?"

He shrugs. "You. Me. The doctor. The gardener. Grace."

I let his words sink in, and let those words tear down the hurt that I was trying so hard to ignore. It hurts to know Rosalind would think I could do that to her. Me, of all people.

Her words last night—that I was right. Was that from her psychosis, too?

"She wasn't thinking clearly," Marcus says, and his voice is soft, almost tender, like he knows what I was thinking. "She thought everyone was trying to take him."

The echo of his words fills my heart. Everyone. It wasn't just me.

"She's going to get the help that she needs, and that's what matters," Marcus tells me as we make our way to the main house.

"I should have seen it," I say. "I should have noticed."

"I feel the same way," Marcus says, and I hear the truth behind his words as well as the apology. "We thought she was just exhausted."

I lay my arm on his. "You know, I found a note in my purse the other day." The words flow from my mouth before I have a chance to stop them.

"A note? What about?"

"That I'm being watched." I watch for a response, but his face remains blank, revealing nothing. "Didn't Trent tell you? I even told him about the cameras."

Marcus pivots and grabs hold of my arms. "What are you talking about?"

I gently dislodge his hold of me and rub my arms where his fingers will no doubt leave a mark on my skin.

"I found two cameras in my cottage."

He lets out a very long, frustrated sigh. "Why didn't you tell me?"

"I told Trent."

He waves that away and pulls out his phone. I notice he has his notes app open. "All the signs were there, I just didn't see them." He adds whatever he was thinking to that note and closes it. "Is there anything else I should be aware of?" he asks. "I know you two are close, but now isn't the time to protect her."

Am I supposed to believe him? "Who would have left me that note, though?"

"I don't know," Marcus says. "The cameras are gone, right?"

I nod. "They disappeared just like they arrived. Unannounced."

When we reach the back porch, Marcus guides me up the steps. "The house is really quiet without the girls, have you noticed that?"

The second the door opens to the kitchen, that quiet is gone. Jack's cries from the monitor are ear-bitingly loud. Mabel's quiet *shhh, I'm here* can barely be heard.

FORTY-ONE

A week has passed. A week of endless nights, of exhausted mornings, and of a full heart. I feel so happy, so at peace, I could burst. At the same time, I'm full of immeasurable guilt knowing Rosalind is at some clinic getting help for her broken soul. What kind of friend does that make me?

But this week with Jack has been everything I thought being a mother would be. I love holding him, washing him, feeding him, seeing all the looks on his face as he watches me, watches the world.

This is heaven.

My heart is fuller with Jack in my life, and I can't imagine how empty I'll feel when Rosalind and Trent return home. Marcus keeps asking for time, but what more does he need to realize that Jack is our son?

After taking Jack for our daily walk, I hold him close as I climb the stairs, losing myself in the soft rhythm of his breathing, the gentle weight of him against my chest as I take each step. To the left is the office and the door is slightly ajar. At first, I don't hear anything, but then I do, and the male voice I hear is sharp and demanding.

Dr. Harmon's voice crackles through the speaker, unmistakable and urgent: "I need the money by end of day, or I'm going to the authorities with proof."

I freeze, heart hammering in my chest, careful not to make a sound, terrified of what I've just heard and more terrified not to hear more.

Money. Authorities. Proof. What is going on?

I tighten my fingers on Jack's swaddled shoulder and pull him close, like I can protect him, or maybe because I need his strength. The breath rushes from my lungs, fast and shallow as I stand motionless and try to keep the panic from bubbling up.

The next thing I hear is Marcus, his low, dismissive laugh, like the threat is just another nuisance in his over-scheduled day. He has no idea I'm right outside, I'm sure of that. He knows my schedule with Jack and probably assumes I'm still out on the walk. I press myself flat against the wall, holding Jack close, straining to hear anything else.

What does Dr. Harmon mean? What proof is he talking about? Then it hits me. The birth and death certificates I found.

You were right. Rosalind's words rush back. This must be what she was talking about.

My grip on Jack's small body is so tight, I'm afraid he'll squirm and make a sound, and yet no matter how hard I try, I can't relax my body.

Jack is mine. My heart races with a wound that won't heal. The edges of the world close in, narrow, squeezing the breath from me. Marcus's voice fills the room. His laugh, low and dismissive, snakes its way around my certainty, and that's when I know for sure.

He did this. He stole my baby and gave him to Rosalind. But why?

I've been so angry with her, but it's all on him. The truth pushes against me, a dark and suffocating weight. I try to fight it, but I can't. I try to breathe, but I can't. I try to think, but I can't.

The words I heard echo in my mind, over and over, my own certainty growing stronger and stronger. More money. The authorities. Proof. There is proof out there that Jack is mine. Proof that others know it too.

I feel like prey, cornered and helpless as I remain pressed against the wall just outside the office.

A phone rings. I catch myself flinching and glance down at Jack, now asleep in my arms. Good.

"Yes, I got it too," I hear Marcus say, so smooth but clipped and certain, like command is his natural state. "This is my problem, so I'll handle it."

His assurance is bone-chilling.

"I don't know what proof he has—we took care of all that, didn't we? You burned those documents, right? Right?" A pause. "Then he shouldn't have any other copies. Any proof that is left is here, in our possession." He pauses again, then sighs. "No, they wouldn't have said anything. We paid them too much money for them to squeal, and they got their baby, didn't they? You need to stop visiting her as much as you do—people are bound to notice. I told you I'd take care of it. Making problems disappear is my thing, or have you forgotten?"

Another pause.

"Why are you worried about Trina? She won't be a problem. The bond the girls have, there's no way Trina will leave her and take Jack. Being Jack's nanny is basically the same as being his mother. She's the one raising him, and who knows when Rosalind will be well enough to be released?" He pauses again, and I hear the chair being pushed back. "One problem at a time, big brother." His words slice the air, and I feel them twisting, wrapping around me like a net. I am caught, and there is no way out.

"Listen, before you go, are you sure Rosalind never told Trina about our arrangement? And she hasn't told the doctors either? The only way this works is if we all stay silent... You know that, right?"

Arrangement? Why do I feel like I'm caught in a web of deceit that I'll never be untangled from?

The shock from hearing Marcus is paralyzing. My stomach knots so tightly I can hardly breathe. The hallway closes in around me. Everything is spinning, and I'm not sure how long I can stay quiet before the truth explodes inside me and I give myself away. I'm suffocating, drowning in the weight of what I heard. My free hand flies up to clamp over my mouth, holding in the gasp that wants to tear from me.

I slowly back away and head to the nursery, where I very gently lay Jack down in his crib and sit in the rocking chair. This is where Marcus finds me, rocking back and forth, back and forth, trying to make sense of it all.

"I didn't realize you were back," he says. He walks over to the crib and checks in on Jack. "I spoke with Trent today," he tells me. "There's been no change with Rosalind." I hear the regret in his voice, but I no longer believe it.

The man is like a freaking Emmy-winning actor right now. I won't ever believe another word from him.

My whole world has been upended, and I'm barely able to find anything to grasp onto.

I'm on the worst rollercoaster in the world. I've gone from being told my child was dead to believing he's actually alive, to being told it was all a mistake and to keep grieving, only to now know the baby I thought was my baby is my baby after all.

What the hell is going on?

"Everything okay?"

I want to laugh from the insanity of that question.

No, Marcus, everything is not okay. In fact, it is far from okay. But saying all that is a waste of breath and energy. No matter what I say to Marcus, how many questions I ask, he will never admit the truth to me.

Rosalind would, though. I need to talk to her. I need to find a way to see if she knows what is going on, if she is just another problem Marcus had to make disappear.

I need those certificates, the real ones, and then I need to figure out how to get him away from this man who I'm beginning to realize stole him from me.

Chills run across my body at the thought.

"Marcus?" A voice carries up the stairs.

"Ahh, right on time," he says, glancing at his watch. "Will you be okay for a bit? I have some things to discuss with Grace before she heads back to her old life. Some documents she needs to sign and such."

I wave him off. "Do what you need to do." It takes everything in me to keep the smile on my face.

I stay in the nursery as Marcus calls up Grace and takes her into his office. Eventually, I hear a sharp voice being raised. Intrigued, I make my way across the upper floor and stand outside the office, where the door isn't fully closed.

"... so that's it?" Grace's voice, smooth but trembling underneath. "You bring me here, make me lie, give me a name that isn't mine—and now you're finished with me?"

My chest tightens.

Marcus's reply is quiet, controlled. "You've done your job. Trina is here now. There's no reason for you to stay."

She laughs, bitter, broken. "You think you can just dismiss me? I know your secrets, Marcus. Remember?"

The silence is heavy. I can't believe she just threatened Marcus.

"Yes, you've held that over our heads for years, haven't you? Seems to me like you've gotten everything you wanted. You wanted security, you got it. You wanted a fresh start, I gave you one. One, I might add, that comes with a hefty paycheck too. Your bank account is quite full, isn't it? You may know a secret of mine, but you've also benefited, haven't you?"

Silence.

Marcus continues. "My son doesn't need you anymore. Neither of the boys do. You're free to go anywhere. Start over. Do whatever your twisted heart wants to do, as long as it is far away from my family, is that clear?"

"I've been with this family since before Matty could walk. I've raised him, stayed hidden from sight, all while you pretended like he wasn't yours. I raised him like he was my own, and you're kicking me out?"

"Matthew doesn't need you anymore."

It doesn't take me long to piece this puzzle together. Matty is Marcus's son? And she's been with him since before he could walk? Does that mean...

I don't move. I don't breathe. My heart slams against my ribs as it all comes together. We always knew our foster mom was responsible for taking Rosalind's son from her, but we always assumed he'd died.

Did she give him to the Eatons to raise instead?

So then Mabel... I get dizzy as the web of secrets fleshes out in front of me.

Does Rosalind know?

The sound of a chair scraping pulls me back from my thoughts. The footsteps toward the door have me rushing into the shadow of the hall, pressing myself flat to the wall as Grace storms past, her face flushed, eyes wet with fury.

She doesn't see me.

Neither does Marcus when he steps out moments later, his jaw tight, muttering under his breath as he heads downstairs.

FORTY-TWO

With Jack sleeping, I make my way to the kitchen for a fresh cup of tea. My mind and heart are racing, and I need to find a way to calm myself before I hit full-blown panic mode.

Marcus's voice during that call is a ghost I can't shake. I think about Jack's pale hair with a tinge of red, of his denim blue eyes, of his distinct birthmark on his shoulder, and my heart blooms with love.

Mabel stands by the counter, slipping small containers of food into a bag. She doesn't see me at first, and I can't help but wonder if she knows about what happened that night.

She was there. I remember that. Did she slip something into my tea? Or is it her hand I remember on my back? No, I can't picture it being Mabel. And yet, at the same time, it wouldn't surprise me either. Mabel, who is loyal to the Eaton boys. Mabel, who runs this house and the people in it with such finesse that no one realizes she's doing it. Mabel, who constantly reminds me that the Eatons are not my family.

Why, though?

I clear my throat and she looks up, startled. "Trina," she says, "are you coming to join us?"

"Join you?" I glance toward her bag, then back to her.

Mabel wipes her hands on her apron. "Mr. M gave us all the weekend off. There's a big rodeo, and everyone is eager to go. I hope you'll come on down to the grounds too"—she hesitates—"make it a family affair. Jack is young, but he can't miss his first rodeo, not as an Eaton."

Make it a family affair? Does she know then? "When will you be back?"

"Some time on Sunday," Mabel says. "A few of the Eaton trailers will be on the campgrounds there and I'll bunk in with some of the others."

I muster a smile. "You'll enjoy that."

She grabs some items from the cupboard and adds them to the bag. "The rodeo is one of the highlights of my year; it always has been. Can you manage without us for a few days?"

I nod, a quick, automatic motion. "I'm sure we'll be fine," I say. I'm trying to give off the facade that the idea of no one being around doesn't stress me out, but the reality is I'm a little worried. *Making problems disappear is my thing.* I can't get that out of my head.

Is this all part of Marcus's plan? Am I becoming a problem that he has to make disappear? When Mabel and the rest of the staff return, will I be gone?

"Mabel, how's your granddaughter?"

"Oh, she's fine. Right as rain." She glances around before sliding so close our shoulders are almost touching. "You need to be careful," she says.

"What do you mean?"

"Did you get my notes?" Her voice is now low, so very low that I almost didn't hear her.

"They were from you?"

She glances around and then nods. "I wasn't sure if you—" She pauses. "What he's done, it's not right. I can't stand by anymore."

"Hey," Wyatt says, causing me to jump. "Whoa, sorry, I thought you heard me stomping down the hall. Where's the little guy?"

I turn to look at Mabel but she's gone.

"I, um..." I lift my hands and drop them, feeling at a loss. Mabel left me those notes?

"Baby girl, what's going on?" He steps forward and takes me in his arms. I lean in and relax, knowing of all the people left on this property, this is the one I can trust the most.

"Please don't leave me," I ask, almost begging. Everything is crashing on me at once, and I'm about to drown in the ocean of fear I'm being swallowed up in.

"Hey, hey, it's okay," Wyatt says softly, his hands rubbing my back in a gentle motion. "I'm not going anywhere. Don't you worry about that. It's been you and me for way too long now for me to leave you, you hear me?" Wyatt pulls back and tilts my chin up. "What is going on? You look like you've seen a ghost. Is it Rosalind? Is there an update?"

"Marcus says she's fine." I swallow hard. There's so much I've been itching to tell him, but he's been busy, and other than waving in passing, this is the first time I've seen him in days. "You're not going to the rodeo this weekend?"

"Well, maybe if you come with me we can make a night of it, but otherwise, no. I'm staying behind to keep an eye on things. The others can let loose a little without watchful eyes on them all the time."

The knot in my chest loosens, and the fear in my mind eases. Wyatt is staying. I'm not alone. Not yet.

I take a breath, a deep, shaky breath. "I can't find my red sweater," I whisper, and I hope he hears me, hope he under-stands, hope he remembers.

Wyatt freezes, and the hand on my arm tightens. I'm about to repeat myself when he gives me a slight nod. He remembers. He understands.

One night, when the stars blazed bright in the sky, he told me that if I was ever scared, worried that something was wrong or that someone was going to or had hurt me, all I needed to do was tell him that I couldn't find my red sweater and he would know something was wrong.

I've only ever had to say the phrase once before, and Wyatt almost went to jail for assault after he took care of a drunk stalker who followed me home late one night.

"Who?" A simple question with a complicated answer.

I'm about to tell him when a presence larger than life fills the room and Marcus is there.

"Wyatt," he says, and his voice is commanding. "There you are. I need you down at the barn before everyone heads out. You can help me hand out the vouchers."

"Sure thing, boss," Wyatt says, but he continues to stare at me, waiting for my answer.

My heart races, my palms are sweaty, and I'm not sure I dare whisper his name, but somehow, I do.

"Marcus." My voice is so soft that I'm hoping only Wyatt hears. His brow rises, and I can tell he's not sure if he believes me or not.

"Did you say something, Trina?" Marcus asks.

Damn it.

I reach for a bottle of water left on the counter and take a drink to hydrate my parched throat. "Just wondering if you were going to the rodeo at all this weekend." Somehow, by some magic, my voice is steady and doesn't highlight anything I'm feeling.

He nods. "With Trent not here, I need to make an appearance. We're sponsoring one of the tents, so I figured I'd go and show my face. Would you like to make a day of it tomorrow and join me? It wouldn't be too much for Jack, would it?"

Wyatt backsteps out of the way. "I'll check in on you later," he tells me, and that simple phrase eases the bands around my heart.

Wyatt leaves, and the room feels bigger, emptier, and all I want to do is leave. It's just Marcus now, just Marcus and me, and I'm finding it really hard to breathe.

"I gave the staff the weekend off to enjoy the rodeo," Marcus says. "The three of us can enjoy the day together." The three of us. Marcus, me, and Jack. Our son. The son he took from me. The son he's making me raise for someone else. I'm still struggling to understand why.

I simply nod. If I were to say anything, he'd hear the fear in my voice, so instead I remain silent. I need to find out those certificates. I need answers, definitive answers, before Marcus believes me a problem he has to make disappear.

My phone dings, and there's a message from Wyatt.

I'll keep an eye out for that red sweater. Let me know if you remember where you left it.

I know he has no idea what's going on but the fact Wyatt is on my side even without knowing all the details means everything to me.

FORTY-THREE

With Marcus down at the barn handing out vouchers to the staff before they leave, this is the perfect opportunity for me to find the proof that I need.

I head to the upstairs office, checking in on Jack first to make sure he's okay.

I already checked the safe only to the certificates I'd found before are gone, but there has to be something else, right? Marcus mentioned something about Trent burning something but he also said they had possession of proof, so... there has to be something for me to find.

I then remember the key. The key Rosalind threw at me and Marcus took back.

I recover the key then head into the spare room and go to the locked door in the closet. I don't hesitate this time. I put the key into the lock and turn. The door opens.

Inside the small storage area are several boxes, clearly labeled *Christmas decor*. Those aren't the ones I'm focused on. Instead, it's the box, larger than a shoe box, that sits on top.

I open it and immediately drop the lid.

Inside is a doll. A baby doll that is wrapped up in a blue blanket.

Rosalind was right. I should have believed her. Marcus and Grace were taunting her with a fake baby, but why? It doesn't make sense, unless Marcus was trying to set the foundation for her psychosis diagnosis.

Seeing this, my hatred for him intensifies.

I place the lid back on the box and relock the door, the fire to destroy him and his lies growing more powerful with each breath I take.

I head to Rosalind's room. She has her own safe that she showed me once. I should have looked here first—the words she whispered to me, that she'd kept it safe, now make so much sense.

This is where she keeps the girls' birth certificates and their passports, along with a few expensive pieces of jewelry Trent has given to her.

I stand at the top of the stairs and listen for any noise below, just in case Marcus is back, and then head to Rosalind's bedroom closet. My hands shake as I move her stack of sweaters to the side, revealing a small safe behind them.

I struggle to remember the combination, knowing Rosalind once told me in case I ever needed it. My thoughts are too wild, too fast, as I try one set of numbers, then another. Time races ahead, the minutes slipping through my fingers like everything else. My panic builds with each failed attempt, knowing at any time, Marcus could return.

I need to remember the code, and the only person who can help me is miles away. With a split-second decision, I dial the clinic. It's a long shot, but maybe I'll be able to talk to Rosalind.

The phone rings, and I ask to be transferred to Rosalind Eaton.

"Trina?" It's Trent's voice, a mix of surprise and concern that makes my heart race. "Is everything okay? How's Jack?"

Caught off guard, I freeze, my mind hiccupping as I struggle to find words. I scrape together a sense of normalcy, like I'm not doing anything and everything to betray his trust. "He's fine," I say, forcing a smile into my voice, shoving the fear out. "I just wanted to check on Rosalind. See how she's doing."

There's a pause, and I think he's caught on, think he's seen through the words, through the lies, through me. But then he speaks again, and the hitch in my shoulders relaxes.

"She's doing better," he says, and his voice is soft, careful, so careful. "The doctors are confident in her recovery."

I catch a breath, hold it, and let it slip away. "Good," I say, truly relieved. I know time is running out, that Marcus could be back any moment and find me in here. But I push the thought away, push it down, down, down. If I can't get the combination from Rosalind, at least I can get a message to her. One that, like Wyatt, will tell her what's going on.

Years ago Rosalind, Wyatt and myself made a pact with each other. We promised to always carry the shovel to dig the grave if it were ever needed. No questions asked. No answers needed. I jokingly said I'd always keep a shovel ready and she told me she'd always have a flame thrower on hand in case we needed to burn everything down and start over.

We've only ever needed the shovel and flame thrower once, and we all carry the burden of what we did.

"I just wanted to let her know I'm thinking of her," I say, my voice shaking slightly.

Trent doesn't seem to notice. "Thanks, Trina. That means a lot."

"Can you give her a message for me?" My tongue races to catch up with my galloping thoughts. "Tell her my favorite red sweater is missing, I'm looking for those receipts I've lost so I can return some baby outfits, and I've decided to pick up gardening and need some new tools," I say, edging my voice with a little bit of laughter, as if this were an inside joke.

There's a pause, and for a moment, I think I've ruined everything, but then he chuckles. "I know that's code for something, but I'm not even going to ask for what," he says. "I learned my lesson last time."

I laugh along with him, remembering the night a few summers back when he walked in on us having a private conversation. Rosie started speaking in code about the Mily Way and the the lava flow, referring to leaking breasts and heavy periods following the twins' birth, and when Trent realized what we were talking about, he backed away, his face blazing red from embarrassment.

"I'll let her know," he promises, and I thank him before we end the call.

I stare at the safe, and it hits me. Rosalind told me the combination that last night in my cottage. *I've kept it safe for your birthday.* It's in the safe and she used my birthday as the code.

I punch in the numbers for the month and date and nothing happens. Then I try my birth year and almost puke when I hear the slight pop of the lock unlatching.

There, in the safe, is that same envelope with the certificates I'd found before. That's not all, though. There's also a small box with a tiny lock. There's a small key on the key ring I hold. It opens the box.

Inside there are dozens of photographs. I go through them, and they're all of Matty, taken from a distance. The earliest is from a few years before I came here.

Why does Rosalind have them? That's not something I can take on right now. I don't have time. I drop them back in the box and reach for the envelope, pulling it out with shaky hands and opening the flap. Inside are the birth certificates, along with more papers and banking transactions.

First things first, I take photos of the documents and immediately email them to myself, saving them to the cloud before returning them to the envelope. I step out of the closet and listen, but the house bears the whispers of ghosts and that's all. My breath is fast, my chest pounding away like I've run a marathon.

One letter stands out to me. It's a letter from a fertility clinic. I quickly scan it, and it looks like this is a results letter from a standard male fertility test. The word "azoospermia" jumps out. I do a quick search on my phone and learn it means there is zero sperm count from these tests.

No sperm? I scan the letter again and realize it's addressed to Trent.

Trent is infertile? What? Why didn't Rosalind ever mention this? Then it hits me—if Trent can't have children, then who—

The loud slam from a truck door through the open window has me jumping. I freeze. Marcus is back. I rush to Jack's room, envelope in hand, barely hearing anything over the soaring rush of my heartbeat. Jack's small, soft huff of breath is the only thing that keeps me from falling apart.

The front door closes, and Marcus's heavy footsteps vibrate on the stairs. *Thump. Thump. Thump.*

My hands tremble as I scoop up Jack, my son.

"There you are," Marcus says, his tone storm-cloud dangerous. "I should have known you'd be in here."

I hold Jack close. "He just woke up," I say, forcing a lightness to my voice I don't feel. I take Jack to the change table, feeling Marcus's gaze on me, and I know if I were to turn around right now, I'd turn to stone, as if he were Medusa.

"Perfect timing then," Marcus says, and the words are smooth. Almost too smooth.

When I do turn, it's to see him staring at me, and in that stare, I read danger. I swallow and try to pretend like nothing is wrong, like my world hasn't been flipped upside down, that he isn't a liar and a kidnapper all rolled into one.

Marcus smiles, and the temperature in the room suddenly

drops. "He's a special little boy, that one," he says, and I feel the daggers of dread dance down my spine.

My hands tremble as I turn my back on Marcus and focus on Jack. "Yes, he is," I say, and I don't even try to keep the love for him out of my voice. My hand lies on my son's chest, feeling the rise and fall as he breathes in and out, and my smile is full and warm as he looks up at me with the most innocent gaze.

"You know I'll do anything to protect him, right?" There's an edge to Marcus's voice, an edge so sharp that it sinks into my heart, cutting me deep.

FORTY-FOUR

A shudder runs along my skin at Marcus's words. His shadow closes in, the hunter at my back. "You should know I have a plan." His voice is smug, sure.

The panic returns, a living thing, a wild thing. It's in my breath, my heart, my blood.

Marcus's steps are measured as he makes his way toward us. I pick up Jack and hold him tight to my chest, like armor, like I'm his protector.

Marcus holds out his phone. There's a video playing. It's me. It's me in his office.

Other than he knows I was snooping, he has no idea of what I found. Unless he has a camera in Rosalind's bedroom, which I doubt.

"Put him down," Marcus says, each word a dagger which cuts and waits for the blood.

But I don't. I won't.

"You should have known I'd be watching. I've always been watching. I've installed cameras everywhere, or haven't you figured that out yet?"

Everywhere?

"Even my cottage?"

He nods. "I had to keep an eye on you, you understand, right? For your own good and all that." He glances around the room then back at me. "What were you looking for earlier?" Marcus asks.

"He's my son." That's the only answer needed. The heat deep within me rises, pushing out the panic, mixing anger with resolve.

"A minor detail," Marcus agrees with a somewhat chuckling, easy, effortless sound.

"He's my son," I say again, as if that is all that matters, as if that is all I need to keep him. I know it's not. We both know it's not. In this world, I'm a mere speck.

"And mine." He doesn't flinch. He doesn't break. He doesn't even crack. "Don't ruin what's already in place."

His confidence cuts through me, flaying my skin into shreds. "You are the perfect mother for our son. I'm not trying to take him away from you," Marcus says, and his voice drips with victory. "All you need to do is trust me."

"Trust you? Trust you?" I step toward him, anger fueling me, and in the back of my head I know I should back down, be calm, think this through, but I can't. I won't. I will fight to the death for my child, my child he took from me.

"Yes, trust me, Trina." Marcus leans against the crib, composed. My heart races as I realize just how close he is to the documents I hid beneath the crib's mattress seconds before he walked in. I almost thought he saw me.

My gaze wants to dart toward the camera in this room but I don't. Will he look at that video too?

Jack squirms, and I shift with him, holding him tighter. I hold him and the life we should have, the life I have to have, the life I will have. I will not let Marcus take my son from me again. I won't.

"How could you, Marcus? He's our son. How could you make me believe he was dead?"

"You're here taking care of him, aren't you?"

Like that changes anything. How can he say something like that?

"Why?"

Marcus lifts a brow. "Why what? Why pretend our child had died? Why give him to my brother and his wife to raise? Why change your contract to ensure you stay here to raise our son?"

He is the reason Jessica was here? "Yes," I say. "Why?"

I don't care about the contract. Sure, I was surprised by the new clauses—increased yearly bonuses, vacations, stock options, and more—but none of that matters when it comes to my child.

"Blame it on my great-grandfather, who wanted to make sure only the eldest-born's son inherited his dynasty." His smile is a taunt. "As fate would have it, the eldest twin is sterile."

"So the girls..." I mutter, already suspecting the answer.

He lifts up his hands. "Mine. Thanks to the modern age of medicine, I was able to help my brother become the father of three children. The girls were a surprise, I'll say that much, considering our firstborn was a boy, but..." He shrugs like what he just admitted to isn't important, but it is.

I don't say anything.

"Oh, you already knew that then. Well, guess I'm not the only one good at keeping secrets, am I?" A lazy grin spreads across his face. "It's always amazed me she never figured that out." He shrugs. "Since she'd already given our family a son, we figured she could give Trent one too. Them falling in love wasn't expected, but all things worked out, didn't it? My brother has the nice little neat family he always wanted, and now he has a son to inherit this multibillion-dollar empire. Tell me you want to take that away from him?" He leaves the words there, wrapped around me like chains, believing they will bind me to his truth.

His truth but not mine.

He takes a step closer, then another, until he's looming over me, over us. The room shrinks. "I don't want to take Jack from you," he tells me. "Everything I've done is to make sure you stay here, in his life."

"You made me believe he was dead."

"I'm sorry for that. I really am." There's no apology in his voice. No remorse.

"Is that why you came to see me every day? Out of guilt?" My head is spinning like a tilt-a-whirl at the rodeo fairgrounds.

"Do you have any idea how hard it is to juggle the emotional well-being of two postpartum women in one household?"

"Something which you obviously failed at." The words drip from my lips as I think about Rosalind and what she's gone through.

"I did what I had to do, and I have no regrets. Rosalind is more fragile than I thought; that is on me."

"On you?" I choke the words out. "She's broken because of what you've done to her. Does she know her baby is dead? What even happened? Was it your idea to torment her with that doll?"

Marcus rubs his face. He looks tired of this conversation, but I need answers, and I need them now.

"So you found the doll, did you?" He shrugs like it's not that big of a deal. "I'll admit, forcing her to hold a doll and pretend it was real was a low blow, but once I realized just how emotionally fragile she is, I knew I couldn't have her taking care of my son."

My stomach churns at his admission. "You are sick." I can't even keep the sentiment to myself.

"I'm practical. I'm not proud of it, but you should know me

well enough by now. I will do anything and everything necessary when it comes to this family." His words slice, but I don't bleed. Not this time.

"Did you drug me?" I've never been able to figure it out, who would have done that. That's the only thing I can think of to cause all the blackouts, why I can't remember what happened that night.

"Drug you? God no, why would I do that? You tripped over something left by the stairs. Blame Mabel if you need to blame anyone. She should have made sure the house was tidier. What happened to you was purely accidental."

Marcus leans over me, into my space. "Nothing has to change, Trina. You'll be Jack's mother in everything but name. I'll make sure you're always taken care of, that this will always be your home. You'll be here, raising Jack, loving him, being the only mother he'll ever need," he says, and the promise is a poison, a knife, a cut, a twist. "Besides, Rosalind's baby isn't dead. Mabel's daughter is raising her, just like Mabel raised my first son, with Grace's help."

"Tammy Lee." I correct him.

"Ahh, yes, her."

"Why her?" I ask before he says anything else.

"Why not her? We have history and she knows your history and I knew the price tag attached." He says it like it's just another business deal. "She hates you, you know that, right? You and Rosalind. She lost everything when your foster home burned down. She was months from aging out and she'd hidden a stash of money that went up in flames. She was there when Rosalind when into labor and that woman called my mother. My mom came personally to pick up Matthew when he was born. Somehow Tammy Lee convinced my mom to hire her."

"Why?"

"Why what?" He looks genuinely confused.

I think about which question I actually want answered first.

"Why did you hide Matthew like you did and have Mabel raise him?"

He shrugs. "That was my mother's choice. Call her old fashioned. I claimed him as mine but we had staff raise him. What's the big deal? I was raised by a nanny, you're a nanny..." He pauses. "You know, I was worried you might recognize her, but no one really looks hard at the help, do they?" He almost chuckles.

"I recognized her."

"And yet, you let her continue to take care of your son. I wonder why?"

Good question.

"I let her plant the listening device," he continues. "I needed to make sure you'd be good, then when you found that, I had to add the cameras. She's got guts, gotta give that to her. But that's our little secret. Tell anyone, and I'll make sure you never see Jack again, and you know I have the means. Think about it, Trina."

I shake my head, a quick, defiant motion, a quick, defiant loss. I don't care about Tammy Lee and what he just said. I care about Rosalind. "You gave your daughter away."

He scoffs. "She was never mine so why would I want to raise her? Stupid clinic mixed up the vials with some random sperm donor, and you can bet I'm suing their asses too. Mabel's daughter had been trying to adopt and Mabel is family, so... Besides, what matters is the world believes Jack is Trent's son."

I throw up in my mouth. "You must be delusional to think you'll get away with this."

He places his hand on our son's back and smiles. "But I already have, haven't I?" he asks, and the doubt creeps in.

He waits for an answer.

I mouth the word, but it's not mine. It's his. "Yes."

I let it out, let it slip, let it mean what he wants it to mean, even though it means nothing to me.

"I knew you'd see it my way," Marcus says, the conqueror, the victor. He thinks he's won.

"What about Rosalind?" I ask, and my voice is hollow, a whisper of the strength I don't have.

Marcus's smile is almost painful. "Rosalind will flourish living long term at the treatment center, and when she's not there, I'll arrange for her to live in a home that is close enough for regular visits with her doctor," he says, and the words sting. "The girls will stay with my parents for now, so they're close enough for visits with Rosalind when she's better."

"She's this way because of you."

He nods. "I know. If she gets better, there's no reason she can't return here and our lives will go back to normal. Nothing will change, Trina. You'll still be here, always here, with me, raising our son—if that's what you choose to do." I hear the ruthlessness, the confidence, the cold certainty. I hear it, and I feel the room spin, like I'm caught in a summer windstorm I can't escape.

Jack fusses, a small, insistent sound that breaks the tension between me and Marcus.

"He's hungry."

Marcus watches, and his eyes are dark, too dark. "Feed him," he says, and the words are more than permission, more like an order. "I'll expect your answer when I return."

I watch him leave, and the fear follows him, and the hope stays. I hold Jack close, and I head back to the change table, where I grab the phone that I'd hidden in a basket.

I take the phone and look at the screen. Not only is it still recording, but the phone call I made while changing Jack is still connected.

"Did you hear?" I ask Wyatt, the phone tight to my ear.

"I did."

FORTY-FIVE

Jack is mine.

Of all the things Marcus spewed earlier, that is the one I'm focusing on right now. Jack is mine. I have the proof and now I have Marcus's words too.

I snuggle with my son, his warm body nestled against me, and I let my heart fill up with love and rightness. I don't know what's going to happen when Marcus walks back into the room, demanding my answer, but I do know that no matter what, I will not let go of my child.

The phone in my lap buzzes with a text message. Turning it over, I see it's from Trent.

Rosie sends her love. She says to remind you that sisters never apologize, and she had Wyatt burn that ugly sweater of yours. Tell him he needs to buy you a new one, and you can decide the color. She also says she's sure you'll find those receipts safe and sound, and to have fun gardening. Let Marcus know what you need.

I reread his words. Everything that needed to be said is there, clear as mud, but I understand completely.

Trent goes on.

You two are ridiculous. She wants a photo of whatever you go with and will even try to call you tonight. And she says family first.

He then includes an emoji of a man with his hands being held up, as if saying, *I don't know.*

Give Jack kisses from both of us.

My grip tightens on my son, and my breath catches. I wasn't sure if she'd understand what I was saying or remember our code, but she does.

Memories crash over me, vivid and urgent. I remember the worn floors of the group home, the shared fears, the unbreakable bonds. *Sisters never apologize.* That has been our promise, our vow to each other ever since we were teenagers just trying to survive in that group home. We agreed that no matter what happened to us, between us, our bond would never break. We could go low, dark, do the most horrific things to each other if there was a reason, and when it was over, we'd never have to apologize for doing what was necessary. As long as we said our code words first, to give the other a heads-up about what was to come.

Rosie said our code phrase, and I didn't notice it. I think back and remember that day by the pool. That's when she said it. *Sisters never apologize.* Why didn't I catch it then?

Her message to me tells me everything I need to know. I send Wyatt a message; my fingers move quickly, typing the words, sending them like an arrow.

*Rosalind said you burned my red sweater and that you're to
buy me a new one.*

I send the message and wait. Wait for his reply. Wait for the
next steps. My stomach rolls, and a wave of nausea sweeps
through me, but I push it back down.

The memories swirl, vivid and chaotic, of a time before this
fairy-tale life, the time before the lies and the half-truths, the
time when everything was raw and real. The group home with
its gray walls and dim lights, with its sadness and anger. We
were young, too young, but even then, we understood the power
of family, even if it meant we had to make our own. We knew it,
and we promised it, and we held onto it like it was all we had.

Family first. The words cut into me, but they are also a
balm. They cut and they heal, and no matter what happens
next, it'll be okay.

I kiss the top of Jack's head and wait for Wyatt to reply.

The house is quiet, the silence of it thick and heavy and
strangely comforting. Like a weighted blanket when you're
trying to sleep. The silence presses in. I pause. I breathe. I hold
my son.

The screen lights up, and for a moment, I almost don't want
to read his reply.

Red, white, or a black one?

My sharp inhale startles Jack, who jumps a little. His eyes
open wide then he fixates on my face and smiles.

For that smile, I will burn down the world. I will destroy
anything and everything in my path for that sweet smile.

Let's go with black this time.

I rock the chair, and the motion is soft, like a lullaby. I rock and wait, holding my son and envisioning the life ahead of us. What will it look like? How different will it be from this moment?

Marcus is going to want an answer, and I have one.

I will not be separated from my son. He will grow up knowing the power of family, and he will grow up never having to worry about where he came from or where he's going.

As I rock my child to sleep, the house is so silent I can hear the soft rustle of his breath, the soft beat of my heart, the soft sound of hope.

The ringing of Marcus's phone shatters the calm. It is loud and shrill, a sound that makes my heart jump, makes Jack let out a soft wail, and makes the silence explode. I strain to hear what is being said, but Marcus's voice is too low.

I count the seconds it takes for him to leave his office.

One. Two. Three. Four. Five. Six. Seven. His footsteps pound on the floor and he's here, at the door, tense and rushed.

"The main barn is on fire," Marcus says. His words are clipped, his expression is sharp, and his voice is filled with something I've never heard from him before, something almost like fear. "Thank God we put the horses out to pasture already. We only have a skeleton crew, so I need to go handle it with Wyatt until the fire trucks get here."

I nod in reply, knowing he doesn't expect me to say anything. A fire in the barn is a big deal, especially in summer when we haven't had much rain. Thank God the horses aren't there.

My phone dings with a text message. I don't look at it.

"Do you need to answer that?" Marcus asks. He's got a look on his face that is demanding. I shake my head no. "We will talk when I get back," Marcus says, and the warning is sharp. "Stay inside."

The sound of his boots on the hardwood, the sound of the door slamming, the sound of the engine as his truck pulls away

—I hear it all, and I breathe it in. I breathe it in and let it fill the spaces with its finality. Marcus wants a decision and I have one. One I'm at peace with.

Once he's gone I check the message. It's from Wyatt.

Black it is.

I move to the picture window, Jack secure in my arms, and watch Marcus's truck kick up dust as it speeds toward the barn. Smoke billows into the sky, black and thick and alive. There's something about a fire that speeds up the racing of my heart till it's a greyhound on a racetrack. The flames are mesmerizing. The smoke destructive. My hand traces the phoenix tattoo, a colorful bird created to cover the flame scar on my chest as I remember the scorching pain from the last fire I was in. The smoke was midnight-black that day, too.

Marcus's figure disappears into the burning barn, and there's a part of me that wants to scream at him, to tell him not to.

Tammy Lee walks into my line of sight.

She's pacing the gravel like a caged animal, arms wrapped tight across her chest.

I press closer to the glass. What is she doing there? What is she waiting for?

She stops, looks toward the barn where Marcus has just disappeared, then back to the house, her eyes daring as though weighing her options. Her lips move—muttering, whispering, maybe cursing; I can't tell. Her hands rise to her face, scrubbing hard at her cheeks. For a moment, she tips her head back, staring up into the sky, her fists balled at her sides. Then she straightens, sudden and sure. Her whole body hardens with decision.

And she walks. Not toward the house, not toward her vehicle, but toward the barn.

I freeze. Do I warn her? Do I protect her? I press my palm flat to the window, useless, invisible.

She glances up and I swear she sees me.

Then she follows Marcus into the barn.

Wyatt races around the barn from the opposite side, toward Marcus's truck, and then flies into the air as the world explodes. The house trembles. My breath stops.

I hold Jack tight as the windows shake with the force of the explosion. The sound is everywhere, a roar, a scream, a cry that I'm not sure is mine or Jack's. The barn is a fireball, bright and huge and terrible, and I can't see anything—not Wyatt, not Marcus, not Tammy Lee, not the trucks.

The shock wave is a physical thing, a push as it rocks the house and my body. My grip on my son tightens as I stare in horror at the scene in front of me, frozen as the barn burns, a massive fire that is bright and raw and violent. The flames shoot skyward, reaching, twisting, turning. The orange glow fills the space with its flash.

The barn roars, a living beast of fire. The blaze splits the night open and I press my hand to my tattoo, to the ink hidden beneath my shirt. The phoenix. My mark. My reminder.

We all were burned the night we left our foster home, after the flames swallowed the past and left me gasping in the ash. The tattoo means survival, proof I can keep going, that nothing can keep me down.

But now, watching the barn collapse in on itself, I finally understand. Survival isn't enough.

The phoenix isn't just about living through the fire; it's about rising up from it. It's about recreation.

The flames dance, and they twist, and the smell of smoke drifts in, sharp and bitter and real. I stare, transfixed in horror, my world crashing down around me, and that's when I see him, stumbling out of the smoke, bent over, hands clutching his knees.

He's alive. Wyatt is alive. I lean against the wall with a thud, relief spreading through my body as Wyatt stands there, far enough away from the blaze not to get burned. My tattoo throbs against my skin, hot as if the flames themselves have branded me again.

In a way, they have. We all survived that first fire. We will all survive this one too.

That's when I move. I grab my phone and call the emergency line.

"The emergency crews are on their way. Are there any animals or people in that barn?" the operator asks me.

"The horses are out to pasture," I say, my throat parched. "I think... I think my boss ran inside, and one of the ranch hands was nearby when it..." I stop because I realize the truth of what I'm about to say, about what I've done.

"Marcus Eaton is in that barn," I manage to whisper to the operator. "Oh God, please hurry." I hang up the phone, dropping it onto the windowsill with a thud, and hold tight to my son.

Did we get away with it?

FORTY-SIX

ROSALIND

I sit in the serene space, and the world stretches into various shades of ocean and sky. It's wide, like grief, a kaleidoscope of emotions that change with the wind and come in and out like the tide. Every new thought, there's grief. Every old memory, there's grief. Every new experience, the grief is like a riptide, threatening to pull me under. I'm a raw wound in this perfect setting, a broken heart in a five-star resort.

This retreat center is everything Trent promised it would be. Its spa-like atmosphere offers a calm oasis for my shattered heart and soul, a soul I'm not sure can ever heal.

I stare at a picture the girls drew for me. Trent's mother sent me a box of items she thought I might appreciate. Soft slippers, a shawl to ward off the coastal breezes, and new loose tea she thought I might enjoy. My favorite things, though, are my girls drawings. The one in my hand is one they drew together: themselves, Trina, me, and a baby lying on the grass. I know they meant for that baby to represent Jack, but in my heart, it represents the little girl Marcus took from me. This would be the only image I have of her, and it feels right that it would be drawn by her sisters.

I miss my children. I miss their infectious smiles, Addison's saucy attitude, and Riley's quiet spirit. I miss the way they watch the world and everyone around them, how much they understand and see. I miss their twin talk, their side glances, and their utterly frustrating way of speaking for each other.

Most of all, I miss their hugs.

I hear the slight buzz of the door to my suite opening, and from the footsteps, I know it's Trent.

Trent, who rushed out of here a few hours ago after his phone rang with news from Wyatt of the main barn burning down. The first thing he asked about was the horses. Then he asked about the men, and I will never forget the way his face drained of all color, how his hand opened, his phone fell, and then he stumbled until he found a chair to grip onto for support.

Now, Trent enters, his eyes clouded, the fog of shock not yet lifting. He sits in the chair beside me, elbows resting on his knees. I wait to see if he'll say something but he doesn't.

So I do it for him.

"I'll never forgive you." My lifeless voice matches his ghost of a presence. He doesn't look me in the eyes, only stares out toward the Pacific Ocean ahead of us.

I let him stare. I let him grieve. It's more than what he gave to me.

I'm responsible for this heartache he feels, which is only fitting since he's responsible for mine.

I think about the messages between me and Trina and I wonder if, deep down, Trent knew what he was doing when I asked him to send my reply. He'd paused and from the way his fingers hovered over his phone, I almost thought he was going to ask me what I meant. But he didn't. He just gave me a questioning glance, a frown, and then when the message had been sent, he gave me a small kiss on my forehead before he opened the patio doors and stood out on the deck, looking out over the ocean.

Did he know? I think he suspected, and yet, he still typed them. Making him as responsible as the three of us. As soon as she sent her message, I knew what she was trying to say:

Tell her my favorite red sweater is missing: Code for "something is wrong."

I'm looking for those receipts I lost so I can return some baby outfits: She was looking for proof about our children. The same proof I'd found myself after hearing a conversation between him and Marcus, about the money they paid the doctor to falsify the death certificate, the financial transactions to Mabel's daughter, how all the times Trent left to run an errand he was seeing my daughter behind my back. The photos on Marcus's phone just cemented everything together.

Marcus's words replay in my head on repeat, and I'll never forget the satisfaction in his voice when he said it never mattered to him who gave birth to his son, and that's why he'd come up with the backup plan to sleep with Trina. The idea that we'd been used so callously lit a flame in my heart and that's when the plan came into play.

It took me a minute to figure out why she'd bring up gardening, then I remembered our promise about the shovel and flame thrower.

I also hoped that she understood my message. When I reminded her that sisters never need to apologize, I hoped she understood that everything I'd done, I'd done it for a reason, no matter how crazy I looked. Adding Wyatt to the message told her to include him in the next step, and she could choose what to do.

We always used colors to convey our intentions: red was to destroy someone's life but leave a way out if needed; white was to let it be; and black was to burn it all down and start anew.

We'd only ever used black before, and we all have the scars to show for it. My fingers touch the roses on my arm covering my burns.

Trent pulls out a tissue and wipes at his face. I should feel for him, for what he's going through, but I don't. It's been hard to look at him. To hold his hand. To let him be a strength when he is the last person I've wanted around me.

It was hard to fake my outbursts and what he's been calling my episodes. It was hard to pretend not to love Jack, to act like he was a doll in my arms when I knew he wasn't.

What's not hard is being able to hate this man beside me. I hate him for what he took from me. I hate him for not having the strength to do what is right, for cowering to his brother and destroying not only our lives but also Trina's.

I trace the drawing from the girls, colors bright against the dark, colors that blur with the tears that flood my eyes, threatening to fall off my lashes and down my sunken cheeks.

Trent reaches for my hand, a motion full of doubt, of regret, of everything he can't say. I don't pull away, but I also don't turn to him.

"I'm sorry," he finally says, his voice low and raw. "I didn't know, not until it was too late what Marcus did, how he switched the babies and had Mabel take our daughter , and then I didn't know what to do." His voice cracks and breaks. I hear the grief, the exhaustion, and the pleading for me to believe him.

"My daughter."

He shakes his head. "Ours. I don't care what the clinic did. She's our daughter and she looks like you." He swallows hard. "I'm so sorry, Rosie, for everything."

If Marcus were still alive, would he be apologizing?

When I turn to him, his eyes are a landscape of grief, a portrait of everything we've lost. My own tears blur the room, and I want to look away. I want to let the hatred I'm feeling manifest and grow. I don't want to remember the love that I do have for him.

"You should have trusted me with the truth," I say, and the

words are hard, a sharp edge in the soft room. "You should have stood up to him. You should have had compassion for Trina. There is no amount of sorrys to make up for what you should have done but didn't do—you realize that, right?"

He nods, his head down.

"We would have figured it out, but instead, you let your brother tear our family apart. He gave our daughter away and he was going to get rid of me too. You understand that, right? I can't figure out why but I guess it doesn't matter now, does it?" My lips tighten at the thought. I've been trying to understand what Marcus gained by getting rid of me, none of it made sense. And now I'll never know. "You broke your promise to me. You promised me our family would always be the priority. Do you remember that?"

Another nod.

"I'm your partner, Trent. You should have told me the truth. Trusted that I could handle it."

Trent looks at me then, his expression solemn. "I was afraid," he finally says.

"Afraid I'd break more than I had?"

I see the truth in his gaze and for a moment, I understand. I do, but it doesn't excuse him either. "I was broken because I couldn't bond with a child that my heart knew wasn't mine, not in the way I did with the girls. I was broken because of that doll that kept making its way into the crib, the same doll your brother kept forcing me to hold. He was gaslighting me. Him. The doctor. You never being home. None of that helped me." I can't hold back the bitterness, the anger. "How was I supposed to heal when no one would let me? The only person on my side is Trina."

"I didn't know about the doll," he says.

"Yes, you did. I told you. You just chose not to believe me. You ran rather than face the truth."

He hangs his head in shame.

"You need to go home, don't you?" I ask. There are a lot of things he needs to deal with, from the funeral to the arson investigation. "Go." I close my eyes for a second. "When you get back, we need to decide together what happens next. Okay? But let me be clear about one thing: I want my children back. All of them."

He doesn't speak.

I see the conflict, see the struggle, see the regret on his face. It hangs between us, a living thing, and I know my husband is lost without his brother. Now it's up to me to step into that void, to be the strength he needs right now.

"I'm so sorry."

I'm tired of his apologies.

"Of course you are, but it doesn't matter. Not now. I need you to understand something—whatever we do from here, Trina needs to be a part of that decision, too," I say, and the name feels like a wound, like a scar, like a promise.

Trent watches me, not saying a word, and that silence is heavy, heavier than the grief, heavier than the loss, heavier than the life we have to rebuild. This time will be different. It has to be.

My breath is shallow and quick. "You should have trusted me," I say again, and the words are softer now, are real now, are everything now. "You let another child be taken from me, let Trina believe hers had died, and I don't know if I'll ever forgive you for that."

Trent takes a long, deep breath that seems to span the ocean and beyond. "What do you mean, another child?" I hear the question and believe it.

"Matthew." That's all I say. That's all I need to say.

Trent's brows furrow, and I watch as he disappears into his mind, into his memories. "That was you?"

I'd laugh at the incredulity that he doesn't already know the answer, except I almost believe him.

"I... I didn't know. I thought..." He rubs his face. "That was always waved off as an indiscretion, and that rather than have an abortion, the birth mother agreed to let us raise the baby instead."

I want to laugh. I want to call out my husband's naivety, except in his world, where money is readily available and anyone can be bought out, I don't doubt he was left in the dark.

"Marcus never told you."

He shakes his head. "I had no idea. I'm so... I'm so sorry," he whispers before dropping down into a chair.

Trent waits for me to say something, but I don't. I reach for the picture my girls drew, and while I don't know what the future holds, I know whichever direction it goes, it'll be my choice.

"I'm sorry for your loss," I say. It's not our loss. Marcus doesn't deserve my grief or any more of my energy. He thought he was stronger than me. He thought he could break me and bend me to his will, and he was wrong.

That one mistake cost him his life, and I have no regrets.

FORTY-SEVEN

TRINA

END OF SUMMER

Dusk on the ranch is the kind of beautiful that sinks into your soul and doesn't let go.

The crackling fire at my feet dances with the slight breeze, and Rosalind and I stare into its mesmerizing flames. We're flanked by empty Adirondack chairs that could use a fresh coat of paint. We don't say much. We don't have to.

My phone sits in my lap with Jack's sleeping face on my screen; his mouth is pinched in that stubborn baby way, and it makes me wonder what he'll be like as he grows. Will he be stubborn and full of self-assurance like his father was? Will he be quiet and contemplative or loud and spirited like the other two men in his life? I glance down every so often, hypnotized by his features, completely in love with this little bundle that is mine.

Rosalind has a mug of alcohol-free cider balanced on one knee and a toasted s'more in one hand. She's softer now, but it's the kind of softness that comes after breaking, like a bone that recently healed. She's fragile and looks tired, but not the lost, bruised kind of tired from before. It's a good tired. A healthy tired.

She's been home a week, and it's been a busy week with her and her daughters all being back home. Josie, her baby girl, sleeps in the stroller beside her. Rosie hasn't let her out of her sight and I don't blame her.

Trent's laughter bounces from the field behind us, the sound of it so unfamiliar I almost don't recognize it. He's chasing the twins, their two little shadows racing wild through the dusk. The girls are hunting fireflies, shrieking every time one escapes their fingers. Riley runs in loops, Addison zigzags straight ahead, both of them breathless and reckless and so full of energy.

I've missed them. I've missed this. My heart is fuller now that my family is home.

"Addison told me today if I make her go to school, she's going to run away. It made me think about the time we tried to run away as kids." Rosalind's voice is hoarse, a rumble through the quiet.

I almost choke on my drink. That doesn't surprise me about Addy. Ever since Marcus's death, she's been a little clingy. "Which time?"

She lets out a laugh that sounds too big for her ribs. "I was thinking the night we made it as far as the highway, with those plastic ponchos and Wyatt's half-broken flashlight."

I laugh, too, the memory bright and sour. "You stole a whole loaf of Wonder Bread and a can of peaches. We thought we'd last a week."

Rosalind tilts her head, a smile sliding sideways. "I'm glad our children don't have to repeat our lives. I told Addy I'd help her pack her bag if she wanted."

"You didn't!"

Rosalind nods, that smile of hers growing stronger. "I did. I told her I'd have to come too, though." She sighs, a peaceful, so-glad-I'm-home kind of sigh. "That was one of the best nights of my life, you know. Out there, just the three of us, not a single adult to mess it up." She squints at the fire, like she can see something I can't. "We were so sure we could build something better. Family, but on our terms."

"Family first," I whisper. It was our pledge, our prayer, the one thing we made up to save ourselves. Will our children need one? I hope not. I hope they grow up knowing this family will do everything to protect them, to keep them safe. Everything and anything. That's now my own personal pledge.

I glance over at Rosalind, see some tears tracking slow and stubborn down her cheek. She wipes her nose with her sleeve, the way she always has. "I'm sorry I didn't believe you," she says.

"For what?"

"You were right about Marcus from the beginning."

I stare into the fire. I wish I'd been wrong. Every time a little hint of sadness weaves its way into my heart, I remind myself of what he did to Rosalind all those years ago.

"Sisters never apologize," I say softly, letting the crackles of bursting flames drown out my words.

"Family first," she finishes. "Who knew it would be so hard?"

I nod.

"I could wish things had been different, but then"—she glances over to her daughters laughing with Trent—"I wouldn't have them. What we've built, it's not normal. It's a little crazy and dysfunctional, but it's ours."

I follow her line of sight and smile at the girls, still chasing the bugs, Trent now collapsed in the grass with them, laughing too hard to get up. I look at Rosalind, at the new lines on her face, at the fire reflected in her eyes, at the way her hands have stopped shaking. I look at the phone in my lap, at my son, breathing and alive and whole.

"Family is what you make it," I say, "and I think our family, as odd or dysfunctional as it may be, is perfect." I mean it.

Rosalind studies me, the way she used to when we were small and fighting for the last slice of bread at breakfast. "You know what's different this time?" She doesn't wait for me to answer. "No one can take it away from us. We're not kids anymore. We're not..." She trails off, the anger slipping underneath. "We're not powerless."

A moth suicides itself into the flames, and we both watch it, silent. I think about the barn fire as construction to rebuild the structure has started. I think of the lives lost in the flames we've created, now and in the past, and I think about what Rosalind just said. *We're not powerless.* She's right. We're not. We've proven that over and over again.

"We're okay, right?" Rosalind asks, reaching over and touching my forearm.

I lay my hand on top of hers and squeeze. "We're okay. I wish you'd told me, given me a heads-up, though." I think about how scared I felt about her, about her mental health, and what she was going through.

Rosalind makes a face. "How many times did I need to say our code phrase for you to catch on? Sisters never apologize. That's always been our motto."

I sigh. I should have paid better attention. I wish I had. Things might be different. I'm not sure how, and I'm not even sure if it might be better, but...

"Was it all an act then?"

She shakes her head. "Not all of it. I... I wasn't okay, I can admit that. The doll, Marcus... that didn't help, for sure, but I was sick. I can see that now. I never wanted to hurt Jack, though, and I never would have."

"That night you thought I stole him? Please say you didn't believe it."

Her hand drops. "When I woke up and he wasn't in his crib,

I did freak out. When I called Trent, I honestly thought I'd lost him, that something had happened to him. But once Trent told me he'd called Marcus... I remembered by then, but I decided to run with it. I'm sorry if I scared you."

I snort. "Scared? I was terrified. For you, for what you must have been going through. Next time, let's come up with a code word you can add to sentences, okay? Something to give me a heads-up at least."

"I hope there won't be a next time." She leans her head back against her chair and looks at me. "Honestly, I didn't have a thought-out plan with step-by-step details. I just knew I needed to get away from Marcus so I could figure out what to do. I needed Trent away from him, too. I thought we were broken, that something was wrong with our marriage and that it was my fault, but once I found the proof... I knew he'd been part of the reason why we were broken, and if I didn't get him away from Marcus, soon there'd be no fixing us."

I nod, understanding too much.

"Do you miss him?" she asks, her voice breaking with the question.

Do I miss him? I wish I knew what to say, or even how to explain what I feel for Marcus. There's a deep anger seeded within my bones toward him, for what he did, for what he thought he could get away with. But there are moments when I remember what he was like as an uncle, the love in his eyes for his children. I don't accept it. I don't forgive it. But I might eventually get it. A parent will do anything and everything for their child.

I did.

"I miss who I wanted him to be, who I thought he could be for our son. I don't grieve him, but what we lost or I guess, what we could have had, who he could have been for Jack. But what he did, who he was... that's unforgiveable and I have no regrets for what happened. It's weird, you know?"

She purses her lips. "This, us, it's all weird."

I sigh. "And yet, it's us," I say, repeating her phrase. "You. Me. The girls. Trent. Matthew. Jack and Josie."

"Josie and Jack." Their names wrap around us. "We are mothers who will do anything and everything to protect our children."

"Our children." The words catch. "Ours," I repeat. "We will make this work. Us. Our family. It's our choice."

Rosalind nods, letting her gaze drift to the horizon. "I want to believe it lasts."

I reach over and grab her hand. It's cold and damp and solid, and she squeezes back so tight my knuckles go numb. "It will."

The twins shriek as Addison slips in the grass, Riley immediately tumbling after her, neither of them able to stop laughing. Trent lifts them both up, spins them in a wild arc, and for a second I think this is what happy must look like.

Jack stirs on the phone screen. His eyelids flutter, his mouth twitching like he's about to wake, but he settles, his chest rising and falling in time with my breath.

"I thought about burning it all down," Rosalind says suddenly. "After everything, I thought that would be the only way to be really free, you know? Like before."

Like before. When she'd been forced to give birth in a bathtub at a young age. When our foster mother slept drunk in her armchair, her daily soap opera on in the background while Rosie screamed through her contractions.

I've never forgiven myself for not being there for her. For arriving when it was too late.

"Is that who we are now?" she asks. "People who burn and run?"

I think about that. Before, I would have said no. That it was a one-time thing, something that needed to be done and we all paid the consequence. But now, now that it's become a repeat experience—where someone who has hurt us dies by fire—now I'm not so sure.

I squeeze her hand again. "We didn't run this time, though. We stayed and fought. And won. We did what we had to do, but maybe we don't make it a habit?"

Rosalind laughs, soft and fluttery. "You're such a mom."

The label is new, strange. I like it.

The sun's almost gone when Wyatt walks around the corner, Matthew following behind him. He looks taller, all long shadows and heavy strides, blueprints rolled tight under one arm.

The twins barrel toward the two at full speed. They crash into Wyatt's legs and he pretends to stagger, spinning them both in a rough, happy circle before setting them down with a thump and a low mock-scolding: "Gentle on the knees, cowgirls. Some of us want to walk tomorrow."

Matthew watches with a smile and then looks our way. He lifts a hand in greeting, then heads into the house. No one stops him.

"It's going to take time," Rosalind says softly.

Life has changed drastically for the young man since Marcus's death. He lost a father but gained a mother and siblings. That's a lot to take in. He has a room in the house now, but he prefers to sleep in the bunk houses with the other cowboys but comes up to the main house some nights to eat, spend time with the girls, and learn how to be part of his new family.

Wyatt makes his way to us, slow and patient, stopping only when Trent meets him at the edge of the stone patio. Their conversation is muted, just shapes in the dusk, but Trent nods a few times, and Wyatt claps him on the shoulder, a brotherly gesture that says more than the words. Wyatt passes over the blueprints, Trent glancing at them and shaking his head in quiet disbelief. He then glances our way and gives us a thumbs up.

"Those must be for the house," Rosalind says. "I can't wait to see the changes they've made."

"You don't think it's too much?" I ask. I feel bad for all the requests I made, knowing how much they're spending to do this.

"Don't even worry about that. I want it to be perfect for you." The firelight catches in Rosalind's hair, throwing shadows over her cheekbones. "If anyone deserves it, it's you."

I shrug, unable to keep the small smile off my face. "Deserve isn't the right word, but it's the best thing for Jack."

I let myself imagine it: a real place of my own, with Jack's crib in the room next to mine, windows that look out at the pasture, a sense that I'm wanted not just as a fixture but as a part of the story. The kind of family that gets built instead of handed down, the kind that keeps its promises.

Trent herds the twins toward the house. "Five minutes to bath," he calls, and Addison throws her hands up while Riley accepts her fate, grabbing Addison's wrist and dragging her along. They disappear up the steps, the last of their giggling trailing behind them. Kathleen, the new house manager, stands at the top of the porch, waiting for them.

Rosalind met Kathleen at the clinic. She was Rosalind's personal nurse but had expressed a desire for a different life. Rosalind offered her one as Mabel's replacement and it's been a relatively smooth transition since Mabel's leaving.

I still don't know what to think of Mabel. Rosalind will never forgive her for what she did, and I don't blame her. Rosalind also wanted to go full avenger mode and destroy the lives of everyone involved in taking her children away from her, but Trent talked her out of it. Instead, Dr. Harmon was forced into early retirement, and Mabel quietly retired with orders to never set foot on the Eaton property again.

Personally, I don't blame Rosalind for wanting justice.

Wyatt circles the fire pit and drops into a chair across from us. He looks tired—real, all-the-way-to-the-bone tired—but there's something looser about him, a slack in his jaw, an ease in his posture that never used to be there.

Rosalind doesn't let him get comfortable. "Is it done?" Her mouth is set, her arms crossed tight.

"Is what done?" I lean forward and ask. There's a tension between these two but I have no idea why it would be there.

This is the first we've seen Wyatt since the funeral, when he climbed on his motorcycle and drove off. He told me not to worry, that he had some things to deal with, but now I'm wondering if those things had anything to do with Rosalind.

He gives her a slight nod. She leans back in her chair and lets out a long, contented smile.

"Um, guys, is what done?" I repeat my question, not liking being left in the dark.

Wyatt shakes his head, but Rosalind starts laughing. It's a quiet chuckle, but it starts in her belly and winds its way around her until her whole body vibrates.

"Thank you," she finally manages to say when she catches her breath. "Wyatt went on a little trip for me, to tie off some loose ends Marcus left dangling," she says. "That's all."

Wyatt stretches out his legs and leans his head back, staring up into the sky.

"Loose ends?" I feel like I'm pulling teeth trying to get any answers.

"You don't mess with my family and not pay any consequences." There's a harshness to Rosalind's voice that has me sitting up straight.

"What did you do?" I look to Wyatt but he only gives me a small shake of the head.

"Rosalind, what did you have Wyatt do?"

"She stole my baby, Trina. She never once tried to make it right, not with me. She let me believe I was going crazy. I wanted her to feel the pain I felt. Raising the twins, Marcus was like a son to her, you know that. We took that from her, but it wasn't enough. It'll never be enough." She rolls her neck in a slow fashion and there's a pit in my stomach.

"She needs to know what it's like to be treated as crazy."

I close my eyes, my mind going in a million directions of what plans Rosalind put into place.

"Marcus was known for making problems disappear, right? Well, I found out where those problems go, and I made sure there was space for one more."

My hand jumps to my chest and I clutch the hemline of my shirt. "You didn't..." I can't get the words out.

"Kill Mabel? Trina, you know me better than that. No, Trent did promise that I would never see her again. I wanted her gone, but that wouldn't be fair to Matthew, so instead, she's going on a little... vacation. Did you know that Marcus served as a founding board member to a psychiatric clinic and that our lawyer added a clause that as long as the Eaton family continued to fund the clinic, we'd always have a seat? Well, that seat now belongs to me. Wyatt went down as my representative to discuss funding a new initiative toward the elderly and their mental well-being. Thanks to our generous increased donation, Mabel now has her own private room at that clinic with the best doctors at her disposal. The poor girl broke when she found out about Marcus's death, but now she's in a safe place to heal. It's basically a luxury retirement home."

This doesn't sit right with me. Mabel was as much a victim as we were. Sure, it's different, but...

Wyatt's hand reaches out and rests on my forearm. The squeeze of his fingers stops me from saying anything else. I sneak a look at him and he gives me a tight headshake.

"It's all taken care of," he says, leaning forward, elbows on knees. "I suggest we move on from the subject and talk about all the changes you guys made while I was gone." He says it so matter-of-factly, but I breathe a little easier. We'll chat later, I know we will, and he'll explain everything to me.

"You mean the house plans?" Rosalind asks. "I'm excited."

Wyatt smiles at her, his eyes flashing red and gold, like the fire in front of us. "The changes to the house look good. Watching all those home improvement shows has rubbed off on you."

"It was mostly Trina," Rosalind says, giving me more credit than I deserve. "Trent says if we're going to be one big happy family, we might as well have the space. You could even move in if you wanted to." After all, we did it once before when Rosie and I went to college and Wyatt worked at a mechanic shop, and it worked out well.

Wyatt chokes on his laughter. "Yeah, um, no thanks. Once was enough. I'm a bachelor at heart, and it's time I had my own place instead of bunking in the clubhouse with the crew. I will take you up on that offer of moving into Trina's cottage, though. But I'll need to redecorate. That place is too girly for me."

There's a pause that grows, stretches, fills the air with the weight of things unsaid.

"Fair enough," Rosalind says. "Make it a man cave if you want."

He nods, clearing his throat, voice low. "You two look good. You look... whole."

The word sticks in my chest. "I feel it," I say, surprising myself. It helps that we received word today that the official investigation ruled the barn explosion an accident caused by improperly stored chemicals.

Rosalind raises her mug, a lazy salute. "To being too stubborn to keep down."

Wyatt snorts. "Damn right." He leans back, the chair creaking, the quiet settling. The fire burns a little lower now, but the night is still warm. The three of us sit, letting the silence do its work.

After a while, Rosalind looks at Wyatt, face softer than I've ever seen it. "I've missed you, brother."

He looks up, the word making its way through the thick air. He nods, slow, a gravity to it. "I've missed my sisters, too. Glad we're all back together."

The old label should feel childish, but it doesn't. It feels earned. It feels like a key turning in a lock. It's who we are, who we've always been. Thrown together in foster care, growing up, taking care of each other. This is family. Our family.

"Did you ever think we'd end up here?" I ask, mostly to myself.

Rosalind laughs, shakes her head. "Not in a million years."

Wyatt studies us, the lines at his eyes deeper now, but not from frowning. "Maybe not here," he says, "but together? Always."

The fire crackles, the wind picks up. Something shifts in the dark. I feel it, the way you can sense a coming storm—change.

We sit there, three broken things made whole again, and watch the fire burn down.

The night closes in, but it's not cold, not really.

Home, I think.

Family first.

Always.

A LETTER FROM STEENA

Dear reader,

I want to say a huge thank you for choosing to read *She Took My Baby*. If you did enjoy it, and want to keep up to date with all my latest releases, just sign up at the following link. Your email address will never be shared and you can unsubscribe at any time.

www.bookouture.com/steena-holmes

I hope you loved *She Took My Baby* and if you did I would be very grateful if you could write a review. I'd love to hear what you think, and it makes such a difference helping new readers to discover one of my books for the first time.

I love hearing from my readers – you can get in touch through social media or my website.

Thanks,

Steena

http://www.steenaholmes.com

 facebook.com/authorsteenaholmes
 instagram.com/authorsteenaholmes

THE IMPORTANT THANK YOUS

Sometimes saying the words "thank you" feel so inadequate. Especially when it comes to these stories I tell. For this book, it would never have come to light if it weren't for my agent, Gordon Warnock, and my editor, Kelsie Marsden, with her brilliantly twisted brain! I'm excited to work with you and your amazing team at Bookouture.

When it comes to my reader group—Steena's Secret Society—thank you is definitely not enough! I write these stories for you to enjoy and every time I come to you asking for advice, for names, and for support, you are right there!

Amy Coats, if I haven't said it before, I will say it now—the fact you let me pick your brain, ask you questions, float mental health questions your way—saying thank you is definitely not enough. When it comes to cheerleaders, you are the first I reach out to and I appreciate you more than I can say!

As a writer, I always keep readers in mind—I want to make sure you have the best experience possible when reading my books, but even more specifically, I always have one reader in mind: Sherri Gall. From *Finding Emma* to now... you've been there with each story, always being honest, always sharing your thoughts. I hope you like this one too, Sherri!

But most importantly, I need to say not only thank you, but I love you, to my husband and three daughters. This might be my 50+ novel that I've written, but none of them would have been possible without you in my corner. Xoxo

P.S.... this book is extra special because while writing a story about a mother and her child, I found out I'm to be a grandma for the first time and I can't wait! My grandbaby should arrive around the time this book is released, how fun is that! We still haven't picked a name yet—granny, nana, nanny, grandma... but you can bet I've already found a bib that is chocolate themed!

PUBLISHING TEAM

Turning a manuscript into a book requires the efforts of many people. The publishing team at Bookouture would like to acknowledge everyone who contributed to this publication.

Audio
Alba Proko

Commercial
Lauren Morrissette
Hannah Richmond
Imogen Allport

Cover design
Lewis Csizmazia

Data and analysis
Mark Alder
Mohamed Bussuri

Editorial
Kelsie Marsden
Nadia Michael

Copyeditor
DeAndra Lupu

Proofreader
Becca Allen

Marketing
Alex Crow
Melanie Price
Occy Carr
Cíara Rosney
Martyna Młynarska

Operations and distribution
Marina Valles
Joe Morris

Production
Hannah Snetsinger
Mandy Kullar
Nadia Michael
Charlotte Hegley

Publicity
Kim Nash
Noelle Holten
Jess Readett
Sarah Hardy

Rights and contracts
Peta Nightingale
Richard King
Saidah Graham

Dear Reader,

We'd love your attention for one more page to tell you about the crisis in children's reading, and what we can all do.

Studies have shown that reading for fun is the **single biggest predictor of a child's future life chances** – more than family circumstance, parents' educational background or income. It improves academic results, mental health, wealth, communication skills, ambition and happiness.

The number of children reading for fun is in rapid decline. Young people have a lot of competition for their time, and a worryingly high number do not have a single book at home.

Hachette works extensively with schools, libraries and literacy charities, but here are some ways we can all raise more readers:

- Reading to children for just 10 minutes a day makes a difference
- Don't give up if children aren't regular readers – there will be books for them!

- Visit bookshops and libraries to get recommendations
- Encourage them to listen to audiobooks
- Support school libraries
- Give books as gifts

There's a lot more information about how to encourage children to read on our websites: **www.RaisingReaders.co.uk** and **www.JoinRaisingReaders.com**.

Thank you for reading.